FORCE OF
NATURE

SUSAN JOHNSON

FORCE OF NATURE

BRAVA

KENSINGTON PUBLISHING CORP.
http://www.kensingtonbooks.com

BRAVA BOOKS are published by

Kensington Publishing Corp.
850 Third Avenue
New York, NY 10022

All Kensington titles, imprints and distributed lines are available at special quantity discounts for bulk purchases for sales promotion, premi-
ums, fund raising, educational or institutional use.

Special book excerpts or customized printings can also be created to fit
specific needs. For details, write or phone the office of the Kensington
Special Sales Manager: Kensington Publishing Corp., 850 Third
Avenue, New York, NY, 10022. Attn. Special Sales Department. Phone:
1-800-221-2647.

Brava and the B logo Reg. U.S. Pat. & TM Off.

ISBN 1-57566-807-6

First Kensington Trade Paperback Printing: March 2003
10 9 8 7 6 5 4 3 2 1

Printed in the United States of America

FORCE OF
NATURE

Chapter

1

Helena, Montana
April 1888

Two women were standing on the windswept porch of the Braddock-Black mansion, their luggage at their feet, the carriage that had brought them from the rail station a receding shadow in the stormy night. Brushing away the snowflakes swirling about her head with an exasperated gesture, the younger woman scowled into the blustery night.

"This is impossible! How can it be snowing in April?"

"The climate is more unpredictable than Florence, darling." The well-dressed woman's voice was mild, as though they were actually discussing the weather.

Spitting out a flurry of snowflakes that blew into her mouth, the dark-haired woman's scowl deepened. "Which is where we should be—not here and certainly not *now!*" She jabbed a finger at the carriages lining the street. "For heaven's sake, Mother, these people are entertaining!"

"We needn't stay long. As for us being here now"—a distinct firmness insinuated itself into her tone—"I daresay, we have as much right as anyone to be here. More perhaps."

"Have you no shame, Mother? You'd confront these people in full view of their guests?"

"Nonsense. We're not here to confront anyone. We've come to visit your father. I see no shame in that."

"Perhaps some of those inside might disagree."

"Darling, there's no need to carry on so. I'm sure I know most everyone in town and this is simply a visit, no more."

"It's been twenty-three years, Mother. I doubt you know anyone at all, although that might be the only saving grace in this debacle," the slender, young woman muttered. "At least we'll be embarrassing ourselves before strangers."

"No one is going to embarrass anyone, my dear. Now, straighten your bonnet. It's awry as usual." Ignoring her daughter's dissent with her usual disregard for any view other than her own, Lucy Attenborough turned to the door, lifted the knocker and let it fall with a bang onto the polished brass plate.

Hazard and his wife, Blaze, were hosting a dinner party that evening. After glancing at the calling card his major domo handed him, Hazard excused himself. Walking down the hall toward the drawing room where he'd been told two women waited, Hazard unconsciously braced himself for trouble. This was hardly the time of day for making calls, especially after twenty-three years. When he reached the door to the drawing room, he paused for a moment with his hand on the door latch. His pulse was racing. Every nerve was on alert—like going into battle, he reflected with a certain irony—just like the old days.

Taking a small breath, he pushed down the latch, entered the room and immediately recognized Lucy Attenborough.

"You've done well for yourself, Jon."

Lucy's tone of voice did nothing to assuage the misgivings her name had evoked, nor did the sight of the young woman at her side. Closing the door behind him securely, as though he could contain the approaching scandal with so small a gesture, he turned back to the women. "What brings you to Helena, Lucy?" he asked. As if he didn't know, he thought, taking in the familiar features of the young lady with his former lover. As if Lucy didn't know he owned half of Montana.

"I wanted you to meet your daughter."

He didn't move from his position near the door. "You waited a long time."

"For heaven's sake, Mother, will you stop this ridiculous game." The young woman rose to her considerable height, lifted the chin that matched that of the man regarding her and met his gaze with similar dark eyes. "Please forgive us for intruding. My mother is without pride. Come, Mother. You saw what you wanted to see."

"There's no doubt she's mine," Hazard murmured, struck by the remarkable resemblance. "If you need anything, it can be arranged." Moving forward, Hazard put out his hand to the daughter he'd never seen. "Welcome to my home."

The young woman hesitated for a fraction of a second before taking her father's hand.

"I'm Jon Hazard Black," he said with a smile.

"Giuseppina Attenborough. Call me Jo," she replied, withdrawing her hand from his grasp.

Hazard's dark brows arched upward. "An unusual name."

"She was born in Florence," Lucy interposed, with an easy familiarity, as though their conversation was of the most banal nature.

"And raised in Florence," the young woman added, "until Mother decided it was improper for me to work for a living, which I'm perfectly capable of doing." She shot her mother an exasperated look. "I could have supported us very well." Turning back to Hazard, she said with a hint of defiance as though she'd had to parry criticism for her choice of profession before. "I'm an engineer."

"It's just a whim for which Father Alessandro has much to answer!" Lucy retorted, tartly. "She's no such thing!"

Jo's gaze was cool. "Mother thinks it's unfeminine."

"The world's changing. Why shouldn't you be an engineer?"

Hazard's daughter looked at him with genuine warmth for the first time since he'd walked into the room. "Exactly."

The door into the drawing room suddenly opened and a beautiful woman with flame red hair stood on the threshold.

Hazard immediately moved toward his wife and taking her hand, drew her into the room. "Darling, come meet our visitors."

The look that passed between husband and wife was difficult to interpret, so quickly was it shuttered.

As Blaze and Hazard approached, Lucy measured her competition with a discerning gaze: obviously a Worth gown. She coolly calculated the price of such luxury with an eye for her own personal gain. The diamonds Hazard's wife wore were worth a king's ransom, her beauty undiminished by the intervening years. And she had a fortune of her own as well, Lucy thought with the bitterness of someone who had lost hers, along with a lover who had required a sizable income to maintain. Her handsome cavalry officer, however enamored, had succumbed to family pressures and married the little heiress selected for him.

So she was here now to repair her fortunes.

And perhaps take back what was hers.

Although their visit to this little backwater town might turn out to be more enjoyable than she'd anticipated. The fact that Hazard was as handsome as ever added a delightful fillip to her enterprise.

In contrast to her mother's dégagé attitude, Jo was mortified to be here. Not that she hadn't been curious about her father, but if her mother hadn't gone into hysterics, she would have stood firm and remained in Florence. She'd lived twenty-two fatherless years without any undue distress. And unlike her mother, she had no wish to be a rich man's petitioner. She doubted as well, that there was a wife alive who would graciously welcome her husband's by-blow and ex-lover.

As for Blaze, after one glance at Lucy and the young woman, there was no question why they were here. The girl's resemblance to Hazard was startling: the same eyes and chin and beautifully defined mouth, the same dark, silken hair. She'd inherited his height as well. As a half blood, her skin was a shade lighter, but in all else she bore Hazard's mark.

"You remember Lucy, don't you?" Hazard said, the gaze he turned on Blaze a plea for forbearance.

"Of course. How are you, Lucy?" Blaze could afford to be gracious; she had no insecurities apropos her husband's affection.

"I'm a bit fatigued after our long journey." Lucy rested against the sofa back in a languid pose that brought her fine bosom into prominence. "But otherwise I'm well. I'm looking forward to renewing old acquaintances," she added, smiling at Hazard.

She looked so smug, Blaze briefly considered throwing her out.

"And this is Jo," Hazard quickly interposed, hoping to deflect Lucy's blatant provocation. "A very pleasant surprise," he said kindly.

Jo's discomfort was so patent, Blaze took pity on the young woman. Surely she couldn't be faulted for her mother's affrontery. "How nice to meet you, Jo. You look so much like your father; you must have felt as though you were looking in a mirror. Has Jon invited you ladies to join us for dinner?"

"I hadn't yet." Nor would he have.

"You both must be hungry," Blaze remarked, cordially. "Please join us." There was no point in trading discourtesies. The girl was well mannered. Lucy was Lucy. And their guests would learn the facts concerning Hazard's daughter soon enough in a town the size of Helena.

"No! We can't!" Jo exclaimed. "That is, no, thank you, we couldn't impose," she added more calmly. "We're not dressed and the journey *was* fatiguing."

"Perhaps some other time." Lucy's winning smile was directed at Hazard. She had no intention of meeting her former friends without a proper toilette and a full array of her remaining jewels.

Jo offered up a silent prayer of thanksgiving, although she knew her mother's reply had nothing to do with good manners.

Jo wasn't the only one to experience gratitude. Hazard stifled a sigh of relief.

An uncomfortable silence fell, the wailing wind and snow pelting against the windows suddenly were conspicuously loud.

"Our luggage is in the foyer," Lucy said into the hush. "And we are dreadfully tired, aren't we, darling?"

The swift look passing between husband and wife was obvious this time.

"Let me see that you have rooms at the Plantation House." The authority in Hazard's tone quelled even Lucy's urge to object.

"I should be getting back to our guests." Blaze's smile was forced. "You won't be long, will you, dear?" she added, turning away in a whisper of shimmering black moire and sparkling diamonds.

"No. I'll have Timms make the arrangements. If you'll excuse me." He dipped his head to his guests. "I'll be right back."

Hazard overtook Blaze in the hallway, caught her around the waist, turned her around and offered her a rueful smile. "Please, don't be angry."

She brushed his hands away. "I'm not sure I want to talk to you right now."

"I don't blame you, but I can't refuse to see my daughter," he said, quietly. "I just can't."

Adjusting her diamond bracelet that didn't need adjusting, Blaze concentrated on centering the rosette design on her wrist. "Of course, you can't," she said with a sigh, her gaze coming up to meet his. "But Lucy's just so bloody annoying.

She hasn't changed one whit. And she's looking forward to renewing old acquaintances." Her brows arched. "How perfect for us all."

"You know as well as I do that Lucy's a bitch through and through."

"I think perhaps you know her just a little bit better than I."

"Lucy's here because she needs money." Hazard prudently shifted the direction of the conversation. "I doubt I would have ever seen my daughter if not for that. You can see that Jo is clearly embarrassed."

"At least she doesn't take after her mother. Lucy's too brazen to be embarrassed. As I recall, she pursued you relentlessly—not only under her old husband's nose, but before the entire town."

"That all happened long ago, before I knew you." There was no point in arguing about Lucy's pursuit; it had been shameless.

Tight-lipped, Blaze stared at him. "How many more children might there be from 'before you knew me'?"

"None, I expect . . . or we would have heard long since."

Her brows rose at his male pragmatism. "I'm not sure that's what I care to hear."

"I can't change what happened before I met you." He touched her hand, slid his finger over the soft white kid of her long evening glove. "I wish I could; I don't like to make you unhappy."

The hum of conversation from the dining room was audible in the abrupt silence, the clink of dinnerware and glasses evidence of another course being served, a strident high-pitched giggle suddenly shrill above the muted sounds of social intercourse.

Blaze groaned. "Claudia will relish hearing the news. She thrives on scandal and gossip."

"I'm sorry. I wish I could change things"—Hazard bent low so their eyes met—"but they're here. And she's family."

Blaze blew out a small breath. "I know . . . I know." She made a small moue. "Go and do what you have to do," she murmured. "I'll make your excuses to our dinner guests. Although it's going to be up to you to explain Jo and Lucy's appearance when you return. And don't even think about dissembling. The entire city will know by morning."

"It shouldn't take long to explain that I have another daughter," he said with male succinctness. "Come morning, we'll see what Lucy wants—or rather, how much she wants. And unless I miss my guess, the moment Lucy has her bank draft, she'll be on the next train east." A faint smile lifted the corners of his mouth. "Jo's very lovely, though, isn't she?"

It was impossible not to agree. "She's beautiful, darling. Very beautiful. And if Lucy Attenborough wasn't looking at you with such fondness, I would be more than willing to let the girl stay here. But—"

"God, no. You're too trusting. Lovely as she may be, let's first see what's brought them so far from Florence after two decades—or more to the point what two decades in Florence may have wrought."

"You know best, dear."

Hazard's eyes narrowed. "I'm not sure I like that patently false acquiescence."

Blaze grinned. "Then we're even, because I'm not sure I like having Lucy Attenborough lusting after you."

"Good God, she's not lusting. That was over years ago."

"I know what I saw. Lusting, darling. Without a doubt."

He groaned.

"Fond memories?" Her gaze was amused.

Lucy Attenborough was the most unnervingly brash woman on the face of the earth. She'd had absolutely no discretion years ago, nor had she now. Who, but Lucy, would arrive in the midst of a dinner party? "No, fond, wouldn't be my choice of words," he noted, brusquely. *Harrowing, maybe,* he thought; she never took no for an answer. He nodded in the direction of the dining room. "I suppose Timms is supervising in there."

"I'll send him out."

"I'd appreciate it. He can see our visitors to the Plantation House." Hazard grimaced faintly, not looking forward to further conversation with Lucy. "I'll go and speak to the ladies and join you shortly."

"You can't say our dinner guests won't be entertained tonight," Blaze murmured, a teasing light in her eyes.

Hazard's gaze narrowed. "I'm glad you're amused."

She grinned. "I couldn't resist. But, darling, consider, it's not as though we're unfamiliar with scandal in our lives. Our son, for instance, has led us a merry chase of late," she pointed out. "And at base, it's only money. We have more than enough to share with your daughter." Her brows arched slightly. "I wouldn't wish, however, to set up Lucy in too much style. I'm not that magnanimous."

"Nor I," Hazard muttered. "She was left a half million when Attenborough died. Although she didn't get her settlement without a fight. Attenborough's first wife and children together with the trustees weren't inclined to be generous to the judge's new young bride."

Blaze shrugged. "Perhaps she lived too well in Florence."

"No doubt. We'll see what she wants and then the lawyers can do the haggling."

"Including Daisy?"

Hazard frowned. "No, not including Daisy."

Hazard's daughter by a previous relationship had been a part of their family for the past fifteen years. Absarokee culture was loosely structured; relationships were easily defined. So when Daisy's mother and stepfather had died in an accident, Hazard's home had become hers. A lawyer now, Daisy was conservative by nature. Unlike her half brother, Trey, who was cutting a very wide swath through the eligible and not-so-eligible females in Montana.

Like his father before him, those with long memories recalled.

"We'll talk to the children first thing in the morning."

Hazard nodded and then gently kissed Blaze's cheek. "Thank you for your understanding."

"My understanding stops at Lucy." Her gaze was sharp. "Just so we're perfectly clear on that point."

"Of course. With luck, she'll soon be gone."

"I suspect the 'soon' part will cost you."

Hazard's brows rose. "If she guarantees me a speedy return to Florence, I'll be more than happy to oblige her mercenary inclinations."

"Do you want a speedy departure for Jo as well?"

He shrugged. "It depends." Raised in a warrior culture where vigilance was the key to survival, having lived in a frontier society where avarice and greed were swaggering credos of empire building, he was inherently wary. "Why don't we see what kind of person Jo turns out to be."

Chapter

2

"I think we're going to be extremely comfortable here." Lucy waved her hand in an airy arc that encompassed the elegant sitting room of the Plantation House Hotel's largest suite. "I'd forgotten how charming small towns can be." Happily ensconced in the Louis Quartorze suite, the hotel manager suitably cowed, a splendid dinner being prepared for them despite the late hour, the champagne she had ordered being poured, Lucy lounged with royal languor on a much-gilded chaise upholstered in azure brocade. "I think we might stay in Helena for some little while after all," she murmured, gesturing the waiter out. "Now bring your maman a glass of that lovely champagne, darling, and we'll drink to our success."

Jo didn't move from her chair, her gaze on the servant about to exit the room. "You mean money, Mother, not success," she snapped as the door closed on the hotel waiter. "This is all about money. Let's not pretend it isn't."

"My goodness. How testy you are about every little comment I make. But then you've always needed your sleep and it's nearly eleven."

"I'm not tired, Mother, I'm annoyed. You promised me once we met my father, we'd leave. Well, we've met him and pleasant as he is, I don't care to bow and scrape like some servile pensioner to add to our coffers. Not when I can earn a perfectly good living for us."

"I'm sure everything will look brighter in the morning, my dear," Lucy murmured, rising from the chaise and moving toward the table that held the champagne. "You'll see how much better you feel after a good night's rest." She picked up a stemmed goblet and lifted it to her daughter. "I think you'll find this little town very much to your liking."

"Haven't you heard a word I've said?" Jo retorted, a blistering heat in her voice. "I don't want to stay. I hate all this manipulation and artifice. I didn't want to come in the first place. I *shouldn't* have come!"

"My dear Jo, I'm afraid you're laboring under some false illusions as to your wishes and my goals," Lucy declared, each word enunciated with crisp coolness. "I don't *care* to live on the money you could earn, even if I agreed with your outlandish notion that women of quality can work, which I don't. Furthermore, I have no intention of living like some impecunious Frau in some seedy apartment somewhere, which is the only thing we could afford if you were to provide our livelihood. We will get what we came here to get and if you *don't* wish to cooperate, I'll do it myself."

"Then do it yourself," Jo said, sullen and resentful, jumping to her feet. "I'm going to bed."

"Well, of all the ungrateful brats! Is that the thanks I get for spending all my money to raise you like a lady of quality!"

Already halfway across the room, Jo spun around. "Let me refresh your memory, Mother!" she said, heatedly. "I believe the bulk of your money went to support Cosimo and his polo ponies, not to mention his tailor. He dressed better than either one of us. And *I* wasn't the one who dined every night at the most expensive restaurants in Florence. Nor was *I* the one who insisted on a premier box at the opera. I don't even *like* the opera. As for my education, it was *gratis* thanks to Father Alessandro. And *thank God* I have an occupation so I don't have to beg men for money. So please don't test my credulity," she spat, grim-faced and furious, "about who most benefited from your money."

As the bedroom door slammed behind her daughter, Lucy stood motionless for a moment, her mouth pursed, and then she shrugged, brought the goblet to her mouth and drained the glass in one unladylike draught. Jo *was* right about Cosimo. He'd been terribly expensive—but so deliciously handsome and *ever* so accomplished in bed. And if she hadn't listened to Vicenzo and his stock scheme that he'd promised was sure to quadruple her money in six months, she might still be enjoying Cosimo's superb body and splendid sexual talents.

But Cosimo was in Florence, unhappily married to a sweet virgin bride selected by his family for her fortune, not her looks, Lucy mused, refilling her glass. And who knew, if Hazard turned out to be generous, perhaps she might respond to Cosimo's wickedly licentious pleas to return. On the other hand, the visit she'd had from the bride's father warning her off had been unsettling. The man didn't even have the decency to buy her off; he simply ordered her away from Cosimo as if she were some lowly peasant. She had half a mind to ignore his threats and show the brutish count she wasn't so easily intimidated. On the other hand, she wasn't entirely sure he wasn't serious about tying her up and throwing her into the Arno.

Not that his rudeness mattered thousands of miles away. The dreadful old goat looked no more like a count than her gardener did, she vindictively reflected. And poor Cosimo, his wife favored her father's looks.

It served him right. Perhaps after several months with his plain-faced wife, he might be more appreciative if she were to return. Although, at the moment, she wasn't overly concerned with returning when she had one of the very best lovers she'd ever enjoyed practically on her doorstep.

Hazard had looked devilishly good in full evening rig.

She'd forgotten how magnificent he was, wildly primal, dark and virile, like his black cougar namesake. A little shiver raced through her senses at the heated memory of their flame-hot liaison. And he was delectably rich now, an additional enchanting allure.

It was going to be such fun seducing him again.

At the sudden knock on the door, she sailed across the room in superb good spirits. Very, very soon she would be renewing her warm friendship with the handsome, wealthy father of her daughter; it made her quite giddy.

She welcomed the servants bringing her supper with an especially gracious warmth.

Apprehensive after their last contact when Lucy had ruthlessly berated them for their every move, the waiters hurriedly arranged the food on the table and hastily departed.

"Jo, darling! Supper!" Lucy trilled as the door closed on the hotel staff. Whether it was her champagne consumption or the surety of seeing Hazard again, she was flushed with exhilaration.

This trip to Montana was going to be very pleasurable indeed.

Chapter

3

It was near midnight when Trey rode into town. Jeb Crawford's stock auction had drawn such a crowd, the bidding had extended well into the evening. But the prime horses he'd purchased had been worth it. Rather than accept Jeb's hospitality, Trey had opted to ride home despite the nasty weather. Satchell's was having some high-stakes games tonight and he felt lucky.

After handing his horse to a boy to be stabled, Trey entered Satchell's saloon and blinked against the legendary crystal chandeliers ablaze with electric lights. Satchell Mumford had been the first saloon owner in Helena to put in electricity in '82. He'd sent to New York for his Venetian-glass chandeliers that shimmered and glittered tonight over a barroom filled with rowdy drinkers, gamblers hoping Lady Luck was on their side, and a piano player fighting a losing battle against the roar of the crowd.

Stripping off his wet gloves, Trey advanced into the room, weaving his way through the standing-room-only-crowd at the bar on his way to the stairway leading to the second floor. He moved quietly for a man his size, nodding occasionally to an acquaintance, exchanging greetings here and there, not sure any of the people he spoke to would remember seeing him in the morning. At this time of night, there wasn't a sober person in the room.

Taking the stairs two at a time with long-legged ease, Trey's worn boots left wet prints on the plush red nap of the carpet. He was soaked through, the spring snowstorms always heavy with moisture. Coming to the top of the stairs he shook his head, ran his fingers through his wet hair, smoothed it behind his ears and strode down the hall. He was looking forward to a stiff drink after his miserable ride.

Satchell's office was at the end of the corridor, a burly guard standing before the door. He smiled broadly as Trey neared. "Jus' about gave you up fo daid."

"It's hard to shoot a moving target my daddy always says." Trey grinned at Donny McGregor whose southern accent was thick as a Georgia native even though his family had come West almost two decades ago.

"Ain't that jus' so. Go on in. I 'spect it's jus' gettin' inter-estin'."

Trey hadn't worried about the time. The poker at Satchell's went on all night. Especially the high-stakes games. And beneath the most colorful of Satchell's Venetian-glass chande-liers reserved for his private quarters sat a half-dozen men focused on their cards. No one spoke until Trey shed his wet jacket and took his place at the table. A variety of grunts and nods were exchanged as Trey settled back in his chair and waited for the next hand.

George Peabody won the round with his usual reticence and as Satchell opened a new pack of cards, conversation re-sumed. It was male conversation: brief declarative sentences or queries; briefer responses; an occasional comment of three or four sentences—the talk of cattle, horses, the price of cop-per and the venal stupidity of "the damned Republicans." Montana was a Democratic state thanks to the heavy influx of southerners to its gold fields during and after the Civil War and territorial politics followed the casually corrupt standard of the rest of the country.

Anyone who was rich enough to sit in on these games was rich enough to buy off a legislator or two with a campaign donation.

And anyone rich enough to sit in on these games was also immune to the censure of lesser men.

Drinks were refilled, cigars relighted, new cards dealt out before Neal Atkinson looked up at Trey. "Hear you have a new half sister come into town."

Trey almost spilled his drink. Carefully setting it back down, he stared at Neal with a faint smile. "You're drunk."

"Didn't say I wasn't. You still have a new half sister."

Trey's dark brows arched high. "Here?"

"Right here. Lucy Attenborough's daughter. Your pa explained it at dinner tonight."

There was no need to say explained what? But it had to have happened long ago because his father was devoted to his mother. "Did you see her?"

"Nope. But Lucy left town after the Judge died in Sixty-five."

Trey did the calculations quickly. The girl would be near his age. Glancing at the clock on the wall, he realized it was too late to visit his parents. He reached for his cards. "Looks like she's going to bring me luck," he said, surveying the straight flush he held. "I'll start with ten thousand."

Since gossip traveled belowstairs at lightning speed, Daisy heard the news about Jo on waking. Her maid blurted out the news the moment she opened her eyes.

Not that she doubted Bessie's information, simply needing a moment to absorb the news, Daisy pushed up on her elbows. "How do you know?"

"Your pa said so at dinner last night."

A dozen questions raced through her mind, none of which

she cared to ask her maid. All of which required an answer from her father. "Take the coffee away," Daisy said, briskly, throwing back the covers. "Set out my blue suit—the wool serge with the pleats. I'll have breakfast with my parents." And rising from her bed, she quickly washed and dressed and walked the short distance to the Braddock-Black mansion on Homer Street.

Chapter
4

Trey and Daisy met on the sidewalk outside their parent's house.

"You heard," Trey said.

Daisy surveyed his disheveled state. "And you've been up all night."

"You say it like you're surprised."

"Do you ever sleep?"

"You sleep enough for both of us. Do you ever go out at night?"

"My social activities are none of your concern." Daisy was twenty-seven, intent on her career and very discriminating about the men she allowed into her life.

"Nor are mine, yours."

"Too late, brother dear. Your social activities are common gossip. Ask Papa sometime how many irate fathers he has to appease on a weekly basis."

"Now why would I do that?"

"Perhaps to take some responsibility for your wild ways."

He tipped his handsome head and smiled. "I repeat . . . why would I want to do that?"

"You're incorrigible," she said with a little sniff.

"And you inherited all the dutiful family graces, Daisy darling."

"Save your 'darlings' for someone less immune to your charm."

"Who are you saving *your* 'darlings' for? I hear you sent Dustin packing. How many is that now who haven't met your exacting standards?"

"At least I have standards."

Trey laughed. "Can I help it if I have a democratic eye?"

"If you could confine yourself to only looking, Papa wouldn't have to pacify so many furious husbands and fathers."

"Now what's the fun in that?" he said with a grin.

The door opened and the servant standing in the doorway curtailed their argument.

"Someday, you're going to find a woman who won't put up with your dissolute ways," Daisy murmured, moving forward.

"No, I won't," Trey muttered under his breath. "Because I'm not looking for that kind of woman. Good morning, Teddy," he said in a normal tone of voice. "I hear we have a new member of the family in town. Are we too late for breakfast? I'm starved."

Hazard and Blaze were still in the breakfast room when their children entered.

"You heard," Hazard said, looking up from his paper.

Trey's smile was sunshine bright. "Hasn't everyone? I'm sure the telegraph lines have been humming since your dinner party last night. Even the London office has heard by now." Pulling out a chair, he glanced at his mother, his gaze affectionate. "How are you taking all this, Mama?"

"Your father is being particularly obliging," Blaze replied with a teasing smile in Hazard's direction.

"Sensible man."

"Perhaps you could take a lesson from this." Hazard's tone was sardonic. "Considering the trail of broken hearts you're leaving in your wake."

"But to date only broken hearts, Papa." Dropping into a chair, Trey grinned at his father.

Blaze sent her son a warning glance. "That will be enough of your impudence. Your father is still trying to deal with this very untidy situation."

"How much do they want?" Unlike her brother's lounging pose, Daisy sat at the table with ladylike composure, her hands folded in her lap.

Hazard smiled; his daughter's query was posed with her usual calm. "Knowing Lucy, quite a lot."

"Will they be leaving when they have what they came for?"

Hazard shrugged. "I would assume so."

"Your new half sister seems very pleasant, however," Blaze interposed. "Unlike—well—"

"You may say it, darling, unlike her mother," Hazard pronounced with a slight frown. "Without getting into personalities, let's just say, Lucy Attenborough is typical of women who marry for money. And in that respect, she's at least predictable."

"She received a considerable settlement from her husband's death, did she not?" Daisy had made a few pertinent phone calls before leaving home.

"Yes, not that it's relevant to this situation."

"Is the girl"—Trey half-raised his hand toward his face—"like us?" He and Daisy bore their Absarokee heritage with unadorned grace.

"The resemblance is quite remarkable," Blaze answered. "No one would mistake her for other than your father's daughter."

"And you said she was pleasant?" Trey grinned. "So when do we see this pleasant young lady?"

"For heaven's sakes, Trey." Daisy cast her brother a censorious look. "She may be trying to extort money from Father."

"That remains to be seen," Blaze remarked. "She was quite uncomfortable about having come. But that may have nothing to do with their monetary goals. By the by, she's an engineer."

"You're kidding." Trey slid upright in his chair. "Both my sisters are career women?" It wasn't as though Trey disapproved of females in the work force; everyone in the Braddock-Black family contributed to the family businesses and Trey was an exemplary partner. But he wasn't driven like Daisy.

"So it seems," his mother replied. "Jo would prefer to support her mother, but Lucy is offended by so déclassé an occupation."

"Her name's Joe?"

"Giuseppina. J-o."

"So when are we going to meet our engineer half sister?" Trey's curiosity was piqued by more than the circumstances of her birth.

More circumspect, Daisy gauged her parents' expressions. "Or would you prefer we didn't?"

"No, not at all. Your father and I were going to talk to you both this morning. You simply heard the news first. By all means, we'd like you to meet Jo. She gives every appearance of being agreeable doesn't she, dear?"

Hazard nodded. "Although I'm reserving judgment until we get to know her better. With Lucy for a mother . . ." his voice trailed off. "In any event," he went on briskly, "your mother and I were planning to speak to our visitors this forenoon and perhaps we could all plan on meeting later."

Daisy lifted her chin a fraction. "Are you talking to them with or without your lawyers?"

"Without."

"Do you think that's wise?" Daisy always erred on the side of caution.

Hazard had carved an empire for himself on the frontier where violence was a way of life; he wasn't easily intimidated. "It won't hurt to begin informally," he said. "But whatever the direction of our discussions, I'd prefer not involving you in this."

Daisy's mouth firmed for a brief moment. "I'm perfectly capable of dealing with these negotiations."

"Of course you are. Not wanting you involved has nothing to do with your capabilities."

"I think your father feels it's too personal," Blaze interjected. "He'd prefer someone outside the family handle the arrangements."

"Everyone knows you're the best lawyer in Montana," Hazard noted. Daisy had passed the bar with the highest scores every posted. "I'd just like to keep the haggling over money separate from family. Then socializing with Jo won't pose any problems."

"We were thinking of having them over for tea this afternoon," Blaze remarked.

Trey groaned.

"I'll have something alcoholic for you and your father, so you needn't break your bad habits for me." His mother swept a glance over his range clothes. "But I will insist you find yourself some more decent attire. Surely with your tailor's bills, you have something more appropriate to wear."

"Yes, Mama." When his mother spoke in that tone of voice, it never paid to disagree.

"Good. Tea then—say at five?"

And the conversation turned to less tumultuous matters as the servants brought in fresh servings of breakfast for Daisy and Trey. The family was even able to forget for brief moments during the lively conversation concerning their many businesses and activities that a ten-ton elephant in the guise of a young lady from Florence was hovering in the wings.

But once Trey and Daisy had gone, the potent question of birthright returned, as obdurate and difficult as ever.

"You don't actually want to go and see Lucy in action, do you? And I'm not saying that to avoid taking you." Hazard's dark gaze was open, but he knew how little his wife liked controversy and whenever possible, he shielded her from the more turbulent issues in their lives.

Blaze wrinkled her nose. "Of course I don't wish to see

Lucy anymore than I have to, but I'm curious—I can't say I'm
not. On the other hand, I know what she wants"—her brows
rose—"and I don't mean just money. So I suppose it's a question of whether I care to watch her try to seduce you." Her
sky-blue eyes twinkled with mischief. "Which now that I
think about it, I'm sure I don't. So, no, I won't go. I would suggest, however, that you keep your daughter, Jo, out of the negotiations. There's no point in exposing her to all the . . . er . . .
titillating details of your liaison."

"I agree, but how do you propose I accomplish that? Jo didn't
look like the type who takes directions."

"An inherited trait, no doubt," Blaze said with a faint smile.
"Perhaps I could go to the hotel with you and invite Jo to go
shopping. If she doesn't like shopping, we have one of the
better bookstores in the West. A studious young woman may
find that an appealing alternative. And I suspect, if Lucy sees
an opportunity to get you alone, she'll find a way to send Jo
with me."

"No question there," Hazard said, drily.

"A better question is, Can you defend yourself?" Blaze
teased.

"I'll bring Sheldon along." Although knowing Lucy, it
wouldn't matter if God himself were on the sidelines. She was
brazen as hell. "Between the two of us, we should be able to
hold her at bay," he said with more conviction than he was
feeling.

"Perfect. Sheldon has excellent mediation skills. He saved
us at least a half million on those copper leases last year."

Hazard smiled. "We'll see how he fares against Lucy."

Blaze held her husband's gaze for a potent moment. "Just a
reminder—I'm more than willing to be forgiving . . . up to a
point. I even understand how Lucy Attenborough might have
been appealing when you were young and without ties. However—"

"You needn't say more, darling. I'll see that Lucy understands." But he almost felt like crossing his fingers behind his

back as he spoke, because Lucy was not only bold as brass, but without scruples.

If he had his way, she'd be on the next train heading east no matter what it cost.

Chapter
5

On that same morning, while family matters were occupying the Braddock-Blacks, Flynn Ito's thoughts were consumed with vengeance. He was standing on a windswept hill a day's ride north of Helena, gazing down on the Sun River valley below. His ranch house, barns, bunkhouse, and outbuildings lay in an untidy sprawl along both sides of the river, the buildings' rooftops covered with a light dusting of snow. Smoke curled up from the chimneys into the clear blue sky. The storm had blown over, the strong winds sweeping east into Dakota, and unlike the violence of his thoughts, the scene below was one of tranquility and calm.

He was standing in the small cemetery where his parents were buried; it was his place of solitude when the burdens of the world became onerous. And after yesterday's standoff with the crew of the Empire Cattle Company who was found three miles inside his borders, and after his men had discovered a score of his cattle slaughtered at the Aspen ford this morning, he needed the peace of the graveyard to clear his thoughts.

To plan and prepare his reprisals.

He and his men would be riding out come nightfall.

The remittance men who ran the Empire Cattle Company needed to be taught a lesson.

Standing before the simple headstones, the granite unembellished except for the names carved into the rough stone, he spoke to his parents as though they were still alive.

"They keep coming, Father—like you said they would—the Sassenach devils," he murmured, a small smile forming on his mouth. His Irish mother had detested the English.

Like many of the large cattle companies, the Empire was funded by English nobles looking for profit in the American West, and on occasion for a distant locale to send their scapegrace sons until their scandals died away. Remittance men, they called those ne'er-do-well sons, and tonight, Flynn would face those running the Empire Cattle Company. Not that blue bloods from England were worth a damn as fighters. But the brutal men they hired to maintain their range lands were quick with a gun and dangerous.

And like his samurai father before him, Flynn had fought a constant battle to guard his land from men like that. In this outland beyond the arm of the law, the strong took from the weak. An eye for an eye wasn't just a biblical injunction, and justice was determined by the number of armed men who rode at your side.

Flynn's men were loyal, their fighting skills well honed. He'd learned the art of war at his father's knee. The military arts were the highest form of study in Japan, the way of the warrior a philosophy of honor and loyalty his father had always lived by. A *ronin* or "wave man" (wanderer), his father had been set adrift when the feudal system had been replaced by a central government and the samurai class disenfranchised.

Ito Katsakura had sailed for the goldfields of California to mend his fortunes, taking with him his samurai swords, the badge of his class, and the principles of Bushido that had guided his life.

Flynn's mother, Molly, an Irish immigrant, endured the drudgery of a scullery maid in Boston for three scant months before seeing the advertisement heralding high wages for mule skinners in California. Who hadn't heard the glorious tales of striking it rich in the goldfields? Hadn't she seen a team driven a thousand times? How hard could it be?

She'd learned to drive by sheer audacity and wits, holding her own against the male drivers, working the route from San Francisco to the goldfields for almost two years. By then, she'd saved up enough to stake her claim, and on her first day panning for gold, she'd met Katsakura. She'd known immediately, she'd always said, that she'd found a man as strong as she.

The young couple worked a series of claims up and down the Sierra Nevadas, making just enough to keep their appetites whetted for more. But the big bonanzas were few and far between eight years after the Sutter's strike. And when word arrived of the new gold discoveries in Montana, they'd followed the rush to the virgin fields.

Their luck turned in '63—maybe it had to do with the fact that Molly had called their claim Flynn's Luck, after their five-year-old son. She'd always said it had, but whatever the reason, that patch of real estate near Diamond City lay over a gold vein rich enough to enable them to buy vast acres of prime land, make them good friends with the bankers in town and give them a life free from want.

With bowed head, Flynn stood at his parents' graves, asking their blessing as was his habit before he rode off to face his enemies. "We leave tonight," he said, his harsh features in repose, his long black hair blowing in the wind. "The moon's full—your favorite kind, Father . . . a raiding moon." He smiled, remembering all the times he'd ridden with his father. His father's samurai swords were thrust through his belt—a long sword and short one, their cutting edges uppermost, the fearful blades, strong and sharp enough to cut through armor. "Give me your strength and courage." He lifted his head as though listening and his mother's voice echoed in his ears. "A Flynn can take on a hundred Sassenach devils without breaking a sweat, my darling boyo . . . and don't you forget it."

His father's calm voice seemed to resonate in counterpoint: "Attack when your enemies least expect it." *And attack your enemies' weak point,* Flynn silently added; his father's wisdom had become his own.

He missed his parents—as if they'd left him yesterday although almost a decade had passed since the choking disease put them in their graves.

And had he not been young and strong, it would have killed him, too.

Almost from the first, he'd had to fight to hold on to his land. He'd been attacked on the day of their burial—and the struggle had never ceased.

It made one cynical and if it didn't break you, it made you strong. He had a reputation now for violence. Swaggering young gunfighters wanted to take him on to prove their manhood—arrogant, stupid, impatient young men—all of them dead. Although someday he knew, he'd meet someone who could outdraw him; it happened to everyone.

But until that day, he thought grimly, he still owned twenty thousand acres of the best grazing land north of the Sun River. And tonight, he'd see that the Empire Cattle Company understood exactly who owned that range.

Chapter

6

"You needn't be polite," Jo said when Blaze invited her shopping.

"Nonsense. If I wanted to be polite, I could have sent you a gift and been done with it. Come, we might as well get to know each other. Hazard is your father, after all. You're part of the family." Blaze took Jo's hand, waved to those in the sitting room at the Plantation House Hotel and left Hazard to deal with Lucy's avarice.

She'd never been part of any family, Jo reflected, following in Blaze's wake, unless you considered her flighty mother and moody, self-centered Cosimo a substitute. Which she couldn't unless she suspended credulity entirely.

Her mother had always been primarily concerned with her looks and her entertainments. Jo had understood early on that a daughter was a liability and more often than not, overlooked. A fact the monks at San Marco had taken note of one day when she was found wandering in the monastery gardens without her nursemaid. She'd been four at the time and Father Alessandro's offer to tutor her free of charge had turned out to be an unaccountable blessing for which she would always be grateful.

Keeping pace with Blaze as they moved through the hotel

corridor, Jo said, "You're very gracious to include me in your family. I hardly expected such kindness."

Blaze smiled at her. "What happened in the past has nothing to do with you or me, now, does it? We can simply enjoy each other's company and leave all the talk of business to others."

"I really want to apologize for my mother's—er—presumption."

"I'm sure your mother has the best of intentions." Blaze's tone was one of exquisite politesse.

You don't know my mother, Jo wished to say.

"Although, I must confess, my husband is under orders to behave."

Jo flushed. Had she read her mind? "I wish I could say the same of my mother," she replied, deciding to answer with frankness of her own. "She's rather bold on occasion."

"I'm sure everything will work out," Blaze said, blandly, deciding Hazard's daughter had his gift for understatement. "In any event, we needn't worry ourselves over anything more taxing than whether we want to go to Swanson's Bookstore first or second. Do you like fiction or nonfiction best?"

While Blaze introduced Jo to the shopping establishments of note in Helena with the aplomb and immunity to gossip that enormous wealth conferred, Hazard and Lucy faced each other across a marquetry tea table. Sheldon Whitney sat off to one side, as though understanding he was there as duenna and referee.

"I'm finding Helena most charming, Jon. Thanks to you," Lucy purred. "I can't believe you have grown children. You look so wonderfully virile . . ." The last word was the merest of whispers as she leaned forward to show off her cleavage.

Lucy had dressed for the occasion—provocatively, rather than appropriately—in a lacy pink froth of a gown more suitable to the boudoir than a morning visit. Carefully focusing his eyes well above her partially exposed bosom, Hazard expected Sheldon was enjoying the view. Personally, she wasn't his style—nor had she ever been—but in his youth, he rarely said no to a woman.

That conduct unfortunately brought him here today.

Not that he begrudged Jo's existence.

He begrudged Lucy's use of their daughter to line her own pockets.

"If you didn't need money, would I have ever seen my daughter?"

It took Lucy a moment to reply. She'd not expected such bluntness. "I didn't think you so uncivil, Jon," she said with a pettish toss of her head. "Our visit is purely social."

"Ah . . . then, we won't be needing Sheldon." Hazard tipped his head toward his associate. "Sheldon brought the company checkbook with him."

Lucy shot a quick glance at the man she'd barely acknowledged when they'd been introduced and silently chastised herself for being so obtuse as to not notice that lovely black leather folio he carried. "Jon, you needn't be so crass." She made a pouty little moue. "I'm sure our discussion needn't be ungracious or venal. Would you like some tea? Would you, Mr. Sheldon?" she queried, offering the man with the checkbook a charming smile.

"No tea," Hazard said, brusquely, "And Sheldon's here to keep your price down, so you needn't smile at him."

"My goodness, how surly you've become. I don't recall you being ill-natured at all. In fact, you were one of the most accommodating men I've ever had the good fortune to meet," she murmured, sweetly.

"If you had thought to tell me about my daughter sooner, I might be more accommodating," Hazard muttered. "Twenty-three years is a long time to wait for the news."

"Well, we're here now," Lucy said, brightly, as though their presence was enough to erase all the years she'd kept him in ignorance. "Don't tell me you're going to hold a grudge against me because I didn't inform you in a more timely manner. Actually, I didn't think your wife would appreciate the information," she added, coyly, thinking herself very clever to have devised such a good excuse. "I'm sure I wouldn't if I were your wife."

The thought of Lucy being his wife was terrifying enough to put everything about their visit back into perspective. And just because Lucy was as avaricious and self-centered as ever needn't obscure the fact that he had a lovely daughter. So it was only left for him to give Lucy what she wanted and see that she departed as soon as possible. "Why don't you tell me what you need to say, live comfortably once again," he offered, mildly. "I'm not *au courant* on prices in Florence."

His sudden *volte face* was disconcerting and Lucy debated how best to answer. Was he being sly? Was he trying to disarm her with politeness? How much could she reasonably ask for without jeopardizing the negotiations? "My little villa wasn't too expensive," she said, trying to read his expression. "Jo had her own small apartment as well," she lied, thinking to influence him with her concern for her daughter and add to her expenses in the bargain. "The darling girl is really quite serious about her career." She smiled, hoping she was conveying a proper maternal solicitude. "Sometimes I do wonder if I've been a trifle unsympathetic about her vocation." She uttered a theatrical little sigh. "But you know how men feel about blue-stocking women; I simply feared for her future. Call me old-fashioned, but surely I'm not remiss in wishing my daughter to marry well, am I?"

Lucy's melodrama was grating; she was a very poor actress. In an effort to scotch any further thespian exertions and minimize his irritation, Hazard said, abruptly, "Would twenty thousand a year maintain you adequately?"

She could live like a queen in Florence on twenty-thousand U.S. dollars. But it would never do to appear overanxious, and a first offer was by definition a *first* offer. Her brow creased in a slight frown. "If you were willing to allow us thirty thousand we could buy an occasional gown as well." She offered him a smile as though of shared commiseration. "You know how young girls are about gowns and fripperies. And perhaps if you could allow us just a bit more income, Jo could continue the violin and voice lessons she so adores."

Hazard hadn't seen such lamentable acting since Trey played the part of a frog in grammar school. "Why don't we say forty thousand and be done with the dickering. Sheldon will write you the first check. You may receive payments either yearly or monthly, whichever you prefer."

For a split second she wondered if she could get more, but one look at Hazard's grim expression changed her mind. "Yearly would be very nice." She was already planning on investing in the new railroad stocks that were—according to gossip—paying such excellent dividends. "How very generous of you," she murmured, sensible of the level of enthusiasm forty thousand a year required. "I told Jo you were the most wonderful, *wonderful* man and now she will see for herself how unselfish and caring you are."

"Speaking of Jo," Hazard said, keeping his voice deliberately mild, "would you object if she were to stay with us in Helena for a time? Our family would like an opportunity to get to know her better." He was careful not to express undue interest. Lucy's mercenary antennae would be put on alert, and if he were inclined to give additional funds to anyone, he'd prefer giving them directly to his daughter.

"What a very nice idea." A fortune hunter at heart, Lucy immediately saw her stipend increasing in direct relation to the charm her daughter could exude. Smiling warmly, she made a mental note to give fair warning to Jo; the girl could be vexing. "We'd *love* to stay," she cooed. "I've always felt that spring here is unbelievably beautiful."

For a second Hazard questioned whether he would regret being chivalrous, whether he should insist she leave immediately as part of their bargain. But a moment later, he decided a few more days of Lucy couldn't be too alarming. "It's settled, then. If you and Jo would care to come for tea this afternoon, we'd enjoy having you. Say, at five?"

"Thank you, we'd love to!" Once more marvelously solvent, she was in excellent spirits. "And thank you, too, for this really magnificent suite," she added with a charming smile. "Although I'm not sure I didn't like that lovely little room you had in Diamond City better. We had such fun there, didn't we?"

That room in Diamond City had just cost him forty thousand a year, although, in truth, Lucy wasn't to blame for the intemperance of his youth. He could have refused her those days in Diamond City; he could have sent her away. "It was a long time ago," he replied, neutrally. "Diamond City's a ghost town now."

"It can't be!"

"I'm afraid so. The last gold was taken out years ago." Not inclined to reminisce about the past with Lucy, he came to his feet and glanced at his associate. "Are we ready?"

Sheldon wasn't too old to appreciate Lucy's voluptuous attractions but old enough to be wary of her artful flirtation. He also had a lawyer's cynicism about human nature and an accountant's reluctance to spend money. Hazard had overpaid her; his employer hadn't even attempted to negotiate, a grievous sin in his estimation. But he wasn't paid to give unwanted advice and no one had asked him for his opinion. Walking over to the marquetry table, he set the check next to Lucy's teacup.

"Thank you, Sheldon," Hazard said.

"Thank you, Sheldon." Lucy's tone was warm and silken, her gaze lifted to his, beguiling. "I do hope we have an opportunity to meet again." Any man who had access to the Braddock-Black checkbook was a friend of hers.

"Yes, ma'am."

"Call me Lucy," she purred.

"You're on your own, Sheldon," Hazard said with a grin. "I'm leaving."

There was the smallest hesitation before Sheldon followed.

Lucy noticed and her smile a moment later as she perused the check in her hand wasn't entirely about the money. Sheldon could turn out to be very useful.

Chapter

7

In the following days, Lucy contented herself with looking up old friends and dispensing some of her new funds at the better dress shops in town. It would never do to be seen looking dowdy in a backwater town like Helena. She even indulged herself in a new carriage, which purchase caused Hazard a degree of apprehension; it gave the appearance she might stay.

Once properly outfitted, Lucy began accepting invitations from all her old friends and like a duck to water reentered the frivolous round of social entertainments so dear to her heart. She didn't mind that Jo spent more time with the Braddock-Blacks than with her. In fact, it turned out to be quite convenient to be independent of her daughter. A great many prominent Helena men were apparently bored with their wives, not an unusual circumstance in the urbane lives of the rich. They were looking for new amusements at the same time Lucy was looking to be amused.

A truly peerless match of motives.

The servants at the Plantation House Hotel kept a running tally of her male visitors and the gifts delivered to her from expensive jewelers. Their vigilance was partly in retaliation against Lucy's continuous threats to have them fired for a multitude of frivolous infractions—and in part because a young, well-dressed man paid them for the information.

In short order, Lucy's social calendar became so crowded, she scarcely had time to scan Cosimo's increasingly pitiful letters when they arrived. Could she help it if he was lamenting his marriage? Did she care about his pathetic existence in his fifty-room villa? Could she help it if he preferred a well-endowed bank account to a well-endowed wife? He *could* have married her and ignored the wishes of his noble family. What good was a title, anyway, if you didn't have two centesimi to rub together? Well, he'd secured his fortune, she supposed, but she'd secured one as well and her transaction didn't require marriage to a gargoyle. Should she decide to return to Florence, she might deign to see him—he *was* adorably handsome. Now what was she going to wear to Estelle's grand soiree tonight? The new embroidered silk surah or the pretty silver tulle? Stepping over Cosimo's last letter that languished unopened on her dressing room floor, she opened her armoire and surveyed her much-improved wardrobe.

Jo's social schedule was equally busy for Hazard and Blaze included her in all their plans and they entertained often. She also was offered an engineer's position at one of their mining companies if she wished it and much as she'd tried to ascertain her mother's feelings on the subject of staying or leaving, she'd not yet received an intelligible reply.

"There's no rush to make a decision," Hazard had assured her. "Enjoy yourself first."

And she did, spending many hours every day in the company of her half sister and brother who responded to her with varying styles of friendship. More conventional and immersed in her work, Daisy enjoyed Jo's intellect, quick wit and modern notions of a woman's role in the world. They rode together and attended charity events that Daisy supported; they talked at length about the Absarokee culture that had become a part of her life literally overnight and visited a number of relatives who still lived in the tribal way. Her Absarokee heritage was at once intriguing and so strange from what she'd known living in Florence, that Jo found herself feeling occasionally as though she were straddling two worlds.

In Trey, she found an instant boon companion, their temperaments and sense of adventure well matched. Having come of age in Florence's informal, expatriate society of writers, poets, artists and dilettantes of every stripe, Jo viewed personal freedom as a right, nonconformity as admirable and intellectual stimulation as the piquant reason for living.

She was not her mother's daughter.

Something her father took note of with delight and at times chagrin. She was too much like him to rest easy. And on those occasions when Jo and Trey kicked up their heels in youthful pleasures, he and Blaze did their best to keep gossip within bounds. It helped, of course, that he was a man of wealth and prominence, that Blaze's personal fortune had long made her immune to censure.

It helped that Jon Hazard Black generated a measure of fear.

Perhaps more than anything though, everyone remembered Hazard in his youth and shrugged in resignation. Blood will tell, they would say with a half smile and a nod. It's a fact of life.

Chapter

8

The first week in May, Flynn Ito rode into town with a dozen of his men. Stewart Warner was being honored for his work on behalf of the Indian schools and Flynn was not only a friend but an important benefactor.

News of the attack on the Empire Cattle Company had preceded him and while everyone understood the Empire's infringement on Flynn's land required retribution, two men were dead—one of them the Earl of Elmhurst's son. There would be an inquiry of course. But the results were inevitable. Not a judge in the territory would rule against a large landowner. The encounter would be ruled self-defense and in a way it was. If you didn't defend what was yours, you wouldn't have it long.

As Flynn entered Stewart Warner's home that evening, he took note of the servants' diffidence with an inward wince. He disliked seeing that look of fear, as though he were going to call them out for not greeting him with enough deference. Although he should be used to apprehensive looks by now. A man his size and heritage was bound to be viewed with alarm regardless of his reputation.

Running a finger under the starched collar of his shirt as he moved toward the drawing room, he cursed the necessity to dress in evening rig. He was uncomfortable out of range clothes. He was also mildly uneasy being here tonight so soon after his assault on Empire land. Everyone would want to question him; the boldest actually would. And he'd have to field those queries with as much politeness as he could manage, because tonight of all nights, he didn't want to embarrass Stewart. The man deserved every honor he was being accorded.

Ignoring the sudden hush that descended when he entered the drawing room, Flynn made straight for Stewart. He walked slowly, familiar with being scrutinized—for his long hair, the oblique tilt to his eyes, the fact that he could outdraw anyone in Montana. He discounted his handsome face, although the ladies who watched him with such longing did not, and they were all hopeful because Flynn was staying in town tonight. Louise Butler had seen him arrive at his town house and the titillating news had spread like wildfire. Which no doubt accounted for the great number of women who went out of their way to smile and bid him "Good evening" as he moved across the room.

"You should come into town more often," Stewart said with a grin when Flynn reached him. "I can practically hear the female hearts beating from here."

Flynn didn't pretend not to understand and his smile held a distinct touch of Irish charm. "If every bloody cattle baron didn't want my land, maybe I could. Congratulations, Stewart. You deserve this celebration."

"Glad you could make it."

"I wouldn't have missed it. Thanks to you, there's hundreds of kids going to school who otherwise wouldn't."

"Couldn't have built those schools without generous donors like you, my boy. You deserve a medal too," the heavy-set, older man replied, tapping the gold medallion pinned to his lapel. "Right purty, ain't it? Lillibet designed it," he added, proudly. "And if'n you should ever get it in your head to take the plunge and get hitched, I might be willing to cede over a couple of copper mines for the right son-in-law." He guffawed at Flynn's sudden discomposure. "Jest a thought, my boy. It ain't as if I haven't offered you her hand afore."

Stewart's daughter Elizabeth was sweet and pretty and so utterly innocent she'd make a perfect wife for any man looking for pure unadulterated wholesomeness. A shame he didn't have an eye for innocence. "If I ever decide to marry, Stewart, you'll be the first to know."

Stewart winked. "I jus' want last bid, Flynn. That's all I ask." Since Lillibet adored Flynn with a schoolgirl's crush, her father wasn't offering his daughter without her consent. "Think about it. You wouldn't have to fend off those Empire renegades everyday. You and Lillibet could retire to Europe for all I care."

"You're tempting me, Stewart," Flynn said with a grin. "You mean I could sleep again at night?"

"Since when do you want to waste your time sleeping," Trey interposed, coming up on the men. "There's better things to do at night. Not that I have to tell you that, Flynn."

The two men were not only good friends, but also the most eligible bachelors in Montana. Their good looks and wealth, along with their reputed stamina in bed, occasioned a steady supply of women in hot pursuit.

"I don't know about you, Trey, but on a working ranch we go to bed early."

"You may go to bed early. As for sleeping"—Trey's brows rose—"that I doubt."

"Well, boys will be boys; that's the way of the world," Stewart noted with a grin. "But you'all are going to have to settle down someday. And I'm a patient man. Now how about some bourbon and branch water. We're all too sober."

Even in the hard-drinking frontier society, Flynn drank more than usual that evening—always out of his element in tie and tails, not in the mood for all the ladies looking for an invitation to join him in bed later, not sure himself why none of the women appealed. Perhaps he'd been up country too long and was out of touch with city flirtations, perhaps there was a sameness about the pretty faces that elicited ennui rather than interest. Whatever the reason, he found himself watching the slow-moving hands of the clock, hoping the after-dinner speeches wouldn't be too lengthy, and planning to leave as soon as courtesy allowed.

He barely touched his food, his conversation was minimal, his constantly refilled glass systematically emptied as though it was his mission to outdrink everyone in the room. With luck, Lillibet wouldn't corner him before he could escape. Although, he could already hear the orchestra warming up in the ballroom and she always insisted on the first dance with him. She was so clearly adoring, he was running out of polite excuses to her invitations; church socials, Grange picnics and the like weren't high on his list of priorities. In the meantime . . . oh, God, Clara Moore was getting up to sing.

He waved a waiter over to refill his glass.

Chapter

9

Jo arrived as dessert was being served.

She stood in the doorway for a moment scanning the room and catching sight of Trey, smiled.

As Flynn followed Trey's gaze and saw the glorious, dark-haired woman, even Clara's strident voice faded into oblivion. That's why Trey had been saving the chair on his other side— for her. Struck with an inexplicable surge of jealousy, Flynn begrudged him her beauty, her lush smile, the sensual pleasure such a woman would accord.

She was resplendently female, strikingly voluptuous, moving toward them with a long-legged, almost mannish stride. But no one would mistake her for a man in that pale ivory gown that bared her shoulders and the half-swell of her breasts visible above the low décolletage; her tightly corseted waist was so narrow, he found himself unconsciously flexing his fingers in anticipation. An obvious half blood, her skin tones lured the touch; her exotic dark eyes held a hint of sexual promise; and her full mouth, half curved in a tantalizing smile, was definitely made to be kissed.

She arrived at the table in a wafting drift of violet scent. It suited her rare beauty. And her smile at close range held a delectable warmth. Trey introduced her to those she didn't know; Flynn and a woman from Chicago were new to her. After she was seated, Trey leaned in close, one arm around the back of her chair and murmured something in her ear that made her laugh. He saw that her champagne glass was filled, that she had a dessert of her choice. And then he sat back and smiled at her like a connoisseur admiring his newest purchase. "Is there anything else your little heart desires, darling?"

She struck his arm playfully with her closed fan, said, "Behave," and then turned to speak to the woman on her left.

More resentful than he would have thought possible, Flynn shot Trey a gimlet-eyed look. "She must be yours."

Trey's brows flew up and then he grinned. "Hell, no, she's my sister."

Flynn tried not to smile at the gratifying possibilities. "Is she available?"

"Depends what you mean."

"She's very beautiful."

"You're not her type," Trey said.

"Are you her chaperon?" Flynn's voice was mild.

Trey scowled. "What if I said I was?"

"Maybe I'd have to ask her whether you were?"

"Ask me what?" Jo inquired, leaning forward enough to see around her brother.

Flynn's dark gaze held hers for a small heated moment. "Whether you liked Clara's singing," he said, husky and low.

"I do—very much." Jo smiled at the most beautiful man she'd ever seen, patently aware that he wasn't talking about singing.

"Just a minute here," Trey muttered under his breath, sandwiched between a scandal in the making. "Just a damned minute."

"How old are you?" Flynn's voice was hushed.

"Old enough," Jo replied, equally softly.

"Do you want to dance?"

She glanced around; everyone was still seated, Clara was singing. "Now?"

"Not here."

"Where?"

"Does it matter?"

"What the hell do you two think you're doing?" Trey growled. "Jesus, Jo, behave for Christ's sake."

She smiled. "I'm sorry. Am I embarrassing you? I didn't know it was possible."

"Very funny—and yes, you are. Stewart is about to speak. Calm down, Flynn, or Lillibet will complain to her father."

By this time, everyone at their table was staring at them. Regardless of the fact that their exchange was inaudible, clearly an argument was taking place. And neither Trey nor Flynn were known for their mild manners.

"I would appreciate it if you would both conduct yourself like adults," Jo murmured, silkily, as though she'd not been the cause of their grim expressions. "Have some respect for Stewart."

"Bitch," Trey muttered, but he was smiling.

A *luscious, teasing little bitch,* Flynn thought, wanting to pick her up and carry her off without a damn for appearances. But he knew better; his mother wouldn't approve, he facetiously thought. She'd drilled good manners into his head with the same kindly tyranny that she'd controlled an eight-mule team. And while Stewart thanked everyone for helping him celebrate, offering kudos to all who had contributed to his cause, Flynn tried to make sense of his outrageous reaction to Jo Attenborough.

By the time Stewart concluded his remarks and Clara ruined another good song, he'd talked himself out of any rash behavior. He wasn't in the habit of acting like an adolescent in heat; he definitely wasn't in the market for more than the most casual of amours. Which meant Trey's sister was a highly inappropriate object of his lust.

Pleased that he'd sensibly curbed his ill-advised urges, he took note of the nearest exit with an eye to flight. The minute he could politely leave, he would. As Clara's last note died away, and the other guests began rising from their seats to move into the ballroom, he came to his feet, bowed to the table at large, and strode away.

Exiting through the terrace door, he felt an immediate sense of relief. Moving away from the lighted windows, he stood on the flags imported from a quarry near Turin to match the elaborate fountain in the garden and marveled at Stewart's tolerance for his wife's expensive and flamboyant decorating taste.

"Pink marble isn't my favorite."

He spun around and the scent of violet enveloped him. "Mine either. Go back in."

She didn't move. "I'm of age. I don't take orders."

All he heard was, "I'm of age," the simple phrase shocking license for his unbridled lust. "You really should go back in." He spoke more kindly this time.

"I don't want to. You interest me."

"Why haven't I met you before?" He didn't dare consider the provocation of the words *you interest me.* Not yet. Not until he knew who she was and what she was and whether the Braddock-Blacks would skin him alive for what he wanted to do to her.

"I just arrived from Florence last month." Her gaze was unutterably direct. "Why haven't I met *you?*"

"I live up north."

"How far up north?"

He smiled; you couldn't say she wasn't direct. "Not too far. A day away."

"Are you staying long?"

He didn't answer for a moment. "Maybe."

"You must not be familiar with women who ask questions."

His mouth twitched into a half smile. "You look like you're more in the habit of giving orders."

"And you don't like women giving orders?"

He shrugged. "It depends."

"Why don't we talk about it?"

"Mostly because I don't feel like talking."

"What do you feel like doing?"

His smile flashed in the moonlight. "You already know."

"So?"

"I'm trying to decide if your father will cut out my heart in the morning and eat it for breakfast."

"I can guarantee he won't."

"You've done this before then?"

"Not exactly."

"Meaning what?"

"Have *you* done this before?"

"Yes"—he hesitated—"and no. Not like this."

His answer pleased her, perhaps he was feeling the same ungovernable desire. "I haven't slept with anyone since I've come to Helena if that's what you wanted to know. Apparently you do quite often according to Trey. He warned me off."

"You should listen to him."

"I don't want to. Will you require written permission from my father? It might embarrass him, but I'm more than willing to get it if need be."

"Jesus," Flynn breathed, wondering if anyone would notice if he fucked her standing up against the ivy-covered wall.

"I was raised in Florence by a mother who was too busy with her own pleasures to worry about me. I didn't run wild, but I'm not a virgin. I'm an engineer. I hope you don't mind either. Some men do."

"Don't say, some men, like that. It's damned irritating."

"Look, mia cara." She laughed. "My goodness, I frightened you. Don't be alarmed, you may be mia cara just for tonight. And there weren't any men if it makes you feel better. Now, don't be cruel, Flynn, say yes." Her smile was delectable. "I won't make you say sweet things to me in the morning."

The way he was feeling right now, he might even be willing

to say sweet things to her in the morning, provided he had the breath left to speak. "Let me talk to Trey, first."

"He can't tell me what to do."

"I understand. But we've been friends for a long time. If you'll wait, I'll be right back."

"I'll go with you." At his obvious hesitation, she added, "Do you mind?"

"No." Clearly he was losing his mind; he blamed it on his whiskey consumption, not wishing to acknowledge the fact that he might be losing his mind over a woman he barely knew.

"Good, because I have this unaccountable need to flaunt you. I want to cling to you and show every woman in the room that you're mine tonight." Her grin lit up her eyes. "Obviously, I'm delirious."

"I wanted to pick you up and carry you away the moment I saw you. This delirium must be contagious." He touched her for the first time, slipping his finger under her chin, lifting her face, trying to control the tremor in his hand. "I do have to talk to Trey," he said, gently, his gaze very close. "You're his sister."

Her hands came up and she lightly framed his face with her palms. "May I cling to you?"

"You may do anything you want to me," he whispered.

They stood utterly still for a moment, lust electrifying their senses.

More familiar with carnal sensation, Flynn overcame the stupefying shock first. "Let's get this over with," he murmured, lifting her hands away from his face. "Come. I'll tell Trey I want"—he paused, choosing his words carefully—"*would like* your company tonight."

"And I, yours," she murmured.

He smiled. "Yes," he said, husky and low. "I noticed."

But they were both more circumspect than to make a spectacle of themselves. Flynn was cautious out of respect for

Trey's sister, and Jo would never consciously embarrass her new family. But she did smile up at him once as they crossed the dance floor, a needful, perhaps unconscious gesture, quickly overcome. And when he smiled back those who saw the impatience, the striking and amazing longing in his eyes said later, the heat of that moment would have warmed every home in Helena the winter through.

At Jo and Flynn's approach, Trey excused himself from the group of ladies besieging him and drew them aside. "Thank God, you've decided to be sensible."

Flynn shook his head. "Sorry, I'm here to ask for your permission to—"

"I said he didn't have to," Jo interrupted. "And don't you dare say no," she added heatedly as Trey's expression turned forbidding.

"Don't you think it might be wise to know each other for more than ten minutes?" Trey muttered, his gaze flicking from one to the other.

"Like you do?" Jo had attended a number of soirees with him of late and seen him in action. And even Daisy who didn't subscribe to her brother's profligate behavior, believed in equal and impartial freedoms for women.

"This is different."

"I hope you're not stupid enough to say because I'm a woman," she said, coolly.

"I don't want to argue about this." Flynn spoke with quiet restraint.

"Then don't," Trey growled.

"I'll have her home in the morning. You know where I live." And taking Jo's hand, Flynn walked away.

It turned out to be a minor spectacle no matter how soft-spoken the argument.

Everyone could see that Flynn Ito had come as a supplicant. It was unprecedented.

But that girl of Hazard and Lucy's was exquisite.

And as independent as the rest of the Braddock-Blacks to walk out of Stewart's ballroom hand in hand with the dangerous Flynn for all the world to see. She couldn't have known him for more than an hour.

What was the old saw about an acorn not falling too far from the tree?

Chapter
10

"Do you mind walking?" Flynn asked. They'd come out onto Stewart's porch, the buzz of gossip that had erupted at their exit still echoing in their ears. "Or I could carry you if you like," he said with a smile. "This is an abduction, is it not?"

"If it makes you feel better," she replied, lightly. "Personally, I don't care what any of them think. Sex is sex—that's all. Plain and simple."

"Or not plain and simple."

She grinned. "Better yet. And you have to carry me, darling Flynn."

His brows rose. "Have to?"

"Have to." Her smile was lush with promise. "And if you do, I'll do something for you."

"You already have." His gaze flicked downward to the bulge in his trousers.

"How nice. You're interested."

"You might say that," he replied, mildly, swinging her up into his arms. It was a vast understatement for a man who had never considered carrying a woman anywhere, who was not given to romantic gestures. "In fact, I'm thinking about keeping you."

"Of course you will."

His stride didn't alter at her words, although in the past, such language would have guaranteed a woman instant dismissal. But nothing was the same tonight. "You let me know when you have to go home."

"I don't really have a home."

"We'll have to talk about that," he said, dipping his head to kiss her lightly. "I have an empty apartment in Helena."

"Can't I see your ranch?"

"Maybe someday."

"That's not very nice." She wanted to live in his pocket; she wanted him to carry her always. It was astonishing, like discovering fire.

"It's too dangerous."

"You have men. Trey told me."

"Not enough sometimes. When it's safer, you may come."

"Stay here, then." Not yet completely lost to all reason, she stopped herself from saying, *forever.*

He laughed. "I will as long as I can."

"I know how to keep you here," she purred, stretching up to kiss his smiling mouth.

"I'm glad to hear it. Then I won't be wasting my time tonight."

"Or I, mine," she replied with a playful grin.

"True," he said, modestly, this man who was known as the Mighty Flynn by all his grateful bed partners.

"We could experiment to make sure you wouldn't be wasting your time. I've read any number of pillow books. They were all the rage in Florence."

His brows rose faintly, not that Jo Attenborough didn't appear to be a thoroughly liberated woman. "You'll have to let me know what you think about Roc Soaring over Dark Sea," he whispered, bending to kiss her again.

And the couple they passed reported the next morning that Flynn Ito had kissed Hazard's daughter so ardently they had to hurry away before they became unwitting voyeurs to something scandalous.

"I hope you can deal with the gossip," Flynn murmured, looking up at the fleeing couple, wondering if he dared threaten Fred Baxter and his wife.

"*I* can. I'm not so sure about my father and Blaze." Jo made a small moue. "They've been very kind. I wouldn't want to embarrass them."

"We'll talk to your father in the morning." Flynn resumed his pace.

"I don't think that's necessary." She smiled. "Not really."

"Out of courtesy then. He's not a man you want to cross."

"You didn't mind a few minutes ago."

He shrugged. "And I don't mind now either. But we'll talk to him anyway."

"*Ummm* . . . I adore that delicious authority in your voice."

His gaze snapped down and he was reminded of how little he knew her.

"Don't be alarmed," she said, a teasing note in her voice. "I don't like whips and chains."

One brow arched upward. "I'm relieved, since I have neither in my repertoire."

"I'm sure whatever you have in your repertoire will be entirely satisfying." Tightening her arms around his neck, she licked a warm path up his throat.

"Such acquiescence," he murmured, his smile wicked. "And I thought you were going to be giving orders."

"I'm trying to lure you into a sense of security before I pounce."

"Since I outweigh you by at least a hundred pounds, pounce away."

She took a small breath at the delicious thought of his large, powerful body in close proximity to hers. "Are we almost there?"

"Two more houses to go and then I'll ravish you to your heart's content."

"What makes you think I like to be ravished."

His dark eyes were very close and heated. "Let's just say I have a feeling . . ."

His home was a beautiful limestone town house, much like those she'd seen in London, pale and precise, not colorful and weathered like those in Florence. Every window glowed with light.

"You have company?"

"I'd better not."

"Servants?"

"Nope."

"Because you planned on being alone tonight."

"Not precisely alone," he said with a grin.

"And I'm the lucky woman."

"You could say that."

"Arrogant man."

"You're not exactly unassuming yourself. You knew every man at Stewart's wanted you."

"But I wanted *you.*"

"And you wouldn't take no for an answer."

She smiled. "You obviously didn't mean no."

He had no answer; she was right—unnerving thought. Setting her on her feet at the door, he unlocked it, lifted her up into his arms again, carried her inside and kicked the door shut.

Her heart was beating furiously. "Why did you do that?"

"Do what?"

"Carry me inside."

"I felt like it."

"No other reason?"

He didn't know, and if he had he wouldn't tell her anyway. It was too bizarre. "You talk too much."

"Tell me."

"Nothing to tell. Now hush," he said, taking the stairs two at a time. "I'm going to make you climax a thousand times."

The shimmering heat of his words flared through her senses

and she shut her eyes briefly against the sudden rush of pleasure. She wasn't a novice at making love, but she wasn't unduly experienced either and the degree of sensation elicited
by his words alone presaged an extremely satisfying night.
"Thank you," she murmured, in blanket gratitude for the
bliss inundating her soul. "Thank you very, very much."

"I should thank you for coming to Stewart's tonight," he
whispered, reaching his bedroom at the top of the stairs, shoving the door open with his foot.

The scent of pine struck her nostrils and she surveyed the
small room. Flynn's range clothes were tossed on the chairs: a
leather jacket, fringed and embroidered with quills, his cham-
ois trousers and linen shirt. His worn leather boots were half
visible under the bed. He'd brought the scent of the north
with him.

He'd also brought the most disquieting sexual energy into
her life.

She felt rash and reckless, desperate to be ravished; he
was right. The word had never entered her consciousness
before; her lovers had been tender and yearning and grateful. She'd been intoxicated with the pleasure of sex but never
even marginally wild and fevered and necessitous as she was
now.

He moved to the large four-poster bed that must have been
purchased to harmonize with the house. It was a fine early
Chippendale, solid, pure in line, and it dominated the room.
The coverlet was a natural Irish linen hemmed with a small
border of crocheted lace, the only ornament in the room with
the exception of the two splendid lacquered swords hanging
from a hook on the wall. And clearly the swords were functioning weapons and not ornaments.

Without speaking, he placed her on the bed and stepped
away.

She stared at him. "What are you doing?" He was standing
so still, she sat up, his expression grave enough to incite a sudden rising panic.

"I need a second." He flexed his fingers, blew out his breath in a long, low exhalation.

"Why?" Didn't he understand she was in the throes of an inexplicable but highly tumultuous sexual need?

"Tell me your name—or something," he said, taut and low. "Talk to me."

"You know my name. I don't feel like talking. What I feel like is—"

"Humor me," he cut in, "or I might scare the hell out of you." He backed away another step. "Understand?"

"Giuseppina Adelaide Attenborough. I can't think of anything else to say, and I'm not sure who might frighten whom the most right now." She kicked off her slippers. "I hope *you* understand."

He watched the arc of her red silk evening pumps as they soared over his bed and landed at his feet. "Nice," he said, surveying the beaded silk. "Red suits you. Would you like a drink?"

"Everything about you suits *me*. And no, I most definitely would not like a drink."

"Well, I would," he muttered, and turning away, he walked from the room.

Incredulous, she jumped from the bed and ran after him. He was already halfway down the stairs by the time she reached the hall landing.

"I'll be right back," he said, without turning around. "Don't go away."

"Damn you!" she shouted. "I just might!"

"No, you won't." And he turned at the base of the stairs and disappeared from sight.

He sounded unconcerned, damn him, when she was ravenous for sex—an inclination hitherto beyond her wildest imagination. Although, if Flynn's tone was any indication, he was entirely familiar with females in heat.

She really should go.

It would serve him right.

She should march out of here, go back to the party and tell Trey he was right—Flynn Ito was *not* her type.

But she sat down on the top step instead, in a pouf of petticoats and ivory silk because much as she'd like to dramatically take her leave, she was breathless with desire and longing. And the very specific object of her desire was the tantalizing Flynn.

Reason had apparently taken a holiday.

A disconcertingly novel state for her; she was never a slave to cravings. And for an afflicted moment, she wondered if she'd inherited her mother's lamentable infatuation with amour after all.

In the midst of her fretful irresolution, Flynn reappeared, holding two glasses tinkling with ice. "I brought one for you, too."

"I don't want any," she said, testy and resentful. While she was beside herself with longing, he was more interested in quenching his thirst.

"It's lemonade." He began mounting the stairs. "You'll like it. And I promise to make love to you soon."

"Don't do me any favors," she snapped. How dare he sound as though he'd fit her in after his lemonade.

"It's not an unselfish impulse, darling, believe me," he said, gently. "Here." Having reached the top of the stairs, he held out a glass. "It's good . . . an old family recipe of my cook's." When she wouldn't take the glass, his mouth twitched into a faint smile. "Would you like me to feed it to you?"

"What I'd like is you in bed with me, unclothed and not drinking lemonade."

He grinned. "Don't be shy."

"I didn't think it was a requirement."

"It's not." Sitting down beside her, he drank some lemonade. "And I apologize. I'm not reluctant. On the contrary, I feel like making love to you for the indefinite future."

"Beginning—when?" Her gaze was arch and challenging.

He set the glasses down on the carpet, turned back to her

and took her face between his palms in a not altogether gentle way. "I'm feeling very much out of control. I'm trying to deal with it. It's not normal."

"I don't mind you out of control."

His hands tightened on her face. "You probably shouldn't say that."

"I'm not a schoolgirl."

"I'm very aware of that," he said, curt and low. "That's part of the problem."

"Do you think I can't say no if need be?"

"The question is, rather, would I hear you," he replied, very softly.

Her gaze held his. "You don't frighten me."

He took a deep breath. "Good. At least one of us isn't frightened."

He was much too close and much too beautiful and the overwhelming power he exuded was so intensely arousing she could no more sustain her anger than she could walk away. "Flynn, please make love to me," she whispered. "Please . . . I'm desperate for you—an aberration for me like your out-of-control feeling is for you. Do you think I make a habit of propositioning men I barely know? Do you think I make a habit of indiscretion? I've never walked from a room like that when everyone was watching, when everyone knew what we were going to do. I never even had the urge to do something so outrageous." Covering his hands with hers, she leaned forward and brushed her lips over his. "Don't make me wait," she breathed. "I want to feel you inside me."

It was impossible to resist so ardent a plea. Coming to his feet, he helped her up and by sheer will restrained himself from having sex with her right there in the hallway. Taking her hand, he quickly guided her to his bedroom, shut the door, but stopped short of locking it. In his current rapacious mood, it wouldn't be wise to lock himself in a room with her.

She was trembling with need, and lifting his hands, he cupped her shoulders, intending to calm her. But his overwrought desires weren't so easily curbed, and her warm flesh under his palms was a violent trigger to his lust. Inexorably, his fingers tightened on her shoulders.

Her small cry should have stopped him.

But he answered her with a low primal growl instead—an impossibly unnerving sound for a man who only amused himself with love. His hands abruptly dropped away. "Sorry about that," he muttered, disconcerted at the frenzy she induced. He'd been playing at love too long to be wild and raging like this. Deliberately sliding his fingers under the décolletage of her gown, as though a familiar gesture would remind him this woman was no different from the rest, he said with deliberate mildness, "How does this come off?"

"I'll take it off later." She began lifting her skirt.

He brushed her hands away. "Take it off now." He wasn't interested in a quick fuck or so he told himself as though it was a measure of his self-control.

She pouted, her dark gaze sullen. "I don't want to wait."

"It won't be for long. Buttons, hooks . . . what do we have here?"

She was as imperious as he, as audacious, and she'd been living her own life for too long to play the docile maid. "Hooks," she said, slipping her hands behind her back, gripping both sides of the gown closure, wrenching it apart with a quick jerk, ripping the hooks from the fragile silk. "There now," she whispered, shoving the wrecked bodice down with a sweep of her hands, surprisingly corsetless beneath her gown. "Any more questions?"

"Who put you in charge?" he whispered with the faintest of smiles, wondering how he was possibly going to last the night with this goddamned wild woman. He'd fuck his brains out by midnight.

"I put myself in charge," she said, smiling back, sliding her palms up his lapels, shoving him backward. "You're too slow."

He came to a stop against a small chest and stood motionless for a few polite seconds. Then he captured her hands, forced them down, held them firmly at her sides. "You're going to take a little getting used to," he murmured, his gaze drifting downward to her lush breasts.

"I know a good way to get to know each other."

He grinned. "I'll bet you do."

"Are you really as dangerous as they say?" she purred, arching her back, flaunting her flamboyant, thrusting breasts.

"Is that what you want?" Her nipples were hard and taut, the plump swell of her breasts perfect ripe globes, delectable, made to be sucked. Not that he needed any additional stimulus to his aching cock. "You want something dangerous?" he whispered, several lurid possibilities racing through his brain. It wasn't the first time he'd heard that lascivious tone in a woman—the one where she was wondering if there was added fillip to sex with a killer. It was, however, the first time he'd considered responding to that bizarre inclination. "Maybe we could arrange something," he said in a husky rasp.

"Now . . . right now . . . please." The strong grip of his fingers imprisoning her wrists, his potent authority, his brute promise so gently offered further kindled the lust beating at her brain, the throbbing between her legs a hard, steady, feverish ache. She struggled against his grasp. "Damn you, Flynn. I want sex!"

He didn't take orders, no matter how heated. "Undress first." He released her hands. "Then if you're very sweet to me, I might give you what you want."

"I didn't think you'd like sweet women."

"I didn't think you'd like rough sex"—his dark brows rose faintly—"or did you mean something else?"

"Maybe this isn't going to work out," she said, petulantly, unfamiliar with men who didn't fawn over her.

"Suit yourself."

"I could leave."

"You already said that . . . and—here you are," he said with a wicked smile.

On the other hand, fawning men never made her feverish

and insatiable and she'd never in her life begged for sex. Even now, she wondered if it were possible she'd not actually said it. She gazed for a fleeting moment at the beautiful, virile male animal called Flynn Ito smiling down at her and knew that she could no more deny her raging hunger for him than she could deny the steady throbbing between her legs.

"You're damned annoying," she muttered, staring at him for a taut, heated moment, wishing she could tell him to go to hell, wishing she didn't so desperately need what he so casually offered.

His smile was indulgent. "And you're one hot little bitch."

"I don't know if I can manage the sweetness you require," she said, sulkily, pushing her gown and petticoats down, the boned bodice catching for a moment on the puddled folds of fabric.

"I'm flexible." Taking in the delectable sight of Miss Attenborough bent over and disburdening herself of her garments, her heavy breasts swinging gently with her movements, he felt himself becoming more accommodating by the second.

She shot him a testy glance. "How fortunate for me." Coming upright a moment later, she stepped out of the numerous garments and kicked them aside. Beginning to untie the waistband of her drawers, she pondered the degree of Flynn's sexual allure that she was not only willing to comply to his orders, but agree to most anything to feel that glorious hard cock inside her.

It was a conundrum she'd never faced before.

But then, she'd never met a man she craved with such unequivocal carnal longing. She softly swore, lust and intellect contesting for dominance in her brain.

"Do you need help?" With a negligible gesture, he indicated the tie on her drawers she was trying to loosen.

How dare he stand there like some cool observer of the scene and speak with that unabashed calm. "Aren't you undressing?" she asked, nettled and huffy.

"Maybe . . . marginally at least . . . it depends on what I want you to do."

His reply was perversely arousing, as though he were in a brothel somewhere and waiting his turn. "What the hell does that mean?" But even as she spoke, a feverish jolt of desire convulsed her vagina, leaving her breathless.

"It looks like you already know," he said smiling faintly. So she liked to take orders too, he reflected, not just give them. "All you want is my cock. I don't have to get undressed," he said, softly. "Come here. Leave that tie . . . I'll do it. Here—come here and take it out. Take it out if you want it."

Her gaze was drawn to the enormous bulge in his trousers, the soft fabric lifted away like a tent. Her body was screaming, *Go, go, take it;* the pulsing of her vaginal tissue flagrant, her silken passage sleek with readiness, every nerve in her body poised for that resplendent moment of penetration.

How could he stand there so calmly when he'd had that towering erection since Stewart Warner's? How could he possibly remain so cool when she was frantic with lust? She wished she could say, *No, I won't; do it yourself.* And if she wasn't nearly crazed with a sharp-set need to feel him deep inside her, she might have.

"I guarantee you'll like it," he said into the sudden silence, as though he knew what she was thinking.

"I can offer you the same guarantee." But her voice was breathy, her gaze lifting reluctantly as though she were loathe to look away from the object of her desire.

"I wasn't doubting that for a minute," he pleasantly observed, as though they were discussing something ordinary and mundane. "There's something about you, Miss Attenborough. I don't know what it is, but I've never been so fucking hard in my life. And if you really like pillow books, I'm more than willing to try all forty-eight positions tonight."

With a sharp cry of protest, she abruptly climaxed, the thought of experiencing forty-eight positions with that magnificent cock buried deep inside her pushing her inflamed senses over the edge.

"Jesus," he breathed, reaching out to steady her as the orgasmic turbulence shuddered through her body. "Jesus Christ . . ."

Moments later when she stilled, he lifted her into his arms and carried her to the bed. Her eyes were tightly shut, tears seeping from under her lids, and he chided himself for goading her. He had no idea why he'd done what he'd done; he wasn't ordinarily so churlish. "I'm sorry," he murmured, with genuine regret, gently placing her on the coverlet. "I'm really sorry."

Her eyes opened. "That wasn't very nice," she whispered with a hiccupy little sniffle. "That incomplete, stupid . . . nothingness." Her pout was fretful, although the pique in her eyes was deliciously sultry. "You owe me."

He smiled, her pouty demand unutterably charming, her unabashed ultimatum tantalizing as hell in his current state of horniness. "Allow me to oblige you, Miss Attenborough," he murmured, stripping off his coat, beginning to unbutton his waistcoat. "I can see you require compensation."

With such a delectable promise and the beauty of his smile, she was assuaged and the bed was lovely, soft, soft, unlike his magnificent erection—pleasant thought. "I will expect a little extra effort from you this time."

He laughed and tossed his waistcoat aside. "Will I be graded?"

"Of course. In any number of areas."

"Ah . . . a connoisseur of pillow books, I forgot. Then I must live up to your exacting standards," he said with a grin, disposing of his shirt and tie.

"My experience with pillow books is not empirical, I fear."

"Fortunately, mine is," he noted, kicking off his shoes. "Perhaps I can widen your horizons tonight, Miss Attenborough."

She smiled. "How lovely. I just adore learning new things."

He stopped in his unbuttoning of his trousers, unused to such girlish delight in the boudoir. "Perhaps we can both learn new things tonight," he murmured, gazing at the lovely Miss Attenborough gracing his bed. She was one of the more voluptuous women he'd had the pleasure of mounting. She was by far the only one he'd ever felt this curious passion for—quite separate from lust. "Would you like to look at some pillow books while you're waiting?" he asked, because he'd prefer not thinking about passion separate from lust. It was a decidedly outré sentiment in his life, and not one he cared to contemplate.

"I don't plan on waiting," she said, firmly. "I believe you owe me a debt on that score. Speed is my only requirement at the moment."

"Yes, ma'am."

"I'm only referring to your disrobing. Speed is not a criterion in lovemaking."

"Ah," he said, smiling as he resumed his unbuttoning. "Thank you for the information."

"You needn't be cheeky."

"And you needn't give me directions," he said, softly, sliding off his trousers and underwear.

"Forgive me . . ." Her tone diminished into a purr at the end, the entire magnificent length of his arousal revealed, any mild annoyance she might have felt instantly suppressed in the interest of détente. "I'm sure you're very competent."

Her comment elicited a sharp, satirical glance as he bent over to pull off his socks.

And she was instantly mesmerized, the turgid veins on his engorged penis swelling with his movement, the motion of his upthrust erection the merest stirring, its taut rigidity a deterrent to movement. Unconsciously licking her lips at the sight of that lovely hard length, she watched him stand upright and smile at her.

"One tangled knot remains between you and me," he said, approaching the bed. "And I'm very good with knots."

She'd forgotten she still wore her drawers, her mind on more lustful possibilities, but he was already unraveling the snarl.

She watched his nimble-fingered manipulations in fevered anticipation, feeling as though she were aglow with heated rapture. *So this is lust,* she thought with fascination, *this ravenous impatience, this dissolving away of inhibitions and prudence, this eager, burning compulsion that overlooked everything but the insatiable need for satisfaction.* She was engulfed in a veritable torment of wanting that could only be assuaged in one way with one person—this dark, handsome, powerful man bending over her, untying her waistband with a casual competence.

Flynn's broad shoulders were blocking out the light, the taut musculature silhouetted against the glow of the lamps illuminating the room. His hair swung forward as he leaned over her, the silken waves almost brushing her body, its scent, like his, like that of the room reminding her of pine forests and wildness.

And then he said, "Done," very softly, slipped her drawers off and looking up, smiled at her with such beauty she felt as though she'd been bestowed the sweetest of gifts. "Now it's speed that's your initial requirement, right?" Again, that soft indulgence as though she had but to ask and he would oblige.

"Please." She could barely speak, the tumult of her body and brain and quivering senses like a raging storm with no beginning or end, no quiet center that allowed her to think beyond her fevered needs.

A man of experience, he recognized that overwrought incoherence and he knew what to do when a woman was beyond the most fundamental conversation. He moved onto the bed with fluid grace, slid over her in a ripple of muscle and sinew and gently lowered himself between her legs. The ladies' thighs were always spread wide, like now . . . a constant in his experience. Scandalously handsome, virile men like Flynn Ito didn't have to woo like men of lesser attributes.

But tonight, he was equally enthralled; it wasn't the usual

game, and to that purpose, he took special care to please the lady.

He entered her without preliminaries, as she wished, the word *speed*, bringing a faint smile to his mouth as he eased forward, her soft little exhalation of satisfaction as he drove in, echoing in his mind. She was slippery wet, hot, sleek and deliciously tight, so they both felt the leisurely penetration with particular piquancy.

She clung to him, every heated cell in her body welcoming him, every pulsing bit of flesh that came into contact with him experiencing a degree of enchantment she'd not thought possible. He was huge, huge, slowly filling her, the tantalizing progress burning through her senses until he was there, solid and hard and touching her in the shimmering hot depths of her fevered body.

"Stay," she whispered, her nails digging into his back. "Stay, stay, stay."

He obliged her, understanding as she rose faintly against his imbedded erection and sighed and panted that he wasn't allowed to move just yet. But he did after a time regardless that she cried, "No!" because he knew better than a young woman who had spent more time in her studies than in amour, that he could make her feel better. He withdrew and plunged forward and withdrew again in a delicate, slow flux and flow, penetrating deeply for a time, then only marginally, waiting until she was crying in little sobs of longing, before driving in deeply again to the very brink of her womb. When she was taut as a bowstring, he knew and held himself right there where she wanted him while she died away in breathy scream. Her heated cry warmed his cheek and lightly blew through the silken fall of his hair while the flutter of her orgasm rippled down his fully submerged penis like butterfly wings.

A light sheen of perspiration glowed on her face, her silk-stockinged legs fell away from his back a few moments later and eyes shut, she whispered, "I love you more than anything in the world."

He smiled, accepting the superlatives in the manner in which they were given. "Forty-seven more to go, darling," he murmured. "You're going to love me even more before the night is over."

Her eyes flew open.

"That was the most basic Somersaulting Dragons," he said, lightly. "It gets better."

"Forty-seven more," she said, weakly.

His brows flickered faintly, like his smile. "Better ones, too."

"I don't believe you." How could it be better? She'd practically fainted away from pleasure that time.

"I'll show you." He grinned, moving faintly inside her. "You know—empirically."

Her smile was a slow, lazy unfolding of pleasure. "You don't know how glad I am that you decided to come to Stewart Warner's tonight."

"I should be thanking you."

"You don't have to thank me yet. Under the circumstances, I mean—when you haven't—"

"Come yet? I did."

"But"—she shifted her hips to better feel his engorged penis.

"Orgasm and ejaculation don't have to be the same."

Her eyes opened wide.

"One learns," he said, softly.

According to the classic oriental arts of the bedchamber, the female essence is inexhaustible. Around this premise, the sex manuals devised elaborate means to boost the male's sexual stamina and thereby prolong sexual union.

Flynn Ito was extremely well trained and accomplished.

"Let's see if you like Wild Horses Leaping," he gently said, beginning to lift one of her legs.

"No . . . no, not just yet." Replete and sated, she didn't want to move.

"I'll go slowly," he murmured, continuing to raise her leg,

setting it on his shoulder, shifting his position inside her, smiling as she softly moaned. "We'll take our time." He lifted her other leg, placed it on his opposite shoulder and withdrew a small distance so the crest of his penis was lodged against the front wall of her vagina.

She gasped and shut her eyes, the fevered sensation almost too much to bear.

"I'm going to move very slowly—like this . . . and this—see you *are* ready again."

She could feel the rush of heat flow through her body, settle liquid and hot in the precise, shuddering spot he was slowly caressing with the protruding ridge of his penis, their most tender, sensitive membranes touching, rubbing until she was trembling helplessly once again, until she came as he knew she would in a few brief seconds more. He kept her there, powerless to resist, coming over and over again, in thrall to his expertise and her hot-blooded passions until even his disciplined emotions gave way and he ejaculated—in the interests of prudence—outside the passionate Miss Attenborough's very pleasurable body.

"My God, Flynn," she purred, her eyes half shut, her arms flung wide in blissful fatigue. "Women must beat a path to your door . . ."

"You liked it then," he murmured, not about to touch the part about women beating a path to his door. Easing himself away, he whispered, "Don't move or you'll drip. I'll be right back."

"I need something to drink, something to eat. I could eat half a cow . . . and to think I was talking about leaving."

He glanced up from the washstand in the corner. "I wouldn't have let you leave."

"You would have kept me here against my will?" She eased her knees up, offering him a tempting view.

"I would have kept you here for my sexual pleasure. I *am* keeping you here for my sexual pleasure," he added with a smile, returning to the bed, leaning over and wiping her stomach dry with a towel. "So you needn't try and seduce me with your luscious cunt. It's mine and I'm keeping it."

"If I allow you to."

He smiled slowly and shook his head. "Even if you don't." His smile widened. "I have ways of changing your mind, if you recall."

"Libertine," she whispered.

"You're keeping up just fine," he said with a grin. "And now for some food and drink. I'm starved."

She followed him downstairs where they raided the pantry, picking out food to sustain their ravenous appetites. Although a brief pause in their selections was required when Jo bent over to pull a tray from a bottom shelf and her pose was too enchanting for Flynn to resist.

"Let me help you," he murmured, reaching around her back to place her palms on the shelf. "We'll get that tray in a minute," he whispered, sliding his rampant penis into her delectably exposed cleft. "I haven't seen you in my kitchen before. Are you new on my staff?"

He was deep inside her in a single hard stroke and the exquisite pulsing began to spread through her body again as though she'd not come for days. "Do you have sex with all your maids?" she said, half breathless with rapture.

"Only the ones with luscious cunts like yours," he whispered, withdrawing for another plunging downstroke. "You can bring my coffee to me in the morning."

"I don't know how to make coffee."

"It doesn't matter," he softly said, his hands hard on her waist, driving in again until he was buried to the hilt, stretching her. "Just bring this pretty cunt when you wake me."

She was panting, her hips moving under his hands, the liquid core of her body slippery around him. "Will you promise to have sex with me when I wake you?"

"Promise," he whispered, driving deeper as she raised her bottom to further tempt him. "You could be my upstairs maid and just stay in my bed and wait for me to fuck you. Would

you like that?" He moved from side to side, forced himself
deeper, holding her impaled on his erection for lingering moments at the extremity of his downstroke while she panted
and cried and sobbed and came. And then he repeated his delectable game with exquisite finesse, and she came each time
until her legs gave way and he took pity on her. "Just once
more," he whispered, holding her up by her waist, his senses
still aflame, his need for her obsessive, violent, pounding into
her this last time again and again, almost coming inside her, almost—when he never did, when he never even considered
coming in a woman for all the obvious reasons.

That near-disaster abruptly cooled his brain and holding
her with one arm, he wiped her back dry with a beautifully
embroidered luncheon napkin and lifting her into his arms,
carried her into the drawing room.

"People might see," she fearfully murmured, glancing at
the windows.

"There are no lights on in here. It's fine," he replied, beginning to lower her to the sofa.

"I'm going to stain the silk," she exclaimed.

"It's my sofa. You have my permission to stain it." And placing her on the pale blue silk, he took his seat beside her and
gently kissed her cheek. "You're irresistible." He smiled. "I'm
afraid that's a warning." For himself as well. "I have this constant erection in your presence."

"How charming . . . and fortunate, since I have this ungovernable urge to have sex with you every few minutes."

"It's very strange," he murmured, half to himself.

"But extraordinarily pleasurable," she said with a warm,
open smile.

"Yes, very," he politely replied, wondering if she'd cast
some spell over him. Recognizing that was unlikely almost as
quickly as the notion had come into his brain, he jettisoned his
ambiguities and decided to enjoy the sexual bounty so generously offered him.

Which, as it turned out, was imminent. As they were making their way up the stairs a short time later—she carrying two glasses and several pieces of roast chicken on a plate, he behind her with a pitcher of lemonade and a coconut cake balanced on a platter—he found the enticing view directly before his eyes impossible to ignore. Jo's lush bottom was delectably close, his hard-on was, as usual in her vicinity, at full mast and he had very little control over his insatiable hunger for her. "Stop just a minute," he said. "You don't have to turn around."

His voice was hushed, heated, and she immediately began trembling as though he had only to say stop and she was ready for sex.

Setting down the objects he was carrying, he took those she held from her and placed them on the stairs. "I'll get them later," he said, smoothing his hands down her plump, smooth bottom, sliding a finger over her drenched cleft. "I think it's time again. Bend over."

She should have taken issue with his abrupt command; she should have said, 'I don't have to do everything you say,' but that soft-spoken order registered in her insatiable, pulsing vagina and she bent over and bracing herself on the stairs, waited for his long hard length to fill her as though she no longer had a mind of her own. As though she were the most wanton, lascivious tart.

"That's a good girl," he murmured, slapping her lightly on the buttocks as she bent over, the distended lips of the gorgeous cunt he couldn't do without wet and glistening with desire. "Show me where you want me to go," he brusquely said, as hopelessly enthralled as she, as unable to restrain himself, wanting to possess her over and over again with a kind of madness he neither understood nor liked. "Show me," he said, harshly, beset with passions he couldn't withstand, blaming her for his voracious lust.

As she quickly obeyed, reaching between her legs to trace her gleaming, pouty vulva with her finger, he still wasn't satisfied. "Ask me to fuck you," he said, gruff and moody, not knowing what he'd do if she refused.

But she didn't refuse. She said the words, haltingly, wanting him too much to ignore his command, her vagina quivering with desire, her senses attuned to his slightest whim.

"I'm not sure I heard you," he whispered, intending to chastize her for her prudery, make her repeat the phrase properly, but tormented by lust, he could no more wait than she. Ramming his stiff cock into her needy, ravenous slit, he drove in fiercely, savagely, his brute force pitching her face down on the stairs, shoving her elbow into the cake frosting. He didn't notice or didn't care, thrusting and pumping into her liquid heat, riding her in a frenzy of resentment and unbridled lust. But their bodies and ravenous senses were immune to their restless rage and grudging assent, to their hampered free will, and they both came swiftly with a particular seething violence that left them gasping.

"Damn you," she whispered, her cheek resting on the stair carpet, her hair in wild disorder on the treads, his weight oppressive.

"I don't like this," he muttered.

"We should stop."

He laughed out loud, a harsh, almost bitter sound. "Yeah, shouldn't we just." Rolling away, he snatched up one of the embroidered napkins he'd been carrying and tossed it on her back. Sitting on the step below her, his penis gleaming wet with her creamy fluids, he scowled into the stairwell.

"You needn't use that tone of voice with me," she said, turning over, wiping her back, finding a place to sit between the cake and the lemonade. "Or sulk like a child, either. You're much more familiar with this carnal lechery than I."

"No, I am not." Clipped, brusque words.

"So rumor has it."

He half-turned his head and gave her a hard look. "This is not sex as usual, Miss Attenborough, in case you haven't noticed."

"Well, that's true."

His gaze narrowed, his dark eyes held hers for a searching

moment more and then his mouth twitched faintly and slowly
lifted into a smile. Reaching out, he scooped the frosting from
her elbow. "Forgive me. It's not your fault," he said, licking
the frosting off his finger. "But you're most unusual, Miss
Attenborough."

"You *could* call me Jo, considering our—well . . . degree of
intimacy. Unless you prefer some semblance of propriety"—
she shrugged—"for reasons that escape me."

"Forgive me again . . . Jo." He seemed to debate some internal issue for a pulse beat more and then shrugged himself.
"What the hell. Are you still hungry?"

"Why wouldn't I be?"

He smiled, thinking this delectable female he was obsessed
with had a cool logical brain—sex aside, of course. "Why not
indeed. I'll bring the food. You go on ahead and make yourself
comfortable on the bed."

"You're sure now? The bed won't be a problem?"

My God, she was delightfully straightforward. "No, it won't
be a problem. I'm quite over my rare fit of judiciousness."

"I'm relieved . . . and hungry."

He came to his feet and began gathering up the food. "After
you," he politely said, as though they weren't both naked on
his staircase. "And thank you, by the way."

"You're entirely welcome. Might I offer you my thanks as
well."

He tipped his head and smiled. "Yes, you may."

Seated cross-legged on the bed a few moments later, Flynn's
rare fit of introspection and Jo's testiness supplanted by more
pleasant activities, they ate the food and drank the lemonade
and kissed occasionally with coconut frosting on their lips and
talked of the most casual, nonsexual things like painters they
liked or books or horses or plays or people who made them
laugh or who didn't. No longer troubled with obsession, or inclined to debate internal issues having to do with discretion
versus spontaneity, they were past the point of caring, more

intent on enjoying the wonder of their mutual and highly charged sexual appetites.

They paged through Flynn's portfolio of Utamaro's colorful prints that depicted the wonders of love with great beauty and charm. The set of shunga prints from 1660 that Flynn owned, showing the forty-eight sexual positions he'd spoken of, was extraordinary, imaginative and breathtaking.

And when they'd finished eating and drinking and their bodies were revived, they took pleasure in recreating a goodly number of those impassioned couplings—with intoxicating rapture and wildness, with irrepressible delight.

Chapter
11

Waking at dawn, Flynn carefully eased himself from bed.
Jo was deep asleep and if he didn't have a point of honor
to deal with, he would be as well. After quickly washing and
dressing, he walked the few blocks to Hazard's home and entered through the kitchen door. Waving away the few servants
who were up, he made his way to Hazard's office at the back of
the house. Hazard was an early riser; anyone who had done
business with him knew that.

Outside the closed door, Flynn ran his hands over his still-
damp hair, straightened the cuffs of his shirt, and briefly
wished he'd thought to put on some cologne. The scent of sex
was still pungent on his skin.

But he was here now; it was too late. And gossip concerning
Jo's whereabouts last night would have reached Hazard long
ago.

Raising his hand, he rapped in a brisk tattoo and opened the
door without waiting, without checking to see if Hazard had
company or more aptly a gun pointed at his head.

A fact he took note of a moment too late.

"Shut the door," Hazard said, brusquely as he entered the
room, the weapon in question pointedly within reach of
Hazard's clasped hands resting on his desktop.

"She's safe."

Hazard's brows rose infinitesimally. "I would hope so."

"She's sleeping. She didn't want me to come."

"But you were more sensible," Hazard murmured, his eyes flinty hard.

It wasn't an adjective often used to describe Flynn. "Yes."

"You sobered up?"

"I wasn't drunk."

Hazard tipped his head in the merest of movements. "I'm relieved."

"She asked *me*, not that I'm trying to avoid responsibility. I just wanted you to know I tried to say no. I actually *did* say no."

Hazard didn't answer for a very long time, his dark gaze unreadable. Then he unclasped his hands, leaned back in his chair and said with a soft sigh, "I gathered as much. Trey told me." He indicated Flynn sit with a jab of his finger at a nearby chair. "She's of age," Hazard noted with another small sigh, "and outside my control. That's not to say, I'm still not concerned about your . . . er . . . friendship"—his brows arched faintly—"for a variety of reasons. I think you know what most of them are as well as I do. The question is, what are you going to do now?"

"Make peace with you."

Hazard wore a white linen shirt open at the neck, the sleeves rolled up, well-worn cavalry twill trousers and moccasins. But regardless of his casual attire, no one would mistake him for anything but a man of authority. "And what about Jo?" he asked, flatly.

"I'll marry her if you wish." The answer slipped out, capricious and unforeseen, shocking Flynn as much as Hazard.

But Hazard's voice was mild as he spoke and his expression gave nothing away. "It's not what I wish. It's what Jo wishes. Did you ask her?"

"No."

"Do you want to?"

Perhaps still infatuated with the events of the evening past, Flynn heard himself say, "I wouldn't be averse."

Hazard's mouth quirked faintly. "She may not find that reason enough to marry you."

Reminded of the necessary courtesies, Flynn tipped his head. "I would, naturally, express myself in more suitable terms."

"I sure as hell would hope so." Hazard shoved the handgun aside and leaned forward slightly. "How long have we known each other—ten, fifteen years?"

Flynn nodded. Hazard had helped his father as well run off intruders on more than one occasion.

"I'm not saying I'm happy about what happened—with gossip being what it is in a small town. But Jo has a mind of her own as you may have noticed, she's a grown woman and I can't tell her what to do. If she wants to marry you after knowing you for less than a day, fine." Hazard smiled. "I rather doubt she will. But don't hurt her or you'll hear from me." Sitting back in his chair again, the man whose power extended throughout the territory, spread his hands wide in a benevolent gesture. "That's all I have to say."

"Thank you, sir. I appreciate it."

The men were a generation apart, but they shared an understanding that the world was far from benign if your skin was a shade different from the norm. And they'd fought to hold what was theirs for as long as they could remember. Both were well qualified to allocate lesser concerns to their proper place.

Flynn's relationship with Jo was not life or death.

And neither man was vulnerable to gossip.

"So you don't think she'd say yes?" Although Flynn had always prided himself on avoiding entanglements, he found himself mildly chagrined at Hazard's assessment.

"Don't take it personally."

"How else should I take it?"

Hazard looked at him from under his brows. "You don't seriously want to marry, do you?"

"Maybe, maybe not."

"Whatever you say," Hazard observed, kindly, knowing what it felt like to want what you want. "Why don't you go home, and bring Jo back for breakfast or lunch if you like. If you have an announcement to make, I'll be the first to congratulate you."

"She might not want to come."

Hazard's dark eyes were suddenly very direct. "Really."

"She said she wanted to stay with me as long as she could. She wants to come back to the ranch with me."

"Impossible." Hazard's tone was curt.

"I agree. I told her it was too dangerous."

"Those Empire boys are out for your skin," Hazard declared, brusquely. "I don't want her mixed up in that."

"Nor do I."

Hazard inhaled deeply, then spoke in a brisk, sharp cadence. "Bring Jo to dinner tonight." His gaze was chill. "Consider it a command performance. If she doesn't wish to come, bring her anyway. I want her to understand she is not to travel north with you under any circumstances. In all else, I'll indulge her whims. Are we clear on that?"

"Perfectly."

Hazard tapped his fingers on his desktop. "Good. Dinner's at eight."

Chapter

12

"You were *where?*" Jo exclaimed when Flynn returned to bed. Coming fully awake, she pushed herself up on her elbows and glared at him. "How dare you! I'm not some ingenue who needs protecting! I can take care of myself!"

"It was a courtesy call. I've known your father a long time."

She looked daggers at him. "And you men had to discuss my life as though I wasn't capable of making a decision without you. God, I hate that! As if my actions require male approval!"

"Calm down. We have an invitation to dinner. No one's upset."

"*I'm* upset in case you didn't notice! I'm *bloody damned well* upset! I don't want you interfering in my life!"

"You didn't seem to mind last night," he said with a faint smile.

"That's completely different and you know it." It wasn't fair that he was so flagrantly virile and so delectably naked; it made it so much harder to focus on her resentment.

"Darling, no one has to be angry about anything." He shifted slightly, half-turning in a tantalizing display of rippling muscle and long-limbed grace. "We're all alone; I sent the servants away this morning and if you get hungry"—his smile

held a lush insinuation that had nothing to do with food—
"Cook left some fresh blueberry scones and a lemon cake."

"Blueberry scones?" Jo murmured, wavering between possible gratifications. "Hot?"

"Hot," he whispered. "Like someone else I know."

"Don't you dare use sex and food to appease me." But the petulance had vanished from her voice.

"Which do you want first, as if I can't tell." He was already rising from the bed.

"Bring the lemon cake, too."

He turned back, magnificently nude, magnificently aroused, his brows arched in query. "All of it?"

"Oh my God," she whispered, feeling herself open in welcome, suddenly beginning to reconsider the importance of food.

His mouth curved upward in a lazy grin. "We don't have to leave the house until dinner at eight. There's plenty of time."

"So I can have scones, and *then* you'll entertain me?"

"At your service, darling."

She smiled. "You're still going to pay for your early-morning visit."

"We'll see."

"No, we won't."

"Let's discuss it after you eat."

The particular hushed quality of his voice when he said the word *eat* caused a tantalizing ripple of response deep inside her, as though her ravenous senses were immune to resentment. As though she had no control over her desire when he looked at her like that. "I should say no," she breathed.

"If you could," he said even more softly.

She threw a pillow at him, but he caught it deftly and set it aside. "If it's any consolation, darling, you're not alone in your feelings; I'm as insatiable. And even if you wanted to go, I wouldn't let you. That's why I had to talk to your father."

"And he allowed it?"

"I told him I'd marry you."

Her surprise almost instantly gave way to a look of displeasure. "Were you planning on asking *me* or have you men already sealed the bargain?"

"Don't get ruffled. As a matter of fact, your father said you wouldn't marry me."

"Really."

"Yes, really."

"Do I get an opportunity to voice my opinion?"

"Of course. Would you like to get married? I can be more poetic if you wish or get down on one knee and offer you my heart."

"It's not your heart I'm interested in, but thank you." In some irrational portion of her brain, a little voice was screaming, yes, but she'd not yet lost all sanity. "I have no interest in marriage."

He should have been relieved; if he wasn't still in full rut, he would have been. "Why not?" he inquired, gruffly.

"Because much as I adore your accomplished, dare I say, gifted sexual talents," she declared with lifted brows, "I don't consider that sufficient reason to marry someone I barely know."

His smile was wicked. "You know me better than most women in town."

"Very cute," she said with a mildness she thought commendable considering her heart was beating so rapidly there was a good possibility it might jump out of her chest. "Nevertheless, my observations on marriage—with the exception of my father and Blaze—don't recommend the institution. Marriage ensures neither love nor faithfulness and surely doesn't guarantee happiness, so why bother?"

"How cynical," he drawled.

She shrugged. "That may be, but you'll thank me when your brains are less addled by lust. Now, bring me my lemon cake and scones."

Overlooking the blow to his vanity, she was right, and for a frightful moment, he realized how perilously close he'd come to disaster. "Milk or tea?" he inquired pleasantly, as though they'd been discussing nothing more important than their breakfast menu.

"Tea, please, with milk." And when he looked pained, she said, "What?"

"Nothing."

"You can't make tea?"

"I'm half Japanese and half Irish. What do you think?"

"I think you like Japanese tea better—without milk. But seriously, Flynn, you can't mean with lemon cake."

"With anything, darling."

"With sex?" He was standing there gorgeously male, and suddenly sex and anything didn't sound so odd after all.

He grinned. "I've found the combination excellent."

And he was right. In fact, no matter what Jo ate that day and for some reason she was ravenous, sex was the natural accompaniment. They had sex before, during and after their lemon cake and scone breakfast. They had sex with their ham sandwiches at noon. They had sex with afternoon tea although it required a degree of dexterity since they were having tea in Flynn's splendid large marble tub. And again as they were readying themselves for dinner, although this time there was no food or tea involved. Flynn had sent for a local modiste and selected a gown for Jo despite her protest. His method of placating was particularly heated, and they arrived, breathless at the Braddock-Black mansion, only ten minutes late and only mildly disheveled.

Chapter

13

When they entered the drawing room, conversation abruptly ceased.

"He asked me to marry him. I said no. I hope that sufficiently clears the air." Jo looked up at Flynn and smiled. "He's very relieved, I might add."

"Not necessarily." Flynn's smile was affectionate.

"I, for one, *am* relieved," Hazard noted, drily. "No offense, Flynn."

"Amen to that," Trey muttered. "Not that I don't wish you the best, sis," he added, lifting his whiskey glass to her. "But you know what they say about marrying in haste."

"Or in your case, marrying at all," Daisy observed lightly.

"I'm too young."

"But not too young to put yourself in the way of a paternity suit or twenty."

"At least we don't have to worry about that with you."

"That will be enough, children," Blaze remarked with the casualness of much maternal refereeing. "I like your new gown, Jo. Is that Lucinda's design?"

Jo glanced at Flynn.

"Yes," he said, looking embarrassed. "She was kind enough to send it over."

"And that beautiful brooch. Is that new?" Blaze inquired, with a smile.

"Flynn had it. He gave it to me—it was his mother's. I shouldn't take it, but I love the sweep of the wings on the crane." She half shrugged and smiled up at Flynn again. "So I was greedy and took it."

"I didn't need it and Jo liked it"—Flynn met Jo's gaze for a heated moment—"and well . . . it seemed appropriate—I mean—"

"Come in and have a drink," Hazard interposed, saving Flynn from further explanation and embarrassment. "What can I get for you?"

Conversation at dinner was occasionally awkward, even though everyone tactfully skirted the fact that Jo had been absent a night and a day. The faintest hint of threat was perceptible beneath Hazard's bland demeanor, as if Flynn were still on probation. And when Hazard made it clear that the controversy between Flynn and his neighbors put the Sun River country out-of-bounds for Jo, she knew better than to argue.

With finesse, Blaze quickly steered the conversation toward less controversial topics, asking Jo about Florence, inquiring of Flynn how his parents had first come to Montana, bringing up the subject of territorial politics, which always elicited considerable interest. As active lobbyists, the Hazard-Blacks were instrumental in keeping the deprecations on the Absarokee reservation to a minimum. They also monitored any new mining laws that could be harmful to their investments.

"It wouldn't hurt you to come down for the sessions, Flynn," Hazard suggested. "It's a game, I know, but a useful one."

"Since Senator Bailey has an interest in the Empire, he's not likely to put his investment at risk, regardless of what I say or do."

"It depends how much he has invested," Trey observed. "Some of these grazing land disputes can be settled for the right sum."

"I shouldn't have to pay someone to stay off my land."

"You can take them to court, you know." Daisy tipped her head faintly, as though saying, "If you were a sensible man."

"That's a possibility." Flynn's tone was polite.

"Their inroads on your land are subject to reparations; the law is quite definitive."

Flynn smiled. "I'm sure you're right."

"You needn't look at me like that, Father," Daisy said, crisply, setting down her fork. "If this territory is ever going to become civilized, it's men like you and Mr. Ito who must set an example."

While Hazard recognized the logic in Daisy's argument, lawyers and courts were too slow to deal with the immediate crisis of armed marauders. "I remember when justice automatically meant a rope strung over a tree branch. Particularly if your skin was a shade darker, not that we've made much progress in that regard with the seven Indians hung on the Musselshell not too long ago. But, perhaps," he added, diplomatically, "with more good lawyers like you, Daisy, and better judges, at least the violence might be curtailed." His dark brows rose faintly. "Although, I'm not so sure."

"But you can't give up, Father." Daisy's voice took on an impassioned tone. "If we don't deal with criminals and tyranny within the framework of the law, there's no hope for a peaceful future. Do we keep shooting until everyone is dead?"

"I'm not sure an injunction will necessarily deter the Empire's illegal use of my grazing lands," Flynn asserted, although his recent attack on their home turf may have dissuaded them. "But if you'd like to represent me"—his smile was conciliatory—"we could test your premise." What did he have to lose?

"I'd like that very much." Daisy didn't quite smile, but it was clear she was pleased. "Thank you, Mr. Ito, for looking to the future."

"Call me Flynn, and I wish you luck."

"It's not a matter of luck, but of the law. Could you be in my office at ten o'clock tomorrow morning and we could begin?"

He knew what he'd prefer doing at ten o'clock tomorrow morning and it had to do with the lush beautiful woman at his side, but under the gaze of Jo's family, he understood there was only one possible answer. "Ten would be fine," he said.

"Would you mind if I tagged along?" Jo asked, her gaze shifting from Flynn to Daisy. "The legalities intrigue me."

"It's up to Mr. Ito—er . . . Flynn."

Flynn nodded. "Please do."

"If you need any help," Hazard said. "Of any sort," he added, the significance of his offer plain. "Just let us know."

"Those men running the Empire haven't quite come to terms with the fact that they're not in England anymore." Trey grinned. "Or that the quarterings on their family crests don't matter when you're looking down the business end of a revolver."

Hazard shot a glance at his wife. "Trey meant that in a hypothetical way," he said, giving his son a warning look.

"I was speaking in generalities, Mama," Trey said, with a disarming smile. "But you know what they're like. Those English lords talk to us as though we're native bearers."

"I agree some of them are beyond bearing. However," Blaze noted, "they're not worth dying over."

Which was the dilemma, was it not—that fine line between maintaining one's sovereignty and dying. Every man at the table understood the distinction.

"Daisy is here to see that we settle our disputes in a civilized way." Hazard's tone was soothing. "Starting with the Empire, right, Flynn?"

"Absolutely."

And the discrepancy between reality and admirable sentiment was smoothed over with well-mannered grace.

After dinner the ladies retired for tea or in this case, champagne, while the men, under express orders not to tarry long, stayed at the table for brandy and cigars.

Jo took the opportunity to offer her apologies to Blaze the moment they were alone.

"You needn't apologize," Blaze replied. "You're capable of making your own decisions. Although, I must say, your father is pleased now that you've taken what he views as a sensible course. He wasn't altogether certain you'd refuse Flynn's marriage proposal."

"Because of my mother, I suppose."

Blaze smiled politely. "I'm not sure."

"To be truthful," Jo said with a faint grimace, "I thought I might be very much like her when I practically carried Flynn away last night. I'm terribly embarrassed in hindsight; I've never done anything like that before."

"Why should only men be allowed to take the initiative." Daisy's cool gaze matched her voice. "It's not fair that we be required to sit demurely and wait for a man to take charge of our lives. So, you needn't apologize to me, although, allow me to reserve judgment on Flynn's propensity for violence."

"I'm not so sure his reputation wasn't imposed on him," Blaze pointed out. "Your father has had to fight more than his share of battles because of his Absarokee heritage. And the Empire is a vicious lot."

"That's true—and Flynn seems willing to try another course of action. Perhaps the stories are—"

"Much exaggerated, I'm sure," Jo interposed. "He's really very sweet."

Daisy politely curbed her response. Flynn wasn't known for his sweetness.

"He's charmed you, I see," Blaze murmured.

Jo arched her brows faintly. "I hope you're not going to say, like all the others."

"Very much *not* like all the others. He treats you altogether differently. He notices you for a start," Blaze said, a hint of amusement in her voice.

"Ah . . . so I've stepped from the amorphous ranks of eager

females," Jo remarked with a half smile. "How fortunate, since I feel as though I'm caught up in a tumultuous whirlwind. Not that I'm complaining. I might as well enjoy it while I may. We both have lives we must return to soon."

"How very practical. You and Daisy are much alike—able to see reality clearly." Blaze surveyed the young women fondly. "I find it commendable."

"Recognizing reality is a necessity in my profession. Engineering is factual and concrete."

"While the law is rife with equivocations," Daisy observed. "In my personal life, however, I prefer certainty."

"Which means Daisy has yet to meet the man who can sweep her off her feet in a whirlwind of any kind," Blaze teased.

"Nor will I," Daisy retorted. "I have no wish to be swept off my feet, thank you."

That topic—although less poetically defined—was being discussed over brandy in the dining room.

"When will you be returning to your ranch?" Hazard asked.

"In a few days," Flynn replied. "I can't be away for long."

"Have you told Jo?"

He hesitated. "Not in so many words . . ."

Trey grinned. "You haven't mentioned it."

"Not yet."

Hazard was lounging in his chair, but no hint of languor was visible in his gaze. His dark eyes were grave. "I'd appreciate your most courteous explanation when the time comes."

"Of course." Flynn ran his finger over the rim of his glass. "It's not as though this is normal for me . . . staying . . . I mean."

"No need to explain," Hazard murmured, eschewing unnecessary details with typical male restraint.

Trey grinned. "Damned if you aren't blushing, Flynn. I never thought I'd see the day."

"Screw you," Flynn muttered, but he was smiling.

"Another one bit the dust." Trey lifted his glass. "Hell, you almost got yourself married."

For the briefest moment, Flynn regretted he hadn't—a transient insanity quickly overcome. "I decided I didn't want you for a brother-in-law," he drawled.

"Or maybe Jo had more sense than you." Trey's silvery eyes were amused.

"Or maybe they both regained their sanity," Hazard noted, drily.

Chapter

14

The time and manner of Flynn's leave-taking was thrust upon him the next morning when one of his men burst into Daisy's office, red-faced from taking the stairs at a run.

"Empire burned down the barn—and stables!" he cried.

Flynn surged to his feet, his expression grim. "Were any of the men killed?"

Out of breath, his chest heaving, the cowboy shook his head.

"How many brood mares did we lose?"

"They got—most o' them out," the man panted. "But McFee thought—mebbe ten, twelve—was caught in the blaze."

"Have my mount brought up."

"Already done, boss."

"I'll be down in five minutes." Glancing at the clock, Flynn turned back to Daisy as his range hand exited the office. "Do you have enough information to get started on the case? I won't be back for some time."

"More than enough. If I have any questions, I'll send a messenger to the ranch."

"If you'll excuse us for a minute," he murmured, his voice almost inaudible.

But Daisy understood and quickly rose from her chair.

As the door closed on Daisy, Flynn found himself momentarily at a loss for words. "I'd planned on speaking to you at a more opportune time," he began, the hesitancy in his voice unmistakable. "Certainly not like this . . ." He cleared his throat. "What I mean to say—"

"I know," Jo said, kindly. "You have to go. I always knew you did."

"I was hoping to stay a few more days . . . explain to you with more gallantry"—he blew out a breath. "Obviously, that's not possible now."

"I understand, really, I do. How could you not leave under the circumstances."

"I appreciate your understanding." Touched by an unfamiliar pang of regret, when in the past taking leave of a woman had always been a relief, he found himself saying, "If you're planning on staying in Helena, please feel free to use my home. The staff is always there."

"I don't know if I'll be staying, but thank you." Jo half-lifted her shoulder in a negligent shrug. "I was going to say it depends on what my mother does, but perhaps she's old enough to manage her own life."

"I'd like it if you'd stay."

No doubt, but she didn't care to be a convenience. "My plans are uncertain." She shrugged again. "I've been away from Florence for some time."

He didn't know what he'd expected, but certainly not this casualness, as though she'd not heard his unprecedented offer, as though the sensational passion they'd shared was so commonplace it could be dismissed with a shrug. "Will you be going back to Florence?" His voice held a faint edge.

"Will you be going back to the Sun River?"

"I have to."

"Maybe I have to go back to Florence."

"Don't."

"Should I just wait here and hope you survive?"

He was comforted by her anger; that he understood. "You don't have to hope. I'll survive."

"Then I should just bide my time until your return."

He ignored her sarcasm. "I'll come back as soon as I can."

"How soon? Days—weeks . . . months?"

"I don't know," he said, a forced mildness to his voice. "When Empire decides not to kill me, I suppose."

"Perhaps I should take up embroidery in your absence and keep a lamp lit in the window?"

He frowned. "What do you want me to say?"

"Ask me to come along and don't say you can't." The mockery was gone from her voice. "I won't be in the way."

"Yes, you will," he replied, gruffly. "We're riding fast and they're going to be waiting for us. I can't put you in that kind of jeopardy."

"I ride well. I can shoot. The monks in Florence hunt; I'm the best shot in ten parishes."

"No," he said, blunt and hard. "I don't care if you're the best shot in all of Italy. Nor does your father."

"Then, maybe I won't embroider," she said, peevishly, annoyed with his misguided chivalry, more annoyed that he might be taking advantage of the situation to dismiss her like all the other women in his life. "Maybe I'll go dancing every night. Maybe I'll meet someone who surpasses you in bed . . . although you were quite extraordinary last night. Perhaps I'll just have to settle for second best."

His frown deepened. "You're beginning to annoy me. I have to go. I should have left five minutes ago."

"I'm sorry I'm not docile and obedient. What a shame for you. Do they always say, yes, Flynn, whatever you want, Flynn, how far should I spread them, darling Flynn?"

He crossed the distance between them in a second flat, gripped the arms of her chair and leaned in so close, she could count the painted quills decorating the collar of his leather jacket. "Go dancing every night," he growled, his long black hair framing the grim features of his face. "Do whatever you damned well please, but be warned—when I come back, I'll find you and drag you from whatever bed you're in."

"That depends, I suspect, on the man with me," she murmured, meeting his gaze with unflinching acrimony.

"You don't understand," he whispered, his fury barely restrained. "I'll take you away, *guaranteed.*"

"I may not be here." Cool as ice, she stared him down.

"Just make sure you stay." Abruptly straightening, he jabbed his finger at her. "That's an order."

"Go to hell."

"That's my plan. Now be a good girl," he murmured, silkily, "and behave yourself while I'm away."

An instant later he was gone and Jo was left trembling with rage. How dare he order her about as though she were another submissive female subject to his whims! Not likely that! Not in a million years! Not in ten million!

But regardless of her mutinous, hot-blooded temper, she was already feeling a sense of loss, as though he'd become an addiction in her blood and she was suddenly deprived. Softly swearing, she reminded herself that she was a rational woman and men like Flynn—too familiar with acquiescent women—were best forgotten. Furthermore, she had no intention of allowing herself to be added to his list of readily available, compliant females.

A fierce wave of longing suddenly overwhelmed her as though in willful contradiction and she fought down the urgent desire flaring through her body. So much for rational thought, she reflected, as images of Flynn in various guises of hot-blooded, rampant urgency made her shiver with excitement.

Dear God, how was she going to exist without the fierce pleasure Flynn dispensed so freely, so frequently—so exquisitely? How was she going to survive until he returned? Was it possible to be addicted to his touch? Or was she crazed?

Or was he just much too accomplished in bed for her peace of mind?

FORCE OF NATURE 97

Resentful of his virtuoso skills or perhaps only resentful of the other women on whom he'd bestowed them, Jo's expression was sullen as Daisy re-entered the office. "I hate him," she muttered.

Daisy smiled indulgently. "You didn't really think he'd take you, did you?"

"Yes—no"—Jo grimaced—"probably not, but that's not the point. I should have been given a choice. But what's much worse," she grumbled, "is the provoking fact that he may have spoiled me for other men."

"I doubt anything so drastic is at stake," Daisy replied, sitting down at her desk, surveying Jo tolerantly. "You've only known him for a few days." While sexual obsession wasn't in her nature, she wasn't unaware of the principle. "If it's any help to your sense of frustration, I can assure you, Flynn had no choice. The Empire wants his land and his life. He had to go."

"Oh, Lord! Will they actually kill him!" Shocked from her self-absorption, Jo imagined Death hovering over Flynn's head, sickle poised.

"They've been trying for a long time." Daisy lifted her hands as though in apology. "With luck, they won't. On the other hand, if we can make it markedly unprofitable for them in court, they might be inclined to give up."

"Might?" Jo's voice rose in alarm, issues of desire sublimated by more fearful considerations. "You never said might, before."

"I'm just realistic. The courts are extending their influence, but"—Daisy sighed—"the judges are unpredictable and at times, corrupt."

"Is it even possible to defeat the Empire in court? Tell me the truth."

"With the right judge, yes."

"Otherwise?"

"We appeal, of course."

"Please, let me help. I'd feel less guilty about my behavior

if you'd let me assist in some small way, although I still blame
Flynn completely. Tell me he has enough men to keep him
from harm. Don't look at me like that. I don't have to make
sense. I'm too distrait."

"Flynn and his men will be fine. They're very good at what
they do."

"Killing, you mean."

"Not always. But sometimes," Daisy said, guardedly, "it's
inevitable."

"I should apologize to him," Jo murmured. "I was outrageously rude when his ranch was in ruins and his future in
peril. And now it may be too late. Lord, Daisy, what if he
should—"

"He'll be back," Daisy said, firmly.

"You're just saying that to cheer me up."

"No, I heard him tell you he would." Daisy grinned.
"Something about dragging you out of bed."

Jo groaned softly. "I don't know why I was so insufferable."

"I'm sure he's had women disagree with him before. You're
not the first." Daisy spoke with a considered calm.

"Because there are always women, and he's always leaving?"

"Something like that. Flynn and Trey are in great demand
and it's not for their conversation. Although, if it's any consolation, Flynn didn't treat you like the others."

Jo's gaze was direct. "You've seen him often with other
women?"

Who in Helena hadn't, Daisy wanted to say. "Once or
twice," she said, instead. "He treated them quite casually, and
I know for a fact," she added with a playful smile, "he never
asked any of them to marry him."

"That was out of respect for Hazard," Jo mumbled. "He
wouldn't have otherwise."

"I'm not so sure."

"Really." Strange how even equivocation could be consol-
ing if you wished it to be. Stranger yet, why she needed con-

soling when the rational portion of her mind understood their liaison was just that and no more.

"I'd bet a new set of law books on it."

That sounded much more certain and jettisoning reason without a qualm, Jo smiled. "I'll send Flynn an apology with your messenger." Or, she suddenly decided, with the confident presumption that had always served her well, she might as well deliver her apology in person.

Chapter

15

"You are not to see that disreputable man again!" Lucy exclaimed later that day, stamping her silk-slippered foot on the Turkish carpet of the Plantation House's best suite. "I absolutely forbid it!"

"Your message said you wanted your accounts balanced." A task Jo had been managing since she was ten. "And even if I cared to wager a guess as to the identity of this disreputable man," she said, disgruntled and annoyed, not moving from her position just inside the doorway, "I'm well past the age when you can dictate to me."

"My accounts are fine," her mother said, dismissively, as though she'd not lured Jo to her suite on false pretexts. "I hear you've quite destroyed your reputation in this town and, I might add, compromised mine in the bargain!" Indignation rang through her voice. "That scoundrel, Ito, is *not* a gentleman and I forbid you to see him again! What will my friends think! How can I hold up my head at the Finnegans tonight?"

"Perhaps Ed Finnegan could speak on your behalf. I understand he's a frequent visitor to this suite. I'm sure he'd be willing to vouch for you to his friends," Jo noted, leaving out the comment concerning his wife she'd like to have added.

"How dare you imply Mr. Finnegan is anything but a very dear friend!"

"And how dare you imply *my* dear friends are any less acceptable than yours. Flynn Ito is ten times the man Ed Finnegan is . . . and richer too. That's all that matters to you, isn't it, Mother? Unless you can trade it for a handsome face. In my case, Flynn is both handsome *and* rich and he's asked me to marry him. Something I suspect, Mr. Finnegan won't be doing." Other than score a point in their argument, she had no idea why she'd mentioned marriage, particularly with a man like Flynn who was apt to turn and run if she said yes.

"You cheeky little tart, I have a good mind to wash your mouth out with soap! For your information, Mr. Finnegan is advising me on the purchase of some stocks!" Purse-lipped and flushed, Lucy added heatedly, "I should have known better than to think you'd take my advice!"

"Yes, Mother, you should have, because your advice, as you so loosely term it, always has to do with protecting your image or wanting me to participate in your latest scheme or substantiate your most recent slander. These little bits of advice you dispense never have anything to do with me. If you're truly concerned with your reputation in this town, my friendship with Flynn Ito is the least of your worries. I'd reconsider the number of other wives' husbands you have up for tea."

"Whom I entertain is none of your concern."

"Then you should understand my feelings. I'm twenty-two, Mother. I'm quite capable of making my own decisions. But if it will ease your mind, I won't be seeing Mr. Ito for some time." Vagueness was always appropriate when dissembling. "Apparently, a portion of his ranch has been set afire by the Empire Cattle Company. He's left Helena."

"Good riddance."

"You don't know him."

"I know of him and that's sufficient. He's a cutthroat thug."

"That's open to interpretation, but whatever he is, he's very wealthy—like Cosimo's father-in law who has an equally ambiguous reputation." Rumor had it the Cavallieri fortune had connections to the Naples underworld.

"Count Cavallieri has impeccable blood lines," Lucy replied, haughtily.

"Some might disagree. I wouldn't contemplate returning to Cosimo's bed if I were you. I hear the old count uses the Arno to dispose of his enemies."

Lucy turned ashen. "Where ever did you hear such rubbish?" Although, it might be wise to meet Cosimo in Monte Carlo or Paris should she choose to see him again, she quickly decided.

"I heard very specific stories, Mother. The maids know everything. You just never talked to them." If she had, she would have known that Cosimo was sleeping with sweet little Lucia who did their laundry and pretty Flora who helped in the kitchen. He was, if nothing else, an aristocrat of democratic tastes. "Are we done with the lecture now? Because I have another engagement." Another of those suitably vague phrases.

Lucy surveyed her daughter with a squinty-eyed gaze. "He's gone? This Ito man has left town?"

"Gone, Mother. Perhaps for good. You'll be happy to hear any number of fine upstanding Englishmen are out to murder him."

She sniffed. "You needn't be facetious."

"I'm not. Although I'm hoping mightily that he survives. And if I decide to accept his marriage proposal, you'll be the first to know." She couldn't resist a last little goad.

"Very droll, I'm sure," Lucy returned, surveying her daughter with a jaundiced eye. "Will you be living on a ranch in the wilderness, then?"

"I might."

"And I might be the next pope."

"You wouldn't be the first pope to enjoy the pleasures of the flesh."

"I don't appreciate your humor."

"I wasn't joking."

"I can see that you wish to be rude when I only have your best interests at heart . . . as always." Lucy's lower lip quivered as it did when she chose to play the noble, self-sacrificing mother.

Jo elected to be merciful and forbearing as usual. Her mother could no more help being self-centered and vain than she could sprout wings and fly. She was pretty, flirtatious and quite sure the world revolved around her. And if men liked her, she saw no reason she shouldn't profit from their interest. "Forgive me, Mother. I didn't intend to be rude. And Mr. Ito is gone now, so you needn't worry."

Lucy's expression lightened. "You see, darling. I do know best. You can be such a sweet girl when you want to. Haven't I always said so? And I just know you'll find a much more acceptable beau and all this rubbishy tittle-tattle will blow over like it always does."

This probably wasn't the time to point out to her mother that the tittle-tattle concerning her affairs was heating up. "I'm sure you're right, Mother." It was easier to agree; hadn't she always? There was little point in arguing with her mother in any event. Lucy had never been wrong.

She had better things to do than argue with her mother anyway.

She had to procure—surreptitiously, of course—a map and directions to Flynn's ranch.

Chapter

16

Flynn had sent scouts ahead on his swift ride north and the ambush he'd been expecting was reported to him as he and his men came up on the south fork of the Sun River. The Empire had upwards of a hundred men concealed in the alder bushes and cottonwoods lining the creek banks.

Which meant he and his small crew would have to swing clear around to the western boundaries of his land to avoid them. He had no intention of riding into an ambush.

He was tempted to pick off some of Empire's hired guns with the high-powered Winchesters they carried, but easy as it might be to use his enemies for target practice, it wasn't sensible to draw their attention. He and his men were badly outnumbered. Raising his hand, he pointed west, wheeled his mount, and lightly spurred his sleek paint. He and his men would take the long way home.

It was almost morning when they rode into the ranch yard, the charred remains of his barn and stables silhouetted against the pale dawn. Home was always his refuge though and he was glad to be back, even dead tired, even faced with certain conflict and an extensive job of rebuilding. He'd been raised here—on the best land in the territory, his father had always said. Perhaps his father was even right. But of one thing, Flynn was sure. Empire Cattle was going to rue the day they'd come to burn him out.

"Get some sleep," he said to his men as they rode past him on their way to the bunkhouse. And he thanked them all for their loyalty. Then, turning his horse, he rode toward the main house, wondering if he would be able to sleep with his thoughts in tumult. Should he attack or defend—where and when and how? How were his horses and cattle? Were they safe? How long would it take to bring in supplies and rebuild? But beneath the practicalities and strategy the constant, looping conundrum racing through his brain was the question of Jo's status. Would she stay or go? And what would he do if she left?

But the moment he lay down, he fell asleep. Two sleepless nights prior to his urgent journey home, no doubt, contributed to his instant slumber—as they did to the nature of his dreams. The romantic imagery was saturated with lush memories of Jo and of the passions they'd shared. It seemed not to matter that he was at risk, under possible attack, that a sensible man would have put aside desire and concentrated on survival.

Nothing mattered in his dream world, but fevered pleasure and blissful consummation. A faint smile graced his face as he slept.

Not so when he woke and heard the extent of the damage he'd sustained: three men with burns, one barn and two stables in ruins, fourteen horses dead, fifty injured. It was a daunting homecoming.

Over lunch, he and his foremen discussed their options.

"How many men are ready for battle?" Flynn asked.

"Eighty, eighty-five. We need to leave some men to ride herd on the cattle," McFee replied.

"We could call in thirty more from Kinnert's crew," another

of his men suggested. "They don't take kindly to the Empire either. Had too many of their fences cut."

"Are there men from other outfits we can trust?" Flynn could hire men like The Empire did, but guns for hire were a certain style of man; he preferred a degree of loyalty when he had his back to the wall. And after the latest attack on his ranch, he wanted unequivocal victory this time. He wanted to annihilate the Empire Cattle Company once and for all.

He was tired of fighting.

He wanted an end to the conflict.

He didn't want to raise children as he'd been raised—in the midst of continuous war. The moment the aberrant thought crossed his mind, he tried to discount it. Children were an anomaly in his world, the notion of a family, madness. But a second later he imagined having Jo with him, here, on his ranch and the degree of pleasure he felt couldn't be so easily discounted.

"How many rifles do we have?" he asked, brusquely, wrenching his mind back to the issues at hand, to survival. "And how's our ammunition supply?"

Before long, a battle plan had been devised and riders had been dispatched to bring in the men they'd need to supplement their crew. If the Empire didn't attack first, they'd ride out in two days, burn the Empire Cattle Company to the ground, dispose of their hired guns and send the blue-blood managers back to England dead or alive.

In a more perfect world, such violence wouldn't have been necessary. Flynn's neighbors would have stayed within the boundaries of their ranches, and the best grazing land in Montana wouldn't have been coveted by those who had no right to it.

But since that ideal world didn't exist, he would need well over a hundred men, triple that number of weapons, several thousand rounds of ammunition, and collective cool nerve and deadly aim to right those imperfections.

Then perhaps someday, he *could* raise a family in peace.

[""]

*   *   *

While Flynn and his men were planning their strategy, Hazard was facing Trey across the broad expanse of his desk.

"Are you sure those gunmen were bound for the Empire?"

"Reilly usually gets his facts straight. They were asking directions for the Empire when they got off the train. Had prime horseflesh with them, too, he said. Those mounts were taken off with scrupulous care. One of the gunmen threatened to shoot anyone who caused them harm."

"The men came in from Wyoming?"

"That's what Reilly said. The Diamond Bar west of Cheyenne runs a rough crew. He was guessing they'd been recruited there."

"The Diamond Bar is another English-owned outfit as arrogant as the Empire," Hazard noted. "They called Tom Burley a nigger at the Cattleman's Club in Cheyenne. Hell, Tom is ten shades lighter than we are. But I guess they don't like dark Irish either."

"And you're thinking about teaching them some manners."

"I'm just thinking Flynn could use some help if the Empire is bringing in trash from Wyoming."

"When do we leave?"

"Late tonight or tomorrow morning. I have to talk to your mother."

Trey grinned. "Good luck."

Hazard smiled. "It's not luck so much as diplomacy that's required. And your mother understands. She would prefer a reasonable solution, of course, as would I. I've never understood why people can't stay on their own land."

"If we knew the answer to that, we wouldn't have to fight to hold our properties, would we?"

"Maybe someday," Hazard said with a sigh. "And in that more charitable future, Daisy might have her wish and the courts can deal with men like those at the Empire."

"In the meantime," Trey murmured, a sardonic edge to his voice, "I'll make sure my Colts are well oiled and loaded."

* * *

"Must you, Jon?" Blaze set her coffee cup down and gazed at her husband over the debris of their luncheon.

"If the Empire is bringing in hired guns from out of state, they're serious. Flynn's going to need our help."

"I thought he had enough men of his own."

"If he doesn't need us, we'll come back."

"When are you leaving?"

"Soon. Late tonight."

"You're already packed, aren't you?"

"I wanted to talk to you first."

"And if I were to say, don't go?"

"Darling, please, you know how important it is to protect one's borders. We've been fighting this battle for years."

She gave him a rueful smile. "You'll be careful, won't you?"

"We always are. Trey and I are bringing thirty men with us—enough to ride north unmolested."

"And Jo likes Flynn, doesn't she?"

"It looks that way. Another reason to help him, I thought."

Chapter

17

Jo had been on the stage to Great Falls for some time when Hazard and Trey discussed their plans, and when Hazard spoke to Blaze at lunch, Jo was enjoying the scenery outside the post stop at Guthrie's store. The map she'd purchased yesterday was carefully folded in her purse, her new saddlebags were piled into the baggage compartment of the stage and she'd been pleased to find that her riding clothes hadn't caused a single raised eyebrow. Her fellow passengers saw nothing amiss for a woman traveling to her ranch to be dressed for riding. Although she'd had to lie about her destination, choosing a vague locale east of Great Falls and hoping no one was overly familiar with the area. But the two salesmen and the elderly lady weren't from Montana. The young couple with them were newlyweds and too much in love to notice anyone; they could barely keep their hands to themselves.

At their most blatant displays of affection, Jo would stare fixedly out the window, struggling to restrain her own desperate longing. Although, in her more rational moments, she chose to characterize her trip north simply as one of apology. That most would view travel into an embattled area as inconsistent with personal safety, she chose to ignore.

Perhaps she had more of her mother's personality than she

acknowledged, for she was intent on having her way. Had she
known her father better, she would have understood that her
heritage precluded a cautionary nature. It would have soothed
her occasional qualms on that long journey to know that natural selection had long ago marked her as headstrong.

Hell-bent as she was to reach Flynn's ranch, she wasn't fool-
ish enough to venture into the wilds unescorted. At Great
Falls, she hired a horse and a guide at the livery stable, the
story she concocted having to do with meeting friends on the
upper reaches of the Sun River. Already late for her rendezvous, she explained, she'd prefer traveling at night if possible. Since she was willing to pay well, her guide saw no reason
to refuse the generous fee.

They left Great Falls at twilight.

The moon was full; the trail well lit.

And Flynn was waiting, Jo reflected with buoyant spirits.

The same moon illuminated Hazard's route as he and his
party left Helena that evening.

It shone as well on Daisy as she walked home after a long
day at the office. Surprised to see her house so well lit, she recognized something was amiss even before she found Blaze
waiting in her parlor.

"Jo's not with you?" Blaze rose from her chair, her anxiety
obvious.

"I thought she was with you. She was going to help me with
Flynn's case, but when she didn't come in, I thought she'd decided to attend Adelia's musicale with you instead."

Blaze frowned. "I haven't seen her all day. Do you think she
spent the day with her mother?"

"Would you like *me* to call on Lucy and save you the aggra-
vation?"

"Of course, I would." Blaze made a moue. "But with your
father gone, the responsibility is mine."

"Do you know if either Father or Trey saw Jo today?"

Blaze shook her head. "I didn't think to ask them before they left. I assumed she was with you."

"Why don't we check with the servants first. If they don't know where Jo is, time enough then to speak to Lucy."

"How clever you are," Blaze declared, clearly relieved. "Jo may have spoken of her plans to Mary."

Jo's lady's maid, however, hadn't seen her all day. "She told me last night she was going to see Miss Daisy, ma'am, bright and early in the morning, so I didn't worry none when she was gone before breakfast."

"And I thought she'd stayed with her mother when I didn't see her this morning," Blaze remarked, worry creasing her brow. "I'm afraid we'll have to pay a visit on Lucy."

"You've lost my daughter! Is that what you're telling me? I can't believe it!" Lucy shouted, her eyes flashing like the new diamonds she wore with her new evening gown and new shoes and everything from the skin out that had been purchased with Hazard's money. "You have the nerve to come here and inform me that you've misplaced my daughter!" She jabbed her closed fan at Blaze. "This is outrageous!"

"We thought she might be with you," Daisy interposed, moving forward enough to force Lucy and her eye-level pointed fan to retreat a step.

"Well, obviously she isn't! As you see!" Lucy exclaimed, in high dudgeon, sweeping her arm back and forth across the room. "I insist on seeing Hazard this instant! Do you hear me? This instant!"

"He's ridden north." Blaze spoke mildly, trying to maintain some semblance of civility when she was sorely tempted to rip Lucy's fan from her jeweled fingers and beat her with it. "I don't expect him back for some time. Did you see Jo at all today? Perhaps this morning?"

"No, I did not," Lucy snapped. She never rose before noon, a fact she chose not to mention. "I want Hazard back in

Helena," she commanded as though she had the right. "Send him word; I want him back immediately. I *need* Jo's father at my side with heartbreaking news like this." Her voice trembled slightly at the last as she slipped into a distraught mother mode. "Tell him, our baby is gone!" she sobbed, forcing out a single tear for effect, pressing her hand to her breast with born stage presence, showing off her new emerald ring in the bargain. "Giuseppina's in some terrible, terrible danger, I just know!" she wailed.

Gritting her teeth, Lucy's theatrics difficult to stomach, Blaze spoke with as much composure as she could muster when she wanted to do bodily harm to Lucy Attenborough or put her on the next train, whichever would be most conducive to her peace of mind. "We'll send our men out to search for Jo," she said instead, the strain in her voice evident. "As soon as I know anything, I'll see that you're informed."

"I'll never, never forgive you for losing my baby," Lucy cried, falling back onto the sofa in an exaggerated swoon, sobbing as though her heart was breaking. "Never, never, never . . ."

Exchanging pained glances, Blaze and Daisy left Lucy to her histrionics.

"She wouldn't want to actively join in the search," Daisy cynically said as they walked from the hotel.

"Jo has essentially raised herself, I understand. Why start at this late date to be a mother," Blaze noted with disdain.

"Men," Daisy muttered in disgust.

Blaze pursed her lips. "I agree. At times like this I'd like to slap your father silly."

"What in the world did he ever see in her?"

"Surely you're not that naive."

Daisy slanted a glance at her stepmother. "You're very understanding."

Blaze smiled. "Your father's had to do penance on more than one occasion since Lucy arrived. And very nicely, I might add. But I didn't know him then and the past is the past. What we must do right now is find Jo. We can deal with Lucy later."

As soon as they arrived at the Braddock-Black home, they gathered a search party and a short time later, their servants set out to comb the town.

Blaze and Daisy set about exploring Jo's room in hopes of finding some indication of her whereabouts.

Jo had few personal belongings on display, even her wardrobe was scant despite Blaze's urgings. But tucked under the stationary in the desk drawer, Daisy found an account ledger and some recent receipts that had been slipped inside.

"An engineer's sensibility," Daisy murmured, surveying the small neatly written columns of numbers in the book recording Jo's expenditures. She held up the receipts not yet entered. "A map of Montana purchased at Harold Lloyd's, another from Mercer's Saddlery for saddlebags and a third for a Colt revolver from Sackett's."

"Are you thinking what I'm thinking?" Blaze asked, softly.

"Of course."

"She's like her father," Blaze said with a sigh. "Without fear."

"And as stubborn," Daisy added. "I should have suspected this. She and Flynn argued before they left. He wouldn't take her with him."

"So she went herself."

"Obviously." Daisy pursed her lips. "The question is when and how."

When they inquired of the grooms though, none of them had seen Jo take a mount that morning. Neither had she rented a horse at the livery stable when they asked. The stage office was closed at that hour, but George Parsons was still up when they reached him at home. He remembered selling Jo a ticket to Great Falls. "She didn't say she were Hazard's daughter. If I'd known, Mrs. Braddock-Black . . ." His voice trailed off in unease; Hazard was a man who generated a degree of fear.

"You couldn't have known, George," Blaze assured him. "Nor can you inquire after every passenger's motives."

"Sure enuf, there, ma'am," he answered with a modicum of relief. The frontier attracted people who wished to escape the complications of their past; it wasn't prudent to ask a person's last name. "The lady was right polite though, spoke real quality-like. That's why I remember where she were goin'. Thought she might be the new school marm up that way. She's there by now, though," he noted with a nod in the direction of Great Falls. "That stage gets in round supper time."

After thanking the ticket agent for his information, Blaze and Daisy took their leave.

"Jo could be at Flynn's by now," Daisy remarked, trying to be reassuring as they began retracing their steps home.

"God willing and the Empire boys notwithstanding," Blaze murmured, her face grave. "Your father and Trey left too late to be of help," she added, biting her bottom lip.

"Jo has a weapon."

"We can only pray she doesn't need it. One woman against who knows what," Blaze noted, nervously. "I wish your father hadn't taken most of his men."

"Jed and Matt are here. They're good trackers. Although, in all likelihood, Father will reach her first, or better yet, she's already at Flynn's," Daisy murmured.

And neither woman cared to contemplate the alternatives.

"We have to tell Lucy," Blaze said, tersely.

"Brace yourself for another tirade," Daisy warned.

But when they reached the Plantation House, the anguished mother they'd so recently witnessed in full tragic form had gone out for the evening.

"She must have recovered from her swoon," Daisy observed, drily.

"How fortunate for us," Blaze briskly said. "We'll leave a note. And if Lucy cares to reach us tonight for more details, she can come to the house."

"Ten dollars says she won't."

"A thousand dollars says she won't. The Finnegans are having a dinner and dance and she and Ed are *very* close, I hear."

"But then Mabel Finnegan has taken an interest in the church choir of late, I understand," Daisy noted with a quirked grin. "The new choir director has more than a fine voice, rumor has it."

"My goodness—*Mabel?*" Blaze looked shocked.

"Who would think," Daisy replied, smiling faintly.

"I can't say she doesn't deserve a bit of fun in her life. Ed's never home."

"Which fact allows for private choir lessons in Mabel's parlor, I'm told."

"My word," Blaze breathed, the image enough to leave one speechless.

Chapter
18

When Jo estimated they were nearing Flynn's ranch, she offered up a long, perhaps slightly too loud, plaintive sigh that pricked up her horse's ears and caused it to whinny back. But intent on her plan, she ignored the fact that her acting was less than professional and said in a less dramatic fashion, "I'm completely exhausted. Is it much farther to the rendezvous?"

Her guide shot her a glance. The truth was not likely to get him his remaining fee, which was to have been paid when they reached their destination. "Mebbe another hour—more likely two," he said about the four-hour ride.

"Oh, dear. Is there a ranch nearby where we might stop?" Jo spoke in a small wispy voice. "Even a brief rest would help."

Her guide hesitated, weighing the danger of approaching Flynn Ito's in the dead of night.

"Surely, there must be somewhere we could find accommodations," Jo insisted, reining her horse to a stop and sighing again.

Her guide brought his mount to a halt. "I don't know, lady." He frowned. "The people round here are apt to shoot first and ask questions later."

"If you could just point me in the right direction," she said, her tone soft with appeal. "I'm sure they won't shoot a lady."

Considering Flynn's reputation with the fair sex, she just might just be closer to right than wrong. "Tell you what." Caution colored every nuance of Howard Nagel's tone. "If'n you don't mind ridin' a piece on your own, I could take you as fer as Flynn Ito's fence line."

"I would be *ever* so grateful." Jo's smile required no pretense, but for good measure she added a further embellishment as stage prop to her artifice. "Do you think my friends may have sought shelter with this Mr. Ito as well?"

"Doubt it, ma'am. He don't take kindly to strangers ridin' in."

"In any event," she said with genuine delight, "if you'd be so kind as to show me the way, I'll take my leave of you there."

"It's a fer piece yet."

"How far?"

"Mebbe five mile or so to the ranch once we reach the fence."

After traveling for hours, surely she could manage a few miles more. "I'll be perfectly fine," she pleasantly said. "Why don't I follow you," she suggested, waving him on.

When they reached the barbed-wire boundary of Flynn's land, a broad valley lay before them in the moonlight, spreading out as far as the eye could see, a silvery ribbon of river visible in the distance.

"That's it, ma'am." Her guide pointed to a barely perceptible flicker of light. "Sun River Ranch. You still got time to change your mind."

"I appreciate your help, Howard, but I'll be quite safe, I'm sure."

"Suit yerself, ma'am." In Montana Territory, it never paid to get too personal. No questions asked was the golden rule.

"Thank you very much for your help," Jo said, handing him the rest of his fee.

"Thank *you*, ma'am." With a dip of his head, he turned his

horse and rode away with a clear conscience and the most money he'd ever earned for half a day's work.

Jo's bay took the fence with a hunter's spring, clearing the top wire with a foot to spare. But the moment she landed on Flynn's land, three riders, one of them an Indian, appeared seemingly out of nowhere and she realized Howard knew of what he spoke. Flynn didn't take kindly to strangers.

"Lookin for someone, ma'am?" It wasn't a polite question and the rifle the man speaking had trained on her was cocked.

"Yes, I am," she replied, careful to use a courteous tone, conscious of the precariousness of her position. "Mr. Ito is a friend of mine."

"He prefers ladies wait for an invitation," the man said gruffly.

"I've come all the way from Helena today. I'm sure if you asked him, he'd want to see me."

The moon was so bright, she could see the three men's eyes as they appraised her, and she caught no glimpse of benevolence.

"I met Mr. Ito at Stewart Warner's dinner," she went on in explanation, feeling a need to breach the uncompromising silence.

The man with the rifle nodded. "Could be."

"He told me about the fire." Three glances narrowed and she realized she may have made a mistake. They were contemplating whether she was a spy for the Empire. "Please, I've been on the road all day. Ask Flynn if he knows me. If he doesn't, let him decide what to do."

The lengthy silence was broken only by the swish of the horses' tails, the men's scrutiny unwavering.

"You have to give up your weapons," the leader finally said. It was a brusque, curt command augmented by three rifles held high and directed at her head.

She quickly complied, handing over her Colt that hung from the gun belt on her saddle horn.

The man who had done the speaking motioned for her to fall in beside him and they all rode in silence toward the lights.

When they reached the ranch house, the men dismounted and signaled her to do the same. Without speaking, they indicated she follow them as they ascended a short flight of steps leading onto a porch that stretched the length of the facade. With the shadowed porch and sense of complete isolation, the heavily armed men crowded around her suddenly took on an ominous note.

As they came to a halt before a heavy timbered door, the leader knocked in a sharp staccato rhythm that may have been a signal.

The sound of boot heels crossing the floor echoed in the quiet of the night.

Jo's heart began beating furiously. For the first time since she'd left Helena, she questioned the intelligence of her plan.

The door swung open slowly.

"This here lady says she knows you, boss."

The light was behind him so Flynn's face was in shadow, but his eyes gleamed with a sharp and lucid animosity. "She does, does she?"

His low growl came from deep in his throat; the harsh, disobliging tone so striking, one of the men immediately seized Jo's arm and began dragging her away.

"Flynn! For God's sake!" Jo cried, struggling to dislodge the man's rough grip as he pulled her toward the stairs. "You can't do this! Tell them you know me! Flynn, damn you, say something or my father will have your head!" she yelled, scrambling to secure whatever leverage she could against Flynn's cold gaze.

"Let her go." The words were without inflection.

"I should hope so," she blustered, shaking off her captor's hand, stalking back to the opened doorway and gazing up at Flynn with blazing eyes. "Who the hell do you think you are!"

"Someone a lot bigger than you," he said in that same neutral tone.

"I'm not afraid of you!"

"You're on my land and my porch—a helluva long way from Helena—and if you had half a brain, you'd have sense enough to shut the hell up."

"I don't have to shut up. For your information, I came up here to apologize, but believe me, I won't now! In fact, I don't ever want to see you again!" Spinning around, she began to stalk away.

She didn't see the faint nod of Flynn's head dismissing his men, no more than she heard his footsteps as he overtook her. But she heard his voice in her ear when he said, "You'll get lost at night, you little bitch," and she felt his hands close around her waist and lift her off her feet.

She was kicking and squirming and screaming at the top of her lungs as he carried her at arm's length before him into the house. Once inside, he dropped her so abruptly, she gasped and waved her arms wildly trying to keep her balance.

Shutting the door, he stood quietly as she found her footing, waiting for her attack. But she brushed her hair back from her face instead and stomped her boots to shake down her riding skirt, a small cloud of dust settling on his carpet with her effort. Then she straightened her belt and shirt cuffs and collar as though it mattered what she looked like at one in the morning in the middle of nowhere. When she finally looked up, her gaze was cool. "I hope you're more gracious to your other guests."

"If I invite them, I am. No one invited you."

"Nevertheless, I'm here."

"So I see."

"You needn't be so rude."

"Pardon, me, who was just screaming at me and trying to unman me with her boot heels?"

"I expected you to be more pleasant."

"And I expected you to stay in Helena."

She looked sheepish for a transient moment before changing her mind, her gaze altering before his eyes into her more familiar straightforward directness. "I felt I should come and apologize for arguing with you in Daisy's office."

"But you forgot about the apology," he murmured sardonically. He knew why she'd come, but regardless she was tempting, she was damned inconvenient at the moment.

"You can be extremely irritating; you know that, don't you?"

"If only you could have recalled my imperfections while you were still in Helena and sent me a note instead."

"I won't be in the way."

"You're already in the way." He'd have to delay his attack while he sent her back and hope like hell the Empire didn't strike in the interim.

"I don't know how you can say that. Your house is so large, you won't even know I'm here."

"Jesus, Jo, could you be any more naive? Yes, I'll very much know you're here because my cock is at full attention whenever you're within ten miles. But my lust aside, this isn't a good time. I told you that in Helena. The Empire might attack any moment. This isn't a fucking game—it's real life; people get hurt. I don't want you to be one of them."

"I'm sorry."

"That doesn't help," he curtly said, trying to think of something other than the exquisite feel of her hot cunt closing around his cock. "I'm going to have to have you escorted home through a countryside crawling with my enemies which overrides about ten thousand sorrys."

"Let me stay," she said as if he'd not spoken. "You look tired."

"I am. You still can't stay."

"I could help you sleep."

He rolled his eyes. "I don't think so."

"I'll be good."

"I'm not interested in good women. Never have been. You're going back."

"Damn you, Flynn, stop being so boorish and rude. I've been on the road all day and half the night, I'm dead tired and all I want is a bath, something to eat and a soft bed to lie on." Her bottom lip began to tremble and her eyes welled with tears. "And if you wish to continue to harangue me, you can do so in the morning."

He tried not to be affected by her distress. He tried not to notice how beautiful she looked even through a layer of trail dust. He definitely tried to blot out any thoughts of her eager, hot-blooded passions. And if her tears hadn't spilled over, he told himself, he might have succeeded. But they did or perhaps he wasn't yet completely delusional about his ability to withstand her allure. "Don't cry," he murmured, reaching her in two swift strides. "Hush, darling," he whispered, pulling her into his arms. "Everything's going to be all right."

The platitude echoed in his brain—jarring and ridiculous— but the lush feel of her effectively stilled his reservations and even the callous savagery of the world and their irreconcilable differences were eclipsed by the wave of happiness that engulfed him. And for those transient moments, he was able to forget what lay before him, what he had to do tomorrow or the next day, how she couldn't be a part of his life in this perilous time.

Her cheek lay against his chest, her body melted into his and she held him tightly, as though the tenacity of her grip would ensure he stay. "Tell me you're happy that I came," she whispered, looking up at him with soulful eyes.

"How could I not," he said softly.

"Then I can stay?" A plaintive, small query so out of character, the words stayed in her brain as though burned there with fire. But she waited for his answer, desperately waited, feeling as though her life depended on it.

When he didn't reply, she said, "Please," in a breathy little sob and he couldn't refuse even while he knew he should.

"For tonight," he consented, unable to send her away.

Understanding she daren't ask for more, she said, "Thank you."

He smiled for the first time since his return to his ranch. "You're the pushiest little bitch I've ever met."

"You like me anyway."

He grinned. "Unfortunately, yes."

"I know," she said with a happy smile. "And I like you enough to travel all this way to hear you say disagreeable things to me."

"We'll call a truce tonight," he whispered, dipping his head, brushing her lips with his in the lightest of kisses.

"I'll take whatever I can get," she breathed.

His smile was instant and very close. "I can help you there."

"I rather thought you might. I expect a special reward for traveling so far."

"How special?"

"All night special."

He glanced at the clock, decided he could sleep some other time and said, hushed and low, "I just happen to have a night free."

"Do we have a bedroom?" she inquired, playfully, surveying the room. "Although, in my current state of sexual deprivation, that couch will do."

"It's not big enough," he replied with the practicality of a large man who also happened to have more in mind than a quick fuck.

"Ummm . . . I like the sound of that."

His grin was wicked. "Little tart."

"Actually, a very dusty tart. Would a bath be out of the question?"

A short time later, Jo was eating a roast beef sandwich Flynn had made for her since his cook was sleeping, a glass of wine was beside her on the small bench and she was watching him set out soap and small wooden tubs in his Japanese bath-house. The building had been constructed over a natural hot springs, the weathered wood smooth as silk, the slatted floor and tub surround beautifully joined with an artisan's eye for wood grain. A folding screen of glass overlooked a small walled garden, the early-spring flowers pale and fragrant in the moonlight.

"It's beautiful," she said. "We don't have anything so gorgeous in Florence."

"Bathing in Japan is steeped in tradition and ritual. It's about entering quiet spaces, relaxing at the end of the day, cleansing one's soul. Father was fortunate to find this hot spring. One reason, I suspect, he wanted this land."

"This experience might turn out to be the highlight of my trip," she said, smiling. "The tub looks large enough for—"

"Eight."

"Don't say that. I'm insanely jealous." She doubted he'd bathed with seven men.

Communal bathing was normal in Japanese households, but he chose not to explain. And in honesty he couldn't deny her assumption. "I've been told it holds eight," he corrected, gallantly.

"That's better. And I've been told you're a virgin."

His gaze flicked up and met hers in a flash of surprise. Then he dipped his head and said, soft as velvet, "Yes, ma'am."

"How did that happen . . . a handsome man like you?"

"There's no women out here on the range, Miss Attenborough. At least, not until you arrived," he added, softly.

It was astonishing how comforting a lie could be. "So you've never seen a nude woman."

His mouth twitched, but he repressed his smile. "No, ma'am."

"Would you like to?"

"Are you offering?" His sham modesty vanished, replaced by a hot fevered impatient glance.

"I might be," she said, a tiny shiver racing up her spine.

"You have some reservations?"

His artless charm restored, he looked at her with such innocence, she wondered for a moment whether she'd imagined
the heat in his eyes. "I wouldn't want the others to know," she
replied, trying to assess his mood.

"My men?"

"Anyone. A woman has her reputation to consider."

"You worry about that a lot, do you?"

"Are you being impertinent?"

"Just asking, ma'am."

"If you must know, yes, I do. I worry about my reputation."

It took enormous self-control to suppress the comment that
came to mind in light of their first meeting. "You can trust my
discretion, ma'am," he said instead.

"I'm glad to hear that, Mr.—"

"Flynn. Call me Flynn."

"You don't look Irish."

"You don't either."

"Mr. Flynn, someone is going to have to teach you some
manners."

"I'm sorry, ma'am. We speak our mind out here."

"A certain chivalry is required when conversing with a
lady."

"I see. Would you like more wine, ma'am?"

"Exactly. How quick you are, Mr. Flynn. And yes, I would."

He filled her glass and then stood before her as though
waiting.

"Is there something you'd like to say?"

"The water's about ready."

"About?"

"If you'd like to undress, I meant."

He spoke with a curiously tantalizing deference as though
he were in fact sexually unawakened. "You're very good," she
murmured, smiling.

"How would you know?" Enticing promise underscored his
words.

"I will soon enough."

"If I allow it."

This time it was her eyes that widened in surprise. "Would you refuse me?"

He shrugged. "I might."

"I can see why you're a virgin, Mr. Flynn. You can be very disagreeable."

"But not so disagreeable as to cause you to leave," he murmured.

Jettisoning any further attempt at play, she gazed at him with resignation. "You really don't want me here, do you?"

"Have I been obtuse somehow?" Each word was pointedly blunt.

Leaning back against the wall, she looked up at him from under the veil of her lashes, suddenly weary beyond measure of his resistance. "Must we continue to fight? Please, Flynn, when I've come so far?"

"You should have stayed in Helena." Hard reality kept getting in the way of the most wishful fantasies.

"But I didn't."

"And I'm supposed to gracefully accept Jo Attenborough doing what she wants regardless of the consequences?"

"I'm sorry, truly I am." She spoke very softly, unable to dredge up any more resentment, worn-out and disheartened. "I shouldn't have come."

She looked so forlorn, a small voice inside his head, said, "The hell with reality." And in his heart of hearts where logic didn't prevail, where the Empire wasn't out for his blood, he wanted her to stay. For a moment more, the rational part of his brain held back the tidal wave of emotion flooding his senses, sexual desire rampant in the forefront. And then he gave in, or perhaps he'd already done so when he'd carried her into his home. "Does that mean we're done playing?" he lightly teased—to hell with reality.

She nodded, glumly. "You're not as much fun as I remembered."

He laughed. "Then I should apologize, surely."

"Damn right you should." But her tone was quiet and low rather than explosive, her eyelids heavy with sleep.

He glanced at the steaming tub, at his house guest about to give way to slumber. "Are you going to stay awake long enough to bathe?"

"No." A barely audible sound.

"I must be losing my touch," he drolly noted.

But she didn't hear him because she'd dozed off. Fortunately *his* reflexes were wide awake because it required quicksilver speed to catch her as she fell from the bench. Swinging her up into his arms, he marveled at the sudden joy flooding his senses at so simple an act as holding her. He'd spent a lifetime studying kendo, the way of the sword, living a warrior's life, cultivating the discipline and vigilant skills that maintained his freedom and protected his land. And now for this, for this moment of tenderness, for the caress of this woman, he was willing to overlook the army poised to destroy him. Calling himself every kind of fool, he shook his head as though to dislodge the rash feelings she evoked. But she suddenly opened her eyes, smiled at him and threw her arms around his neck. Before he could return her smile, she was fast asleep again and he was left reeling.

He knew lust and this wasn't it.

This was terrifying.

But it was also so glorious, he felt invincible.

Which might be useful under the circumstances, he thought derisively.

He undressed her, himself as well, and holding her in his lap sat on one of the low stools and, scooping water from the tub with one of the wooden buckets, poured it over them. He scooped out enough water to rinse the dirt from their bodies and then coming to his feet, carried Jo with him into the tub. Slowly lowering them into the warm water, he held her while they soaked and he marveled at the tranquility that overtook him, how vital this woman he barely knew had become to him. The moon was bright in the sky, the scent of pine pungent and fresh, the purple shadows of night surrounded them. His mind was clear as though the sacred *Yu* had cleansed his understanding and for these moments he and she were alone in the mists of night, bound by some enchantment—far from his enemies.

But an owl hooted in the distance, as if in warning and he was reminded of what lay before him. Lifting her from the tub, he sat down once again on the stool and washed her, shampooed her hair, rinsed away the soap with such gentleness she only stirred from time to time.

Returning to the tub for a last soak, the water felt smooth and silken, and his muscles and nerves once again released their tensions—the ugliness of the world drifting away like ripples on the water. They had tonight at least, he told himself, there was no point in accelerating the onset of morning. On this moonlit night, they had these rare moments of *sukinshippu*, the intimate bond of skin-ship, sharing of a bath and perhaps understanding.

If he had been told even a week ago that he'd be bathing a woman with no ulterior motive other than unaffected kindness and friendship, he would have scoffed. Women were for pleasure—his pleasure—and while he was an accommodating and indulgent lover, self-interest was his prime motive. But tonight was different. Sound was muted, what was sexual and sensual merged in quietude; they were bound in a luxury of feeling, ephemeral and fragile. A rare happiness stirred inside him, and if it were possible he would have stopped time.

He knew better of course and with a small sigh, he rose from the tub, wrapped her in a blanket and carried her to his bed. He lay down beside her—saintly and serene, perhaps noble, disinclined to wake her when she was sleeping so peacefully.

There was no explanation for his conduct, no yardstick in his past against which to measure his benevolence. Lying propped on one elbow, he watched her sleep, no longer questioning his behavior, content to feel the enchanting pleasure.

Her dreams were fractured and disturbing, images of Flynn always just beyond reach no matter how much she yearned for him, no matter what she promised if only he would stay. His stark beauty and smile, his virility and strength lured and enticed her in the fantasy of her imagination, but when she came too near, he'd disappear and she'd be left saddened by his loss. She wanted the warmth of his body beside her, the scent of him in her nostrils; she wanted to feel his touch—like that.

Her eyes flew open, and she saw his hand poised above her, his smile exactly the same, the faint curve of his mouth enchanting.

"I was about to brush this lock of hair aside," he murmured, his touch gentle as he lifted the dark tendril from her cheek.

"You're here." And she saw him as she had that first night at Stewart Warner's dinner—the harsh beauty and intrinsic sexual heat, the competence to take on the world, and best of all that night, the ability to recognize her reckless urges at first glance.

"You've been sleeping."

"Why didn't you wake me?" A small unease trembled through her senses.

He shook his head. "You were worn out."

Half rising on her elbows, she glanced at the drawn drapes. "What time is it?"

"There's time. It's still dark." The Empire crew needed daylight to take to the field.

His words assuaged her unease. He wanted her, she gratefully thought, as though she were a supplicant and only he could bestow the pleasure she craved. "I wish we didn't have to worry about time," she whispered, moving closer, wanting the feel and warmth of him, his body a magnet to her desires.

"Then we won't." He lifted her chin with a crooked finger and smiled. "Good evening, Miss Attenborough." he murmured, with graceful politesse. "I was hoping your dance card wasn't filled."

She giggled. "As a matter of fact, it is."

"I'm crushed."

"You needn't be. I wrote your name on every line."

His dark brows flickered in amusement. "You're a forward little vixen, aren't you?"

"I knew that's what you liked. Rumor precedes you, Mr. Ito."

"Do you know everything I like?" he asked in a particularly enticing way.

She shook her head. "I was hoping you'd show me."

The teasing disappeared from his voice. "You're not too tired?"

"What would you do if I said yes?"

"Suffer in silence." And surprisingly, for the first time in his life, he would have.

"You're much too nice, Flynn." She smiled. "And I owe you a favor for bathing me." She touched her hair. "Perfume, too—I'm impressed."

"If you really aren't too tired, I was thinking I might impress you in another way," he said, a teasing light in his eyes.

"With this?" Her hand slid down his chest and came to rest on the pulsing crest of his erection hard against his stomach.

"With that."

"We seem to be in complete agreement," she whispered, circling the swollen head with her fingertip, gratified to hear him suck in his breath. "Come dance with me . . ."

"Fast or slow," he murmured, lifting her hand away, not certain he could oblige her if her answer didn't suit him. He'd missed her, it seemed.

"Silly question when I haven't seen you for—"

"A very long time."

She smiled. "Indeed, and you're happy to see me after all." She reached for the object of her desire, pulsing taut against his stomach.

"Very happy," he said, warding off her hand. "But I can't guarantee my control at the moment." A shocking admission for a man who prided himself on self-control.

But he was too practiced to be completely selfish and he cared for her more than he might wish. He made love to her with gallantry and finesse—gently, tenderly—their senses more attuned after their bath, their flesh susceptible to the merest touch, even the lightest contact tingling on the surface of their skin, resonating, stealing downward, melting into every grateful, glowing hypersensitive nerve. She felt as though she belonged here when she'd never belonged any-where before, his warmth and power, his gentleness enfolding her, the rhythm of his lower body matching hers, the tantaliz-ing pleasure he offered exceptional, rare—hers alone.

She didn't want to speculate that she may not have been the first to feel that way. Not now when there was so little time, when she wanted this all to last.

And he didn't dare think, because with morning, she would be gone. Shutting his eyes, he buried his face in her hair spread on the pillow, drew in the scent of gardenia and smiled—the fragrance, heavy, so different from the fresh vio-let scent she wore. But she hadn't complained, had even been complimentary. And while something so insignificant shouldn't matter, he found her generosity enchanting. Like everything about her.

"I'm glad you rode so far," he whispered, lifting his head, smiling down at her.

"So *you* could ride me." Her smile was heated, close, her body arching up beneath him, skin on skin, silken friction in-side and out, unalloyed pleasure scenting the air.

"For that," he breathed, responding to her tantalizing un-dulation with a deftly placed downstroke that elicited a soft, low purr. "And this," he softly added, pressing deeper. "And this . . ."

They had both perhaps, for reasons of their own, repressed what could no longer be repressed and they came with a sudden strange stillness, falling over the edge, softly, gently, together.

She noticed what he had not done with winsome delight.

He noticed but didn't care, for the first time in his life.

Neither spoke of his climaxing in her as though by some tacit consent and he kissed her with special tenderness and thanked her.

Her eyes were half-closed in languor and her gratitude was whispered in a sultry contralto that brought a smile to his lips.

He wiped them both dry with the sheet, then lay on his back and stared at the ceiling, silent and utterly motionless.

Adrift in her own shimmering lush afterglow, she didn't take alarm.

"Now then," he said, after a time, pushing himself up against the headboard. And she thought he was going to deal with his blunder because Flynn had in the past always been scrupulously careful. "Would you like to dance?" he asked.

He was sitting beside her, nude and starkly handsome and distracted by his great beauty and the oddity of his question—the even greater oddity of his disregard for what he'd just done—it took her a moment to reply. "Dance?"

"You said, before, you wanted to dance."

"I did?"

She hadn't really, but their relationship to date had been primarily one of all-consuming sex, and he felt an inexplicable need for normalcy in these fugitive moments they had left. And what he had just done couldn't be undone. The way of Zen would say, "Walk on," for death follows life just one pace behind. "We have time for a dance or two," he said instead.

She understood then. It was about mortality and impermanence. About his and theirs. "I'd love to dance with you," she replied, holding her hand out to him.

He took it, raised it to his mouth, brushed a light kiss over her fingertips, intent on ignoring the past or the future, focusing his energy on the moment. "Do you have any requests?" Releasing her hand, he tipped his head toward a phonograph in the corner. "Although I'm not sure my music is the same as that in Florence."

"How modern you are," she lightly murmured, surprised to see a phonograph in the bedroom of a man like Flynn.

"We have all the amenities, Miss Attenborough." His gaze was amused as though he understood her surprise.

"I can see." Her gaze flickered down to his blatant erection, and when she looked up, he was smiling.

"Besides that," he said, his smile broadening.

"Yes, of course, forgive my obsession."

"There's nothing to forgive. Obsession's in the air, I think."

She tried to speak as urbanely as he, tried to deal with the storm of her emotions in an adult, civilized way. But she found herself saying, "You'd better pick out a song quickly or no one's going to dance."

He grinned, slid from the bed and a moment later brought them both sumptuous silk robes, obviously Japanese and precious. Helping her into hers, overlarge and sea green, he slipped his on and drew her toward the phonograph. "I think a waltz would be suitable for our first dance."

In love or in lust, mindlessly, desperately infatuated with him, she watched him as he selected a cylinder, his expression intent, his long, slender fingers deftly sorting through the various boxes. She felt as though she were in heat; she'd left Helena for that exact reason and her susceptibility to his sexual allure hadn't diminished in his presence.

"Liszt's 'Mephisto Waltz'?" He held it out to her. "I'm in the mood," he pleasantly said, as if he'd just met her in the ballroom and didn't know her heart was beating in triple time. "Would you do me the honor?"

Tall and powerful, his dark hair just touching the shoulders of his gray silk robe embroidered with the cranes of long life, he was so beautiful her heart ached.

Unable to speak with her throat choked with tears, she nodded and moved into his arms. The rich melody swirled around them as they held each other, her cheek on the silk of his lapel, both scarcely breathing, their sensibilities awash in a tidal wave of emotions neither had expected or perhaps had thought themselves capable of resisting—bereavement and loss, an inchoate sense of commitment too bizarre to acknowledge and the lurid and perilous word, LOVE, writ large and disturbing.

"I don't want to go," she finally whispered.

"I know," he said, terse and low, but he had nothing to offer her with his life and his future in the balance. "If it were possible," he said with honesty if not complete conviction, "I'd say, stay."

She looked up at him. "But it's not possible."

"No," he gently replied. "Now dance with me because I don't want to think about you going or"—he blew out a breath—"think at all. And I like this song." Having come to grips with his tumultuous feelings, his voice changed at the end, took on a facile urbanity, and lifting her hands from around his waist, he placed one on his shoulder, held the other in his hand and softly humming the melody, twirled her around the room with sure-footed grace.

His dancing was adept like everything he did, she thought—peevish and jealous and too much in love for her peace of mind even while she knew it would never do to be in love with Flynn Ito. He was unreservedly single, self-indulgent, impossibly profligate and all the ladies he'd left behind were testament to his dissolute existence. A shame he could be so affectionate and appealing as well, worse that she didn't have the strength to resist his allure.

When the music came to a stop and the last note died away, it seemed for a moment as though everything was over.

"Would you like another song or should I take this off in-stead?" he murmured, his voice low and silken, touching the sleeve of her robe.

Like a moth to the flame, she thought, eager and impatient, heedless to all but her insatiable cravings. Pulling open the front of her robe, she pushed his aside enough so she could melt against him, so she could feel his hard arousal, flesh to hot flesh.

Sliding his hands down her back, he cupped her bottom, pulled her closer so the imprint of his ardor was unmistakable. "No more dancing, then?" he queried, husky and low.

"Yes, please . . . no more dancing." Her voice was trembling, her gaze imploring, her hips moving against his erection in a feverish rhythm.

He kissed her lightly on the cheek, avuncular and courteous. "Thank you for the dance." And then he lifted her into his arms and moved toward the bed, responding as he had so often in the past when women looked at him like that, when they wanted what she wanted.

But he felt a curious warmth quite separate from sex as he carried her across the room, a tenderness and undefinable gratitude. A feeling of fascination and wonder. He wanted to dance with her again . . . sometime, here, like this—or just like this—anywhere.

Glancing out the window, ever mindful of what morning would bring, he saw the stars fading in the sky.

The gods willing, of course.

Chapter
19

Flynn woke at the first distant rifle shot, heard the second, counted slowly to five waiting for the third. There.

He was out of bed before the echo had faded.

One of his scouts had sighted riders approaching.

In afterthought, he glanced at the bed as he reached for his trousers and was grateful to see that Jo still slept. His mind was focused, the past night no longer relevant regardless of its extravagant pleasures.

He had to mobilize his defenses.

The dogs started barking as he strode through the house buckling on his gun belt. Only partially dressed in trousers and boots, his shirt still undone, he'd shoved his father's swords into the braided silk tied around his waist, and slipped two ammunition belts over one shoulder.

He hadn't had time to leave a note. He hoped Jo would understand. But with riders on his land, he had to forgo the courtesies.

When he came out on the back porch, the stable yard was already filled with milling horses and men in various states of readiness. A groom came running up with his favorite paint, saddled and prancing to be off. Some horses were born for battle, like people he supposed, and Genji was such a mount.

Springing into the saddle, Flynn gave Genji a murmured command and the stallion leaped forward, his nostrils flaring in excitement, his gait shifting from jog to lope to gallop in mere seconds.

With his men strung out behind him, Flynn had just cleared the drive when the sound of rifle shots rang out in the still morning air.

Four shots in quick succession.

All clear.

The troop of armed men surged to a stop, but the dogs didn't cease their barking, which meant they were getting visitors of some kind.

Flynn surveyed his armed troop with a smile. "That was damned good speed, men—under five minutes."

"At least they didn't come in last night and cut into our sleep," one man said with a grin.

"Speak for yerself, Mike," another man drawled. "The boss had a female visitor that kept him awake, I'm guessing."

"As for that," Flynn said, clearing his throat with a rare look of embarrassment, "the less said, the better. The lady won't appreciate being discussed."

A great many eyes widened in varying degrees of shock. Flynn's amorous adventures generally weren't so delicately handled. The women who came out to the ranch to visit him weren't the shy kind. And he'd used the word *lady* as though he meant it.

"Whatever you say, boss," McFee replied, surveying his crew with a quelling glance in the event any of them didn't understand this woman wasn't to be the stuff of gossip. "Will the lady be staying long—I mean—under the circumstances," he added with a wary look.

"No," Flynn firmly said. "She leaves today. I'll need the very best escort for that duty. Twenty men. Armed to the teeth."

"Yes, sir. You're figuring before the Empire comes, right?"

McFee just wanted to make sure Flynn hadn't forgotten his enemies, lady or no lady.

Flynn nodded. "Once we find out who our visitors are, I'd like Miss Attenborough taken to the stage office at Great Falls. The passenger list has to be checked for undesirables before she gets on. If there are any, see that they're removed."

"Yes, sir." McFee didn't so much as bat an eyelash, although he had thoughts aplenty concerning his instructions. This lady must be right fine to be treated like a queen by a man like Flynn who was charming enough to the ladies and generous from all accounts, but never so conscientious and softhearted like this. *Undesirables?* Hell, that could mean half of Montana.

"Be ready in an hour or so." The rifle shots had come from a scout on the fence line, which meant the riders were still miles away. That meant he had time to talk to Jo before they arrived.

She wasn't going to want to leave—that was a given.

Nor would he want her to if circumstances were different.

He sighed. Now, if only wishes were horses . . . as his mother used to say.

Jo was pacing as he quietly entered the bedroom. She wore a robe half draped over her shoulders, leaving a delectable amount of silken skin showing and for a transient second, he wondered if she'd mind living in his basement until he could kill everyone on the Empire crew. His brief lapse in sanity quickly passed; they'd tried to burn him out last time and even a basement wouldn't guarantee her safety against fire.

"That robe looks a lot better on you than me," he said, shutting the door behind him.

She spun around at the sound of his voice, took one look at his gun belt and swords and went motionless. "You're not hurt, are you?"

"No, it was a false alarm." He slipped the cartridge belts

from his shoulder and tossed them on a chair. "However, we do have visitors arriving."

"I'll stay in here."

"That would be best." Unbuckling his gun belt, he hung it on the chair back.

She smiled. "Is that solicitude for me or you?"

"For you." Pulling his swords from his belt, he laid them on the dresser top and tried not to dwell on her lush availability.

"How sweet."

"Don't start." It took enormous will power not to untie the robe she wore, slide it from her shoulders and make love to her—very quickly, he waggishly thought—with visitors on the way.

"May I thank you for last night without getting a rebuff?"

"My gratitude to you as well, darling"—he smiled, a sweet, boyish smile she hadn't seen before—"from the bottom of my heart." Which was all he could offer her at the moment.

"I didn't know you had a heart."

"For you, I do." His expression suddenly turned grave. "But much as I'd like you to stay, you're not safe here as you well know. I'm having some of my men escort you out."

"Is there anything I can say to change your mind?" She had to at least try.

He shook his head. "Sorry. After our visitors leave, my men will take you to the stage office in Great Falls. And as soon as I'm finished with Empire Cattle Company's newest levy of hired guns that seem to come in like clock work, I'll ride down to see you."

"That would be nice, although I'd rather you didn't have to fight anyone."

"So would I, but, unfortunately, they keep coming."

"Then I'll wish you luck and wait in Helena."

His gaze narrowed. "You're usually not so amenable."

"I don't want to put you at risk," she said softly.

He'd been equivocating about his feelings for Jo, hoping to deal with his affection in some sensible manner, but the sweetness of her reply touched him more profoundly than he wished.

"You can't do your best if you have to worry about me. Come to Helena when you can . . . you see I'm without pride." She opened her arms, a vulnerable, artless gesture and when he didn't immediately respond, she whispered, "Hold me, please."

He went to her, unprepared for the tumult of emotions that overwhelmed him as he held her close. He should be feeling only cold vengeance on the cusp of the bloodiest battle of his life, not this chaos of tenderness and passion. "This will be over soon," he said, forcefully suppressing his unwanted feelings, offering platitudes in lieu of more personal pronouncements.

"Be careful." She was terrified for him, for herself now that she knew love existed.

"I have good men."

"But your enemies want *you.*"

"Too bad. They can't have me."

"Promise me anyway," she said as a child might, wanting blanket assurance.

He tightened his hold. "I promise," he whispered.

She gently touched his cheek. "I love when you indulge me."

He smiled faintly. "I'll indulge you in any way you wish when I come down to Helena again."

"And I'll have some slippers embroidered for you when you get there."

His smile widened. "Now there's an incentive to get this thing over with."

Chapter

20

Flynn stood on his porch, waiting for his visitors, braced or resolute depending on the whimsy of his turbulent thoughts.

McFee had reported the identity of the riders five minutes ago, the scout on the stable tower recognizing Hazard and Trey through his field glass.

Flynn hadn't yet told Jo. Nor was he sure what he'd say to her father other than express some form of apology. Hazard had distinctly told Jo not to ride this way. Although, Flynn reflected ruefully, so had he.

After he greeted his visitors, Flynn invited them inside, deciding his explanation might first require a stiff shot or two in his coffee. He was experiencing the apprehensions of an erring adolescent for the first time in his life, a novel sensation for a man who had taken on an adult role early.

Flynn's cook brought in coffee promptly, but the addition of liquor notwithstanding, the subject remained difficult for him to broach. Even with the pleasantries exchanged, he still hadn't decided how to segue into the topic.

"You're well prepared for an invasion from the looks of it," Hazard said. "We heard your signal shots the moment we crossed your fence line. What does that give you for warning—forty minutes or so?"

"Your horses are prime stock. The Empire won't come in that fast. I'm calculating an hour."

"Is your whole perimeter covered?"

"Every foot."

"We didn't see your scouts," Trey remarked. "Are you using some of our clan?"

"Always. The Absarokee are the best scouts." Flynn's crew was extraordinarily diverse, his own heritage predisposing him to look at a man's ability, not his skin. At first his troop had been looked on with derision, but it wasn't long before his men were not only given respect but a wide berth. Dark or light, young or old, each man was brave, competent and willing to follow Flynn to hell and back.

Hazard glanced out the window, the stable yard crowded with men. "How large a crew do you have?"

"With additions from Kinnert's and Bensen's, say a hundred and a half."

"Add our thirty. We thought you could use some help."

"I appreciate it. There's something you should know though," Flynn said, hesitantly, his discomfort plain. "Jo's here. Don't get riled," he hastily added as Hazard's expression turned grim. "I didn't bring her. She came herself—late last night."

Trey was grinning from ear to ear. "She came alone through fucking Otter Creek Pass at night?"

"She hired a guide in Great Falls. Howard Nagel."

"At least she had sense enough to get someone good," Hazard growled, setting his cup down so hard the coffee sloshed over the rim.

"He only took her to the fence line. My men brought her in."

"Howard knew better than to test your hospitality at night," Trey sportively noted.

"Apparently. I'm sending her home, of course. I said as much to her directly she arrived last night, but it was after midnight. She was tired."

"Do you have a way out that's safe from the Empire crew?" Hazard's voice had moderated although his frustration was still evident in the scowl creasing his forehead.

Flynn nodded. "McFee will escort her, along with twenty of my best men. I'm sorry; I know you didn't want her here."

"Not much you can do about it when she shows up in the middle of the night," Hazard said, gruffly.

At Hazard's acceptance however grudging, Flynn came to his feet. "I'll tell Jo you're here."

"And tell her I'm furious."

When Flynn acquainted Jo with the identity of their visitors, she stared at him in shock. "They're *here!*"

"In my study."

"Oh, my god!" She quickly glanced at the cheval glass. "I'd better get dressed."

"That might be wise. Your father is angry, as you might guess."

"Damn, this far from Helena. What kind of miserable odds are those?"

Flynn smiled. "Some people are more lucky than others."

"I'd appreciate a little empathy, if you please," Jo muttered, "and some clean clothes," she added, surveying the room. "Where are my saddle bags?"

"I'll get them." Although knowing it meant walking by his study, it was his turn to experience a twinge of discomfort.

"At times like this I could do without a father," Jo groaned. There were distinct merits to being on your own, she decided. Her life in Florence had been essentially without restrictions unless Father Alessandro's admonitions about hell fire counted.

"I'll just apologize again and refill everyone's cognac and coffee. Don't worry," Flynn said in soothing accents. "Trey's amused, by the way."

Jo's brows rose. "Why am I not surprised? Although, perhaps if I take my time dressing, Father's good humor might soon be restored as well."

If his good humor wasn't fully restored, Hazard had resigned himself to Jo's escapade by the time she entered the study. Reminding himself that his youth wasn't precisely a time of prudence had been instrumental in his newfound acceptance. And Jo's politic and lengthy apology further improved his disposition. When she called him Papa, which she rarely did, he caught a glimpse of her mother's cajoling flattery, but her smile was sincere as was her contrition and he surrendered to her charms. "You could have been seriously hurt. That was my only concern," he did say in the way of a scold. "But as for the rest, do as you like." Her liaison concerned him less than her safety; Absarokee culture recognized adult pleasures as a natural part of life. "Although Flynn assures me you understand now that it's more prudent for him to visit you in Helena than for you to be here."

"Yes, Papa. I understand," Jo said, meekly.

Trey grinned. "If we could only freeze this moment in time—Jo contrite."

Jo glared at her half brother. "I'm not sure I'll live long enough to see your moment of contrition."

"That will do, Trey," Hazard admonished. "Everyone understands the seriousness of the situation. The discussion is closed."

And despite the softness of his tone, Hazard's unmistakable command resonated in the room.

"I, for one, could use a refill now," Hazard pleasantly noted, holding out his cup, putting an end to the critical review of Jo's rash adventure.

Flynn refilled cups, offering Jo unadulterated coffee at that early hour, and the conversation turned to the most casual of events: the spring roundup, the expected runoff from the mountain snows, whether Stewart Warner would have another of his annual picnics after the gunfight at last year's festivities.

Despite the relaxed atmosphere, Jo was well aware that Hazard and Trey were dressed for hostilities—the light sweep of red and black war paint under their eyes and across their foreheads evidence of their purpose and resolve, their fringed leather clothing and moccasins not their usual dress, their well-oiled holsters gleaming on a nearby table along with their cartridge belts.

And Flynn had been fully armed this morning, his numerous weapons the necessary accoutrements to war.

How different these men were from those she'd known in Florence where the judicial system dated to ancient times. On the northern plains, the rule of law was very recent and often a day's ride away. Protecting one's own became a personal mission and only men of courage and boldness prevailed.

The worldly pleasures that had been the staple of her mother's sphere and the backdrop for hers seemed empty and vain in this brutal country where life and death were daily uncertainties. And whether her personal desires were immediately sated or her passionate feelings reciprocated suddenly seemed trivial set against the larger issues of survival.

She was truly contrite.

She gave no further thought to cajoling Flynn into letting her stay and before long she was escorted outside where McFee and twenty men were mounted and waiting. As Hazard spoke to McFee and Trey exchanged greetings with several of the men he knew, Flynn lifted Jo onto her horse. A personal farewell was impossible before so many watchful eyes. She sat stiffly in the saddle, trying to think of something appropriate to say within earshot of everyone, and purse-lipped, Flynn busied himself adjusting the bridle on her horse. His fingers lightly touched hers as he handed up the reins and the contact however lambent, jolted him. Compelled by uncontrollable impulse, he looked up and met her gaze.

She smiled.

He took in a deep breath of restraint and smiled back, a tight, forced smile. "Thank you for coming to visit." His voice was flat, controlled.

"My pleasure," she replied, as capable of cool politesse as he.

"McFee will keep you safe." He stepped away.

"Thank you. You keep yourself safe, as well."

"Of course." She couldn't possibly understand the samurai's resolute acceptance of death.

Flynn glanced away, nodded at McFee and his foreman moved forward to take his place beside Jo.

And it was over.

A kind of brusque finality to the moment.

Hazard offered some last words of warning and Jo listened closely, trying not to cry when she should have known better than to think she would get words of undying love. Trey added his cautions and advice; both men had spent years waging war with men like the Empire. And by the time they had said what needed to be said, Jo had composed her errant emotions.

Moments later, she rode away, five men before and behind her, five on either flank, the extent of her guard, the closeness of their ranks, evidence of their hazardous journey ahead.

Chapter
21

While McFee led his party out on a rough convoluted track through deep arroyos and cut banks, Hazard, Trey and Flynn finalized their battle plan. With Jo out of danger by nightfall, they would begin their assault. If the Englishmen were recruiting in Wyoming, they could expect a stout defense.

But a rider carrying a white flag and a message was brought into Flynn's study late that afternoon by one of his patrols.

Flynn opened the envelope and read the note. The Englishmen at the Empire wanted a parley in three days on a neutral site to be selected by Flynn. The message was couched in conciliatory language and signed by all three remittance men.

When the envoy had been taken away, Hazard and Trey both scrutinized the communication.

"Do you believe them?" Hazard was seated at Flynn's desk, his expression skeptical.

"I don't have any reason to." Flynn stood at the window, his gaze on the messenger who waited under guard. "Given their great kindness to me in the past," he sardonically observed.

Trey shifted in his lounging pose enough to reach the

whiskey bottle on a nearby table. "Is it possible they're considering the vast amounts of money this war is costing them?"

"Not to mention their pathetic lives." Flynn squinted at the rider who'd brought the letter, as though he could decipher the authenticity of the offer by the look of the man.

"I suppose there's nothing to lose by going to a parley," Hazard said, a faint disgruntled note in his voice.

"Or an ambush," Trey submitted, looking up from refilling his glass.

"Well, that's a given," Hazard murmured. "One's prepared for that."

Flynn turned back from the window. "My first instinct is to say no. A three-day wait sends up a lot of red flags in my mind. They could have heavy artillery brought in by then. And have any of the Sassenachs ever operated in good faith on anything?" he added, in cynical assessment.

"Maybe someone's papa in England received a nasty note from his banker and is putting a stop to the money drain," Trey suggested. "Those remittance men live high and the price of cattle is dropping. Hell, I took ten thousand from stupid Hughie Mortimer last month at Satchell's. He's a bloody rotten gambler who shouldn't be allowed near a deck of cards."

Hazard leaned back in his chair. "It's up to you, Flynn. It's your call."

"Do you ever get tired of this—of constantly defending yourself," Flynn asked, grim-faced.

"Always," Hazard replied. "I tell myself it's a matter of honor." He shrugged, the greed of his enemies an unavoidable fact. "You do what you must to survive."

"And until the courts are effective against people like the Empire and the thieves in the territorial legislature," Trey remarked, "someone has to remind them there are consequences to their venality."

Flynn blew out a breath. "So we're the means of justice."

"The alternative appeals even less," Hazard said with silken emphasis.

"You need another drink," Trey cheerfully proposed. "You're thinking way too much. When they push, you shove back, that's all. It's simple."

"Maybe I've been doing this too long."

"If it's any consolation, I've twenty years on you." Hazard maintained a remarkable calm. "You'll never regret doing what's right. The Empire should stay on their own land. When they don't, you have to see that they do."

"After this parley."

"If you wish. Ignore their offer, if you'd rather. I doubt it's an honest proposal."

"And yet . . ." Flynn wouldn't have even questioned replying to such an offer two weeks ago. Two weeks ago, he didn't know Jo Attenborough. Two weeks ago, his life was familiar and focused, his future determined. Now because of a headstrong, audacious, hot-blooded woman who was raising havoc with his emotions, he was thinking about his future differently. Perhaps stupidly. Particularly so when he was considering parleying with scum like the Empire. "This is all so much shit," he growled, frustrated and fractious.

"But the Empire's not going away, not with new hired guns arriving on the train," Hazard pointed out.

"I suppose a parley doesn't mean we can't attack afterward. Our defenses are in place. They can't move onto my land without my knowing." Flynn took a deep breath because he was going against every strategic principle he'd ever been taught. "Very well," he said, exhaling. "I'll agree to hear their proposal. We'll meet them at the Sun River ford. It's open ground."

Hazard nodded his approval; Trey shrugged, willing to go or stay.

Restive, unsettled, his judgment mercurial, Flynn muttered, "I hope like hell I'm not going to regret this."

Chapter
22

McFee and his troop rode into Great Falls midafternoon and immediately went to the stage office. He had his orders and he'd fulfill them efficiently and with dispatch.

He was well mannered as he helped Jo dismount, but his gaze was businesslike and direct. "If you'll wait in the stage office, ma'am, I'll see about a ticket for you."

"I can buy my own ticket."

"The boss gave me orders, ma'am. Would you like something to eat before you leave?" He waved her forward.

A glance at his face and she knew argument would be futile. "Is the stage leaving soon?"

"I reckon it'll leave when you're ready, ma'am."

He spoke without inflection, but she understood no matter how understated his tone, that McFee and twenty of Flynn's men positioned outside the stage office in defensive stances, commanded sufficient respect to set their own schedule. "Perhaps a sandwich to take along," she murmured. "If you don't mind."

"Whatever you want, ma'am." After conveying her wishes to one of his men, McFee opened the office door for her and indicated an empty chair. "This will just take me a few minutes," he said, politely.

The waiting room had a handful of people seated with their luggage at their feet, and Jo navigated her way around several carpetbags and valises before taking a chair. Despite McFee's courtesy, she felt oddly constrained to do his bidding. It wasn't that he was intimidating in size; he was of middle height and lean. He didn't give the impression of violence either; his face was usually without expression, his blue eyes almost innocent. He was perhaps forty, his skin weathered from the outdoors, but his strength wasn't in dispute. She found him likeable even though she felt obliged to submit to his orders. Perhaps it was his quiet loyalty to Flynn that appealed.

She watched him as he talked to the ticket agent, saw him scrutinize a sheet of paper the agent handed to him, wished she could have heard the agent's lengthy responses to his queries. When he walked over to a man, bent down and spoke to him quietly, Jo watched the passenger turn red. But the heavyset man didn't argue, he just got to his feet, picked up his luggage and hurried out of the office. The same scenario was repeated with another passenger and after that well-dressed man exited, McFee walked over to Jo. "The stage will be leaving in ten minutes," he politely affirmed. "Charlie's getting you a lunch to take along."

"Why did those passengers leave?" She couldn't suppress her curiosity.

"I told them they were on the wrong stage," he replied, his voice mild.

"How did you know?"

"I recognized them."

His reply was deliberately ambiguous, she realized.

"We'll see that you get on the stage soon, ma'am, if you don't mind."

What would he do if she said she minded? "Thank you," she said instead, understanding she wasn't in a position to take issue.

"Sit tight, ma'am, and I'll come back for you."

Which he did a few minutes later, after having thoroughly

checked over the stage and talked to the driver, she noted, watching him through the window. He helped her step up into the stage before the other passengers were allowed outside and saw that she had the seat facing forward. "You'll have the seat to yourself, ma'am, seein' as how those other men changed their minds."

She noticed the slight shift in his explanation and knew he'd been assessing the occupants of the stage. Because of Flynn, she thought, and while she should have taken offense at Flynn's high-handed authority, she found herself warmed by his concern. "Thank you, McFee, and thank Flynn as well. Tell him I enjoyed my stay at the ranch."

"My pleasure, ma'am," he replied, putting his finger to his hat brim. "You take care now." And then he stood like a guard at the door as the other passengers filed past him and entered the stage. Shutting the door after the last one was seated, he tipped the brim of his hat once again in Jo's direction and gave the driver leave to depart.

Flynn Ito had more power than she'd suspected, Jo decided.

And the frightened stares of her fellow passengers further attested to that fact. But she was too tired to be concerned. Having slept very little last night, she leaned her head back against the seat and soon was fast asleep.

Chapter

23

When the messenger returned to the Empire ranch that evening, Hugh Mortimer, Langley Phellps, Nigel Breck—three honorables as younger sons of peers—perused Flynn's reply with delight. All three men had come to the States three years ago after they'd been sent down from Cambridge, their carousing beyond even the extremely lax limits tolerated by the college. They had then proceeded to spend their allowances with undue speed in the fleshpots and gambling dens of London until their fathers interceded and shipped them west to gather a modicum of sense and fiscal responsibility. Or perhaps, they simply wanted them out of England for the duration to avoid any further scandal in their clubs.

Whatever the reason, they were raising hell now in the wilds of Montana, offending everyone of reasonable sensibilities, flaunting their lordly antecedents, swaggering like vainglorious caballeros in a land of hard-working cowboys.

"He fell for the bait," Hughie crowed, snapping his finger at the sheet of paper with Flynn's response.

"Which means we have three days to control the site," Langley drawled, half in his cups.

"Which also means we get to use our Maxim machine guns for the first time," Hughie said with a nasty smile.

"And a better use, I can't imagine," Langley murmured, lifting the silver stirrup cup he favored to his mouth and draining it. "The world will be a more civilized place without that colored rabble at the Sun River Ranch."

"I want Ito's swords when he's dead." Hughie waggled his finger at his cohorts. "I said it first."

"We'll cut for the spoils," Nigel said, firmly. "I want his samurai swords myself. They'll look extremely fine next to my pere's tiger head from India."

And for the next several minutes, a drunken argument ensued apropos of the booty they expected to divide when Flynn and his men were all dead. Their voices were raised over the disposal of Flynn's valuable paint horse that had won two large purses at the races last fall, when one of their valets entered with a note on a silver salver.

Hughie grabbed it, ripped it open and cried, "Bring the darling boy in!"

Their visitor must have been waiting in the hall because he appeared in the doorway at Hughie's cry. "I have some news of great interest," he said with a wicked smile.

"Look, look!" Hughie waved the note before his two friends.

"Can't see, Hughie, when you're waving it like a banshee," Langley grumbled

"Tell them, Alistair," Hughie commanded. "Tell them what you saw."

"I need a drink after that long ride from town."

Hughie waved him to the liquor table.

"It must have been cunt," Nigel murmured. "That's about the only thing that will bring a smile to Strathmore's face."

"That and a good bottle of whiskey," Langley drawled.

"They go hand in hand, do they not," their visitor murmured, pouring himself a healthy dose of Kentucky bourbon. "Now, then," Alistair Strathmore cheerfully declared, "where should I begin?"

"Tell us what this female looks like." Nigel gesticulated in

an undulating, downward rhythm. "Does she have big titties?"

"They looked extremely fine beneath her white silk
blouse, as did her legs in her split riding skirt. She had come a
long way, you see, and wished to be comfortable on the trail."

"A long way from where, do tell," Langley whispered, inch-
ing upward on his spine as his interest grew.

"From the Sun River Ranch, escorted by McFee and
twenty men."

"She must be a fucking queen with that kind of troop for a
guard."

"Perhaps an Indian princess would be more apt." Alistair's
eyes gleamed with delight.

"There's only two possibilities for Indian princesses in the
territory and that bitch lawyer isn't likely to catch Flynn's
eye," Hughie said with a wink. "He likes his women hot."

"So . . ." Alistair prompted, waving his liquor glass.

"Don't tell me you saw Hazard Black's illegitimate daughter on her way back from Flynn's ranch," Langley murmured.

"In the flesh." The scandal of Hazard and Lucy Attenborough's daughter was too delicious not to travel across the
territory at record speed. And the Englishmen spent enough
time in Helena at the brothels and gambling houses to be
aware of the gossip.

"What say we have a little taste of that half-breed pussy,"
Hughie suggested.

"And how the hell would we manage that if she's guarded
so well?"

"*Was* guarded so well," Alistair corrected, softly. "McFee
put her on the stage to Helena and headed back up country.
She's not guarded at all now that she's back in civilization, and
I use the term loosely," he sardonically murmured.

"If she was put on the stage, she's back in Helena or will be
very soon."

"Don't you have some more hired men coming in on the
train?"

"Several."

"Why couldn't they bring her up north? Send a rider down with the message and that pretty cunt will be back here in no time. How hard can it be to pluck one woman from the streets of Helena?"

"If that woman happens to be related to Hazard Black, I'd think twice," Nigel warned.

Hugh's thin lips pursed in disdain. "Since when were you intimidated by a redskin?"

"He's not just any redskin."

"Good God, man. He lived in a lodge; he still does on occasion I hear. If an Englishman can't get the better of a bloody, ignorant native, I don't know what the world is coming to."

"He went to Harvard," Nigel pointed out.

"Really, Nigel," Hugh returned peevishly. "As if a college in the colonies is of any consequence!"

"Hear, hear, Rule Britannia!"

Langley's cheer was taken up by every drunken voice, the din rising to a crescendo. They were all inebriated; even Alistair had been well into his cups or he wouldn't have ridden so far at night. And the remittance men were rarely sober, no matter what time of day or night.

When they tired of their patriotic hurrah, Hugh turned his intoxicated gaze on his cohorts. "It would be rather fun to snatch Flynn's little pussy from under his nose," he gloated. "That knave has a good eye for females, you have to give him that. Why shouldn't we enjoy the little tart? I've never fucked a half breed."

But when they called their foreman in and gave him orders to bring Hazard's daughter back from Helena, he warned them off. "I'd leave her alone if I were you. It don't pay to rile Hazard Black and that's a fact."

Hugh gazed at him with the hauteur instilled in him from the cradle and augmented tonight by considerable drink. "I don't recall asking you for your advice," he said with overbearing arrogance. "I don't care how many men it takes," he snapped. "Bring the bitch back."

"Yes, sir." The foreman knew better than to argue, but on his return to the bunkhouse, he chose to give the mission to several of the new hired guns. Since his drunken bosses hadn't specifically assigned the duty, the new men would be less likely to be recognized as members of the Empire crew. "You'd best leave right now," he told the new men. "Those English are in a damnable hurry." And if Hazard decided to shoot them, it would save him the task of replacing working cowboys.

But the unusual assignment caused considerable discussion in the bunkhouse that night.

"It's one thang to work for an outfit what skirts the law here and thar," one of the cowboys pronounced with a Texas drawl. "Scarin' off a few cowpunchers over water rights or grazin' rights, brandin' new calves wanderin' out on the prairies—hell, everyone does that there or you don't work for an outfit."

The ranchers subscribed to the principle of "customary range." The use of government lands for private purposes was a long-standing tradition on the Plains, and it required an occasional gunfight to maintain control of those public grazing lands.

"Amen to that," another man said, rolling his cigarette deftly with one hand. "But no one done ever asked me to kidnap a woman afore, specially Hazard Black's daughter. It makes no never mind to the Absarokee whether she's born in or out of marriage. For them, a kid is a kid and that's it. And if you mess with Hazard Black's kid, you mess with him—no question there."

"Jus' as well, Smithy sent out those new guys," a young man remarked. "If'n they do what they supposed to do, it ain't gonna be my hide Hazard comes alookin' for. And he'll come lookin' sure nuf."

There was a moment of silence in the shadowed bunkhouse, the kerosene lamps offering only small halos of light, the woodstove snapping and crackling, taking the chill out of the cool spring night.

"Anyone ever hear of Hazard losin' a battle?"

Another hovering silence fell.

"Or Flynn. You heard Smithy say Hazard's daughter come from Flynn's place."

"Shit," someone said softly.

"It gets a man thinkin', don't it," an old timer murmured. "'Bout stayin' alive."

This time the silence almost pulsated with apprehension.

Chapter

24

Jo reached Helena in the wee hours of the morning and rather than rouse Blaze, she slept at Flynn's house. Despite the late hour, she was warmly welcomed by a servant. "Right this way, Miss Attenborough," he said, as though he'd been expecting her and he led her to Flynn's bedroom as though she belonged there. "The boss left you a note." He pointed to an envelope propped on the mantle and closed the door.

The message was hastily written and succinct. But then he'd left in a hurry that day, she recalled.

"There's some gowns in the armoire. Pleasant dreams . . ."

And he'd signed his name in Japanese characters, the fluid pen strokes bold and sure.

Opening the armoire, she found a dozen gowns hanging inside and she smiled, even while she knew she shouldn't be tempted by such largesse. It wasn't right accepting so much, she thought with an integrity she'd not inherited from her mother. But she reached out to touch them, tantalized by their beauty, charmed by the gift and the giver.

Perhaps she could accept one, she decided, and pay him for the rest. Or maybe she could try them all on for him when he returned, she mused, a rush of heated pleasure coursing through

her body at the thought. And blissful images of such enchanting play filled her dreams that night.

But with morning, the mundane responsibilities of the
world intruded. She had apologies to make promptly. With
one clean blouse remaining in her saddle bags, she took advantage of her new wardrobe—that she would buy, she told
herself—selecting a spring gown of black India silk strewn
with pink and yellow blossoms. She bathed, dressed, quickly
ate some of the breakfast ready for her in the breakfast room
and set our for the Braddock-Black house.

Rather than an upbraiding, she was welcomed by Blaze
with genuine warmth. "Next time, leave a note," she said.
"And we'll know where to go looking for you."

"I'm sorry, truly I am, but since I was given express orders
not to go to Flynn's"—her voice trailed off.

"I understand. But just for our peace of mind, tell us regardless of your delinquency," Blaze noted with a smile. "And
your father is probably at Flynn's by now."

"I know," Jo replied, with a rueful smile.

Blaze laughed. "So you've already been chastised. Come,
have breakfast with me or tea if you've already eaten, and tell
me what your father said."

Daisy soon joined them at the table for Blaze had sent a servant to her with news of Jo's return and Jo regaled them with
the details of her journey north, her return and her decision to
sleep at Flynn's last night.

"Nonsense, you could have wakened us," Blaze said. "But
I'm sure Flynn won't mind you staying there. And I'm pleased
you understand the seriousness of the conflict in that area."
Blaze surveyed her with a searching gaze. "You do, don't
you?"

"Yes, very much. I count myself fortunate my guide was competent or I may have run into trouble on my ride to Flynn's."

"I wonder whether Howard Nagel might have suspected
who you were?" Blaze murmured.

"How could he have possibly known?"

Daisy snorted. "The question is rather how could he not? Gossip travels as fast as the telegraph."

"Howard may not attend to gossip," Blaze remarked, "but in any event, you were very fortunate to have Howard for a guide. He's the very best in the territory . . . with the exception of your father's clan, of course."

"So you're returned to the safety of town," Daisy said with a smile.

"That everyone is so ready for combat is rather alarming to tell the truth," Jo maintained. "Are all cattle companies so contentious with their neighbors?"

Daisy grimaced faintly. "Grazing rights have always been contentious and the bigger the company, the more aggressive they are."

"Fortunately, Flynn and our family can meet any challenge with the resources at our command," Blaze declared. "The smaller owners aren't so fortunate."

"In time, all the range will be fenced," Daisy explained. "Whether that helps control or escalate the violence remains to be seen."

"With cattle prices down, some of the foreign investors are having second thoughts. Who knows, in time, the Empire may fold up their tents and go home. But regardless of the unsettled times, you're back safe and sound." Blaze smiled. "For which we're pleased. You must let your mother know you're back. I had a message sent to her when you arrived, but I'm sure she'll be pleased to see you."

"Not before noon, she won't," Jo replied with a grin. "But thank you, I will visit her directly I leave here."

"I don't have to ask if you enjoyed your visit with Flynn," Daisy remarked. "You seem in excellent spirits."

"He's much too charming. I'm trying to keep him in proper perspective."

"That may be wise, dear," Blaze murmured. "He does have a reputation with the ladies and I wouldn't want to see you hurt."

"Never fear. I have both feet planted firmly on the ground." But she surreptitiously crossed her fingers in her lap because she was walking on air after being welcomed so kindly by Flynn's servants who no doubt acted on his instructions.

Shortly after noon, Jo went to see her mother, who was having her breakfast in bed. She'd no more than entered the bedroom than she was rebuked for her conduct. "Fortunately, your absence wasn't noticed," Lucy went on in a pettish tone, taking a bite of her buttered toast, proceeding to eat and talk, "but think what people would say if they knew you hied yourself north like some little tramp to see that horrible man."

"Mother, for heaven's sake, will you stop. I just returned. It wouldn't be amiss for you to be pleased that I'm back unharmed."

"Well, of course, I am, dear. What kind of mother do you think I am. I'm just concerned for your reputation in a tiny, little town like this. Come, sit with me." She patted the bed. "And have some coddled eggs and chocolate."

"I don't like coddled eggs, Mother, but thank you."

"Since when haven't you liked coddled eggs?" Lucy inquired with such wide-eyed innocence, Jo didn't have the heart to tell her since always.

"Well, you look as though you've eaten quite enough anyway, darling," she declared, raking Jo with a glance. "It doesn't pay to be too plump. Men like slender women I've found. And that brilliant print fabric rather accents that little extra weight you must really do something about, sweetheart."

"I'll change, Mother, as soon as I leave you," Jo said, to curtail any further discussion of her weight. "I just wanted to let you know I was back."

"What a sweet child, you are." Lucy beamed at her daughter as though she were ten. "But I never worried for a moment, even though Hazard's horrible wife broke in here in a fury wanting me to tell her where you were. But you've always been so resourceful and clever, I just knew you were perfectly fine wherever you were. Although, I chose not to tell that annoying woman a thing because it was really none of her business. And she wouldn't allow me to speak to Hazard just like every petty, jealous little wife I've ever met. She told me he was out of town," Lucy sniffed. "As if I were born yesterday. But never you mind, darling, Hazard adores you and so do I and we'll all manage just swimmingly together. Do take a little peek at my new gown in the armoire, dear. I need a fresh eye. Do you think I'm too old for pink muslin?"

"No, Mother, of course not," Jo automatically said, knowing her opinion was incidental to her mother's taste that bordered on the ostentatious. But far be it from her to apprise her mother of the fact. "You'll look very nice in pink muslin."

"Exactly what I said to the dressmaker who was trying to talk me out of that lovely fabric. I don't look a day over thirty, I told her." She giggled. "Which is a slight problem when I have a daughter your age. But never you mind, because I don't in the least."

Her mother was a well-preserved and attractive forty-one, but she always wished to be younger. But then she wished for a great many things she couldn't have. Although with her fingers on Hazard's fortune now, Jo nervously reflected, she hoped Hazard was capable of protecting his assets. "I'm going home to sleep, Mother. The stage came into town very late last night. I'll call on you tomorrow."

"Not too early, darling. You know I need my beauty rest."

"I know." As she knew her mother would forget she'd even been out of town before long.

Chapter

25

That afternoon while Jo was resting at Flynn's, a man was inquiring about her at the stage office. He wanted to know if someone had been waiting for her when she arrived last night.

"Don't rightly know if it's any of your business," George Parsons replied.

"She's kin of mine."

"She ain't no kin of yours, and I know that for a fact." George didn't care if the man did look like a gunslinger. After letting Hazard's daughter slip through his fingers once, he wasn't about to make the same mistake twice, no matter how nasty the fellow looked.

The Empire cowboys changed their method of questioning after that, posing instead as messengers from Hazard. They'd been asked to deliver a package to his daughter and being strangers in town, they needed to know where she lived. Within the hour, the Empire men had Hazard's address, but even better, they'd found the cab driver who had driven Jo Attenborough to Flynn's house late last night.

They celebrated their good fortune, by having several drinks at Satchell's Saloon, against the long journey back, they rationalized. But their leader hadn't survived ten years as a hired gun without maintaining some personal discipline and after four drinks, he dragged the rest of his crew out of the bar.

It wasn't a subtle operation, but then not a man among them was known for his subtlety. Two men were posted at the back of Flynn's town house, two on the street in front while the leader and two additional men walked up to the front door, knocked and shoved their way in when the door was opened.

The single servant in the front hall was no match for three armed men and he was knocked unconscious in seconds. The leader waved his men forward, one toward the back of the house to hold the servants at bay, one upstairs while he stood watch at the front door.

Jo heard the heavy footsteps on the stairs and for a fleeting moment, she thought she'd wakened from her dream to the reality of Flynn's return. But seconds later, her happy conjecture was brutally vanquished when a rough-looking man broke into her room and pointed his revolver at her.

"Up, lady," he growled. "We got a fer piece to go."

"I have no idea who you are," she blustered, her pulse rate spiking with fear.

"Well, that don't matter much, cuz I know who you are. Some Hazard's daughter and yer comin' with me."

She started screaming, the impulse without thought, terror-driven and ungovernable, and when he lunged at her, she picked up the first thing she saw and threw the bed lamp at him. He ignored the shattering glass as it struck him and kept coming, the crunch of glass under his boots suddenly galvanizing her. She leaped from the bed and bolted for the door, reaching it before him, feeling increasingly more confident of escaping. He was lumbering and slow; she was not and racing into the hall, she ran full-out for the stairs.

"Stop right there," a gruff voice commanded and she skidded to a stop inches from the seven-inch barrel of a Colt revolver.

The man was barely her height, but his face had the hardened look of someone familiar with a loaded revolver. And he was directly in her way at the top of the stairs. Dare she try to kick him down the stairs? Would he shoot? The fleeting thought was curtailed by rough hands grabbing her from behind and holding her captive.

She screamed, a high, piercing shriek that echoed through the house for a brief moment before a filthy hand covered her mouth. And in short order, her mouth was gagged with a sweaty neckerchief, her hands were trussed from behind and she was being carried down the stairs. She squirmed and struggled to no avail. Within moments, she was being rolled up in a large blanket and brought outside where she could smell the fresh air through her shroud. A second later, she was tossed over a horse like baggage, the distinctive odor of the stable pungent in her nostrils.

Surely someone would take issue with a squirming bundle being led away on a horse, she hoped, but the men abducting her must have taken an untraveled route out of town because they proceeded unmolested. After a very long time, when every muscle and joint in her body was stretched and strained in agony, she heard the party drawing to a halt.

She was lifted down and unwrapped. Blinking against the sunshine, she quickly scanned her surroundings, hoping to recognize a landmark. But nothing was familiar.

"You got a choice, lady," the man she'd seen at the top of the stairs said, his voice coarse and brusque. "If you don't scream, I'll take off the gag."

She nodded in the affirmative and a moment later, the disgusting kerchief was withdrawn from her mouth.

"We're puttin' you on a horse here. Untie her hands, bring over her boots," he ordered.

Shaking the blood back into her hands, Jo debated how far she'd get if she tried to leap onto a horse or if she could even manage to reach a horse with so many men surrounding her. The answer was as unpalatable as the look of her abductors, and her conjecture was short-lived. If she hoped to escape, this wasn't an opportune time. Taking the man's jacket and her boots that were offered her, she donned them and mounted the horse given her. After which, her hands were tied to the saddle horn, and the party set out once again.

As the sun moved across the sky, she tried to gauge their direction, but they traveled little-used deer trails and every tree looked the same. Much later that night, she did recognize the lights of Great Falls, but the horsemen skirted the town and headed north-northeast, she calculated, the lights fading behind them. No one spoke except for occasional words of direction from their leader.

She felt as if she'd dropped off the face of the earth and was traveling with a ghost troop. Tired, hungry, thirsty, she dozed off and on throughout the night, so weary as the hours passed that she found it difficult to even conjure up enough energy to sustain fear.

As dawn broke, they rode into a large stable yard, the ranch house on the hill a dark, looming shadow, the outbuildings so numerous, she lost count. Once untied, she slid from the saddle; barely able to stand upright, she tottered behind the man leading her. He brought her to a small shed, opened the door and nodded at her. The small space was sparely furnished. A bed, a chair and, thankfully, a chamber pot, she noted, but the door was shut behind her and she was left in darkness.

Leaning against the door, she heard the key turn in the lock, the sound unmistakable proof of her captivity and the tears she'd kept at bay all day suddenly spilled over. Was there any hope at all of rescue? Did anyone even know she was gone from Flynn's house? If so, were there any clues left behind? Wretched and despondent, she wondered if she had the courage required to face the horrors that might be in store for her.

Florence seemed like the safest of havens now that she was in such comfortless straits—even her mother's brittle world of social amusements, the sweetest of refuges. Perhaps she wasn't as brave as she'd always thought. Perhaps this raw frontier required a degree of courage she didn't possess.

But with the next small sob, she reminded herself that both Flynn and her father were more capable than most; surely, they would come for her. In the meantime, she'd deal with this crisis as she'd dealt with others in the past, taking charge of her life a not unfamiliar task. And if ever there was a time when clear thinking was required, it was now.

Wiping away her tears, she set out to examine her prison, slowly feeling her way around the shed. The walls were solid logs, bereft of windows or any object she might use as a weapon. Perhaps the chamber pot would be a useful defense, she drolly thought. Although, in her present state of exhaustion, she hadn't the energy required to mount an attack or attempt an escape. Groping her way to the bed, she sank down on the rough straw-stuffed mattress and shut her eyes. Whoever her captors were, she reflected, she would discover their identity soon enough.

But beneath her weariness, in a small corner of her brain still operating marginally, a single question repeated itself in baffling puzzlement. *Who would be stupid enough to kidnap Hazard Black's daughter?*

Chapter

26

When the remittance men rose from the fog of inebriation in the early afternoon and wandered into the dining room for their breakfasts, they received news that their captive had arrived.

"Bring the hussy in," Hugh ordered the servant, dropping into a chair like dead weight, leaning his head back, half-smiling in anticipation. "Let's see what this half-breed looks like."

"Now that's what I call a reason to get up. Other than the pounding in my head," Langley muttered, easing himself onto a chair at the table. "I need a drink." And leaning over slowly, he drew a whiskey bottle closer, uncorked it and lifted it to his mouth.

"Are we talking about your cock getting up or a rhetorical rising?" Nigel drawled, lifting a bottle from the sideboard.

"Both," Langley murmured. "Although I'm going to need a drink or ten to make anything move anywhere. Grab me some kippers," he added, waving his hand at Nigel. "And bring over a deck of cards. We'll cut for who goes first with her."

Nigel scowled. "Do I look like a fucking servant?"

"One plate of kippers, for Christ's sake. The lout of a servant left to get the bitch."

"If we're cutting cards, I want a fresh deck." Hugh surveyed his friends with a jaundiced gaze. "Not that I don't trust you," he added sardonically.

The men's sense of honor was less than optimal, all the well-advised schooling on gentlemanly behavior that had been drummed into them in their youth sacrificed to their personal pursuit of pleasure. As a result, the next several minutes were occupied in a heated argument over the correct methodology of cutting cards. At last, all was resolved, that first hair-of-the-dog drink helpful in coming to an agreement. Langley was designated cutter, and Hugh turned up high card.

"It's only fair," he said with a gloating smile. "Since it was my idea in the first place."

"At least the bitch will still be usable for the rest of us. You last about thirty seconds."

"As if you set any records fucking the ladies," Hugh countered, scowling at Langley.

"Don't have to with cunt. They're just there to service me."

"And now, we have Flynn's latest hot piece for our enjoyment. A bit of good luck, what say?" Hughie queried, smirking.

"We'll have to compare notes on her performance." Langley lifted his glass with a mocking smile.

"If Flynn doesn't come for her first." Nigel gazed at his friends, his brows raised in critical assessment.

Hugh flushed red. "Who the hell's side are you on?"

"Just being practical."

"Have another drink for courage," Hugh suggested snidely. "We have more than enough hired gun men."

"You hope. I just don't care to go back to England the way Boyden did—in a coffin." Nigel for all his faults, had a mind that functioned, whereas Hugh and Langley's intellect had been hampered by too many centuries of aristocratic inbreeding. Nigel's grandfather had acquired his title for building canals that had enriched the British economy and that hard-headed Breck intellect hadn't yet been completely diluted in two generations.

"Hell, if you're saying you want to give up your turn with the hussy, what say, Langley"—Hugh's fat lip curled up in a sneer—"there's just more for you and me."

"You won't find me complaining, Hughie." Langley flicked back his long blond hair with the air of a priggish fop. "I'm thinking she might be worth keeping here for the duration. It would save us from riding into town for cunt."

"Ahem."

The soft utterance came from the doorway.

The three men turned toward the sound, to find the servant they'd sent to fetch their captive standing just inside the doorway with Jo. At least a portion of their conversation had been overheard from the embarrassed look on the man's face.

"That will be all, Frank. Shut the door behind you."

Jo's hands were tied behind her back, her toilette sadly lacking after hours on the trail, but she looked at the Englishmen with cool disdain. "Do you know who I am?"

"One fine-looking cunt once we clean you up." Hugh's voice was mocking, but his gaze was lustful. Her voluptuous breasts were thrust forward in the most flaunting manner with her hands tied behind her back.

"This little exploit of yours might cost you your life. Have you considered that?" If she was feeling any apprehension, it didn't show.

"Are you that good in bed?" Langley snickered. "She's going to fuck us to death, Hughie. Damn! I'm looking forward to that."

Jo surveyed them, meeting their eyes with a nervy insolence. "You'll be dying in a less pleasurable manner, I suspect, once I'm rescued." While she was aware of her peril, these contemptible creatures didn't inspire the degree of terror that her abductors had. Those hired guns would have killed anyone for a price. Fortunately, these spineless young Englishmen were in charge.

Hugh slid up into a sitting position and leaned forward. "Are we supposed to shake with fear?"

"You'd do better to get on a horse and ride south as fast as you can."

"Shut the fuck up," he snarled. "No one's going anywhere. We're not afraid of your father."

So they knew who she was. "Then, you're more stupid than you look."

Hauling his corpulent body up from his chair, Hugh moved across the room with a cumbersome tread, fury in his gaze. "The next time you talk back, bitch," he growled, coming up so close she was forced back a step, "I'll show you what happens to a loud-mouthed cunt." Reaching out, he grabbed her breast and gave it a vicious twist.

Suppressing her gasp of pain, Jo fought back the tears that welled in her eyes. "I'm told the Absarokee can flay a man alive," she said, through gritted teeth, "and he doesn't die for days."

"Maybe you'll want to die before I'm done with you." But his grip loosened, and the flicker in his eyes was fear.

"We'll have to see, won't we," she murmured. "I'm ready if you are." A bluff was a bluff was a bluff, but she was in such pain from the malevolent little pig who didn't have the courage to fight his own battles that, at the moment, she wouldn't mind skinning him alive herself.

"I suggest you keep your mouth shut," Hugh whispered.

She held his gaze, unflinching. "When my father finds you, your mouth will be shut permanently."

For all his bravado, Hugh wasn't able to conceal his alarm. His hand fell away and he backed off, although his voice when he spoke was boastful for the benefit of his friends. "We're going to have to teach this bitch some manners."

"Let's see if she's as insolent after we fuck her a few times." Three drinks had augmented not only Langley's courage but also his carnal passions. "But I'd prefer the cunt be bathed first. I can smell her from here." Langley affected the wardrobe of a Wild West show performer: his shirts of silk; his boots, colorful; his trousers fitted so tightly he couldn't have ridden a mile in comfort.

Hugh's brief moment of fear forgotten, safely distant from Jo's fanatical gaze, the thought of ramming his cock into the defiant bitch was making him hard. He turned back to his friends. "Where do we want this little orgy to take place?"

"Why not the billiard room." Langley's sly smile revealed sharp little teeth that gave him the odious look of a rodent. "I've always wanted to fuck some cunt on the billiard table. First one to sink a ball into her wet pussy wins a monkey," he chortled.

Hugh joined in his laughter, getting more excited by the second at such a tantalizing prospect. "With her tied spread-eagle on the table, we can take turns with *our* balls and the billiard balls. Although we're not sure you're going to participate, are we, Nigel?" he jibed. "Are you in or out of this randy game?"

"I'll see."

"He'll see." Hugh giggled. "He'll see if he can get his cock up when he's scared shitless of Hazard Black."

"I don't think the man travels alone," Nigel murmured, twirling his whiskey glass as he gazed at Jo. "Does he?" he added, nodding in her direction.

She smiled, feeling more confident with one out of three considering the probable risk in abusing her. "He travels with a small army. You'll find that out soon enough."

"*Ooie, ooie,*" Hugh jeered. "I'm scared to death."

A good choice of words, Jo reflected, not sure whether the culture of violence was contagious or she was simply responding to their inhumanity with a normal degree of rage.

"Come, come, boys," Langley briskly remarked, his liquor consumption having mitigated the last remnants of his hangover. "Let's move this fucking game along, or should I say this game of fucking," he added with a roguish smile. Rising from his chair with a determined air, he quickly walked to the door,

pulled it open, and roared for a servant. Turning to Jo, he
grabbed her arm and jerked her out into the hall. As Frank appeared in the distance, he barked, "Run, arsehole! I don't like
to be kept waiting!"

When the servant reached them moments later, Langley
shoved Jo at him. "Take this bitch to the bathroom and see
that she gets clean," he snapped. "I don't care how you do it. I
want her in the billiard room in fifteen minutes. Understand?"

"Yes, sir." The elderly man dipped his head in acknowledgment, then glanced up at Jo, his gaze both apologetic and fearful. "This way," he said, half under his breath.

Seeing the trepidation in the man's eyes, Jo wondered if
she'd found an ally. But when she asked, "Can you help me?"
as they moved out of earshot of her captors, he shook his
head.

"My life wouldn't be worth a plugged nickel if I did," he
replied, bluntly. "You've seen the kind of men they've brung
to the ranch. Me and my wife didn't know what we was gettin'
into when we hired on, and now"—he shrugged helplessly—
"no one dares leave."

"Have they threatened you?"

"Not in so many words, but they're right erratic when
they're drunk. And that's most of the time when they ain't
sleepin'. Up these stairs, ma'am."

"My father's Hazard Black. He'll come looking for me."

His eyes widened. "Then I'm between the Devil and the
deep blue sea, ain't I, just."

"Could you get a message out for me?"

"How? The place is crawlin' with hired killers. No one rides
away from here without good reason."

"I don't suppose you could find me a handgun?"

"If'n it were just me, I might think about it, but with my
wife—she can't ride much anymore. We couldn't get out of
here fast enough if they found out. I'm willin' to shut you in
the bath and look the other way, though, if'n that would do
you any good. Turn left here, ma'am," he said as they reached

the top of the stairs. "I wish I could do more, but there's a few others like me here and we're caught right and tight for the duration."

"Duration?"

"Until whatever fight they're plannin' is over. Hired guns been comin' in for almost a month now. Somethin's gonna happen. This is it." He opened a door and waved her in. "There's hot water in the tub. It was brung up for the English gents, but they was too hung over to use it. Should still be hot enough. But you best hurry; he said fifteen minutes and those milords are right ornery. Turn around and I'll cut those ropes," he added, taking a penknife out of his pocket "I'll knock when it's time to go back downstairs."

Free once again, she smiled at him, said, "Thank you," and walking into the bathroom, shut and locked the door. Understanding time was at a premium, she quickly divested herself of her clothing, stepped into the claw-foot tub filled with steaming water, and lay down in the blessed warmth. She allowed herself only a moment to rest before washing, wishing to avoid any repercussions. Brave she might be under ordinary circumstances, but three drunken aristocrats familiar with the prerogatives of their rank were unpredictable. And while she understood her father would come for her, it might not be soon enough.

As she dried herself and dressed once again, she came to terms with the possibility she might be raped by the repulsive men downstairs and steeled herself against the ordeal. The physical misery she could withstand; her only concern was whether they were capable of killing her if sufficiently provoked.

That was the uncertainty.

Against that possibility, she eyed the razors hanging beside the washstand, wondering if she could secrete one somewhere on her person without jeopardizing her life. She wouldn't wish it to be turned on her should it be discovered. But she didn't wish to die, passive and unresisting, either. This thought, brought her to the washstand where she tore a linen towel in strips and wrapped one of the razors in a small scrap of material so it wouldn't rattle in her boot. Slipping the small bundle down the side of her boot, she straightened her gown, ran a hand over her still-damp hair and waited for the servant to summon her.

Her heart leaped when the knock sounded and it took a moment to compose herself. Breathing slowly, she told herself she could triumph over three such miserable examples of manhood, then reached for the doorknob and opened the door.

"Ready?"

Frank looked almost as worried as she felt. "I think so."

"I'm right sorry, ma'am." He motioned her past him.

"It has nothing to do with you," she said, beginning her return journey downstairs. "And with luck, I'll manage. They seem witless."

"But dangerous, ma'am. They're used to givin' orders."

"You haven't heard any recent gossip concerning my father?"

"I went downstairs while you was . . . er . . . washin', but all I found out in the kitchen where the hired men come for food was that they're waitin' for some big battle right soon."

"How soon?" A battle no doubt meant Flynn and her father with all the preparations she'd seen at Sun River Ranch.

"No one's sayin'. But they're armed full up when they come and go. Here we are, ma'am. The billiard room. I'm right sorry."

"Should you have the opportunity to get a message out, see that Flynn Ito knows where I am."

"Oh Lord! Him too!"

Jo almost smiled and if the circumstances hadn't been so dire she would have. Instead, she nodded, then twitched her foot so she could feel the comfort of the razor in her boot, took a deep breath and said, "Open the door."

Her skin turned clammy as she walked in and saw the three

men lounging on the billiard chairs drawn up in a half circle at one end of the table. Each had a whiskey bottle in his hand and a coil of rope lay on the green baize table top.

Feeling her stomach tighten at the sight of the rope, she fought down an urge to scream or run. Neither would be useful. She wouldn't escape no matter how fast she ran and her cries would only give them satisfaction. But she stopped just inside the door. She wasn't willing to make this easy for them.

For a fleeting moment she wondered what would happen if she were to attack them with the razor. With the element of surprise, surely she could do some damage. But what chance did she have of overcoming three men? And what price would she pay for her assault? Perhaps with Flynn and her father near, delay was her best weapon. That and the courage to endure.

"Come here, bitch." Snapping his fingers, Hugh pointed to a spot on the carpet directly in front of his chair.

She moved forward slowly, her hands in fists at her sides, her spine stiff, her expression an impassivity she didn't feel.

"There," Hugh growled, as she approached, indicating a small stool she'd not seen from the door. "Sit."

She did, although it was unnerving to obey, to submit to men she normally wouldn't have even glanced at. And now she had to look up at them as though they were sovereigns and she their docile vassal.

"Unbutton your gown."

"I can't. The buttons are in back."

"Do it or I'll rip the dress from you," Hugh ordered, curtly.

She had unbuttoned it for her bath; she was capable of the function, however awkward, and not wishing to feel his repulsive touch, she acquiesced. Slowly, taking her time, she undid each button until the gown hung loose on her shoulders.

"Now take it off—like you do for Flynn. Did he fuck you often during your stay at his ranch? I hear he's very nice to the ladies—they come and go at all hours of the day or night. You didn't know that? She seems surprised." Hugh murmured, glancing at his friends. "Do you suppose he told her she was the first?" he added with a nasty smile.

"First, last, who cares," Langley grumbled. "She's not moving fast enough and my cock is so hard it's aching. Everything off, quickly now, bitch. Stand up . . . the chemise and drawers, too. I want to see what Flynn's been fucking."

Understanding any further delay was impossible, Jo literally gritted her teeth and yielded, coming to her feet, sliding off her gown, her chemise and drawers, debating a moment before slipping off her boots as well. But she set her boots nearby, just in case.

"Sit," Hugh barked, snapping his pudgy fingers.

She complied, her heart beating in her ears, trying not to show her fear. It was agony to be naked before these men, but more frightening was the look in the fat man's eyes. Brutish and frenzied as though her nakedness fueled some perversity in his brain.

"I think the bitch needs a drink to loosen her up," Hugh murmured, stepping down from the high viewing chairs holding his bottle in his hand. "I don't like tight cunt. Here, bitch, open your mouth."

For a brief moment she debated her options, but he was towering over her, the bottle pressed to her lips and before she could make a decision, he grabbed her hair, jerked her head back and as her mouth opened in shock, he poured whiskey down her throat. Sputtering and coughing, she was forced to swallow the vile liquor or choke on it, the steady stream of whiskey filling her mouth, running down her chin and throat, coursing over her breasts and stomach and legs.

In those first terrifying moments, she silently swore vengeance, wanting these men to pay dearly for what they were doing to her, an incoherent rage filling her brain. But in the next choking breath she understood that her survival depended on compromise or perhaps capitulation—for only a few hours, she reflected hopefully. And with that thought in mind, she swallowed again.

"She's looking good enough to lick now, Hughie," Langley crowed. "Look at all that fine whiskey running into her crotch . . . and over those big tits. Make her stand up. I want to see that cunt up close."

"Up, bitch," Hugh ordered, jerking on her hair, forcing her to rise. "Didn't you hear Langley? He wants to see your cunt up close." He kicked her feet apart so her thighs were spread wide, pulled her arms behind her back with a vicious twist and held her wrists captive.

"I like that pose, Hughie, with those tits jutting out like that." Picking up a gold-handled letter opener from a nearby table, he balanced it for a moment on his palm as he moved toward them. "Such great big tits," he murmured, coming to rest before Jo, running the chased gold hilt around one of her breasts, lifting the weight of her breast slightly with the flat of the handle, as though gauging its size.

Jo trembled, the blade nearly touching her breast, the man's intentions unclear.

"Don't worry, my sweet. I wouldn't hurt such a succulent body. We have better uses for you," Langley drawled. Leaning forward slightly, he slid the hilt down her stomach, slipped it between her spread legs, traced her cleft with one light stroke and then without warning, rammed the metal hilt guard deep into her vagina.

She gasped, frozen in fear, the opener blade only a hair's breadth from her pubis, the filigreed guard her only protection.

"That's a smart little bitch." Langley surveyed her with a faint smile. "That blade could do damage."

Terrified, she stood motionless, scarcely daring to breathe.

"There's no need for me to hold her now," Hugh said with a grin, releasing his grip. "Looks like I have time for another drink." Walking to the table, he picked up a whiskey bottle and put it to his mouth.

"That's what I call a nice showy piece of ass," Langley murmured, taking a step back to survey her. "She'd fetch a prime price in the slave markets of Marrakech, now, wouldn't she? Nice, big tits"—he slapped them lightly, set them quivering, but she stifled her startled response, afraid to move. "And such a high, flaunting mound, just made to lure cock," he added, lightly, stroking her pubic hair for a moment before he slid his fingers downward to trace the verge of her labia encircling the hilt. "Ah, she's getting wet, just like a well-behaved submissive little slave should." He held up his glistening fingers. "She's going to be a tantalizing little sultana for our entertainment, gentlemen. I'm guessing, she'll be able to last for hours."

His words sent a chill through her, but any utterance, any agitation could be dangerous with the blade so near.

Sliding his wet fingers up her stomach, Langley ran his palms over her hips. "Fine, strong hips . . . just made for fucking," he whispered. "You like to fuck, don't you? All Flynn's women like to fuck." Stepping back, he slowly circled her, pinching her buttocks. "And a beautiful ass, smooth and round, perfect for taking the strap." Walking around to face her again, he took her nipples between his fingers and rolled them gently. "You'll like the strap, my sweet. Here, on these plump titties"—he pinched the crests so hard she almost cried out—"and between your legs on your wet little cunt and on your silky bottom when you don't please us quickly enough. You must please us . . . you know that, don't you?" His grip on her nipples tightened. "Answer me."

Bile rose in her throat, but she had no choice. She nodded.

"Say yes; I want to hear you." And he compressed the soft tissue so cruelly, she choked out the word. "I knew you could talk," he said with a wicked grin. "You just need a little encouragement—like this." He stretched the tips painfully. "Is that making you hot? Tell me."

She shut her eyes and gave him the required answer.

"She's going to be such fun," Hugh exclaimed with glee. "She likes to resist. It makes everything so much more interesting, doesn't it?" The exhilaration in his voice was alarming and for a shaky, tremulous moment, Jo wasn't sure she had the necessary courage to endure.

"She's going to be a delicious little charmer," Langley agreed. "Disobedient enough to require frequent spankings and chastisement and a bit of disciplining like this. See how long I can make these enormous nipples," he said, softly pulling on them until she moaned in pain. "Come, Nigel, come closer. You can't see from so far away. Look, I'll do it again . . . and I can lift them. Is that high enough?" he playfully inquired, hoisting her heavy breasts upward by her nipples until she cried out.

"I'll watch from here," Nigel answered, his gaze on Jo's quivering, shuddering breasts as Langley released them.

"Maybe he'll get closer later," Hugh jibed. "When his cock is stiff enough to make him forget Hazard Black. We'll tie her up for you, Nigel, then she won't hurt you. Bring her here, Langley," he ordered, setting his whiskey bottle down, moving to the billiard table. "And careful taking that handle out. We're going to need that cunt in good condition."

It wasn't often Hugh had an opportunity to exercise his depravities free of scandal. The brothels frowned on rough play; they didn't like their merchandise damaged. But here in the wilds, surrounded by his hired guns, he was exempt from social censure.

"We'll teach you a little obedience now," Hugh cheerfully said at Jo's approach, her hands held firmly behind her by Langley. Picking up the coil of rope, Hugh slid the rough hemp back and forth, over and around her breasts, the coarse hemp leaving raw scratches on her fragile skin. Every time she cringed or flinched, he smiled. "Bitches need to be disciplined, made to know who's in charge," he whispered with an evil smile.

The fat Englishman's nasty smile seemed to hover for an instant like a fiendish apparition before her eyes, the image adrift and unstable. Blinking, she tried to clear her vision.

But perhaps she should have been grateful for the liquor. A

few moments later as she was deposited none too gently on
the billiard table, the shock to her senses was dulled. And
when her wrists and ankles were roughly tied, her pain was
lessened by the alcohol coursing through her blood.

Although anesthetized by whiskey, she groaned just enough
to excite Hugh or he'd tied the knots tightly enough to elicit
that utterance from her. But not satisfied, his cruelty requiring
added gratification, he exerted extra traction on the ropes tying
Jo to the table, stretching her arms and legs wider. "There,"
he said with a smile as she whimpered and sobbed in pain.
"Perfect."

Brutally bound and tethered, she existed in drifting consciousness, aware at times of conversations and sights and
pain, at other times inert and torpid. Perhaps her brain wasn't
functioning properly with all the liquor, she understood in
those moments of lucidity, or perhaps her inability to concentrate had to do with her drowsiness . . . she mused, drifting off
a second later.

However, at one point, she was roused by an explosive
shout that she heard very clearly indeed. "You're a bloody
coward, Nigel!" Hugh raged. "Here, I'm offering you goddamned first chance with the cunt and you're refusing! I don't
want to hear you whine or complain later, dammit!" Nigel was
the one who had questioned her father's presence, wasn't
he—that was it—and now he was declining to participate.
Although what he was going to participate in escaped her, she
hazily thought, shutting her eyes again, her mind floating
away, the name *Nigel* strumming in her ears.

"Then, she's all yours, Hughie," Langley generously con-
ceded. "She was your brilliant idea anyway."

Hugh squinted down the table. "Don't tell me the bitch
passed out." Leaning forward, he picked up a billiard cue and
turned it so the leather-bound grip was directed at Jo's exposed vulva.

"Gentlemen, on our stage tonight we have a gratifying ex-
hibition of hot, dripping wet cunt, impaled with a good eight

inches or more of a stiff hard billiard cue. And as you can see, gentlemen, this bitch's copious love juices are sufficient to service a fucking army."

"And we're the current army," Hugh added with a chuckle. "Not that she's completely been put through her paces, my man. She hasn't taken the billiard balls yet. We have to stretch that cunt a little more for the main event." Lining up two balls, he reached out, jerked the sodden billiard cue from her vagina and swung it toward Nigel. "Want a sniff at least, ye of faint heart?"

"Thank you, no." Always uncomfortable with Hugh's brutality to women, Nigel kept his distance as he often had in the past. He and Hugh didn't agree on the pleasures of sex.

Hugh shrugged and flipped the cue around. "Your loss, Nigel. Here goes, ball one." Lining up the cue tip and the ivory ball, Hugh shot the ball straight at Jo's glistening vulva. As the ball struck her damp flesh, it stuck with a soft splat. "That ball needs a little help there, Langley," Hugh brusquely noted. "Shove the goddamned thing in."

"My pleasure," Langley drawled, stretching across Jo's thigh, gently parting her drenched labia and easing the ball in. "That's a damned tight fit, Hughie. An absolute beauty of a fit. Let's just leave it there for a minute while we have another drink and admire how willingly her cunt accepts even something that large."

As they passed the whiskey bottle back and forth, Jo's already stimulated and whetted senses were feverishly quickening. Her sleek flesh was stretched taut around the billiard ball, the cool ivory sphere securely lodged, her engorged tissue pulsing around it, a glowing heat beginning to infuse her body, rippling upward through her vagina in a tantalizing, illusive pulsing that disturbed her torpid languor. She tried to move, reaching for the strangely insistent, inexplicable delight.

A hard knock on the door echoed through the room.

But the restless urgency bringing her awake, altering her

breathing, burning through her body required all her concentration. She took no notice of the intrusive sound.

Nigel nodded toward the door. "We have visitors."

"Not now, we don't have visitors," Hugh said, firmly, striding to the table. "I'm about to mount this wet cunt. Look at her, she's on fire."

As she drifted in and out of consciousness, an eddying frenzy was swirling inside her: carnal urges, powerful lust, a rapt feverish wanting, all converging where the hard surface of the billiard ball met her pulsing flesh, where the solid ivory pressed firmly against her clitoris.

As Hugh began climbing up on the table, some primal sense of survival wakened her and she stiffened and tried to rear back at the sight of the fat man grunting and struggling to reach her.

The rapping at the door had intensified and she heard it for the first time, the frantic tattoo echoing faintly in her beclouded brain.

"Someone should answer that," Nigel said, sober enough to understand that their caller's persistence had significance but not quite sober enough to move.

"Fuck no," Hugh growled, finally managing to heave his corpulence up on the table. "Go away!" he shouted.

"It's urgent, Smith says!" a voice shouted back.

"It better be urgent," Langley muttered. "Stay there, Hugh," he added with a casual wave. "I'll be right back." And turning from the table, he slowly walked toward the door. Opening it a moment later, he listened to the servant and then slammed the door shut. "The machine guns have been spiked," he said, so inebriated his voice registered no concern.

"Bloody bastards," Hugh declared, irritably, sitting down on the table. "They weren't supposed to be here until this afternoon."

"It *is* afternoon," Nigel pointed out with a sweep of his hand toward the clock on the wall.

"Hell and damnation, their timing could have been better. I'm about to fuck this hot bitch," Hugh resentfully muttered.

Langley was making his way back, his stride erratic. "Is it too late to call off this meeting?"

"Shit, yes," Hugh grumbled, his gaze shifting to the clock. "You're going to have to wait for my cock, bitch. Hell, maybe you can watch Flynn swinging from a rope while I fuck you."

Jo heard Flynn's name and galvanized by the sound, her brain came transiently to life, Hugh's sentence replaying itself to her horror. With every shred of will she could dredge up, she tried to concentrate, to bring the world into focus, understanding how critical clear thinking was to that moment.

Nigel gazed at his friend with an incredulous look. "Are you mad, Hugh? You heard the guns are useless!"

"We still have plenty of firepower without them. And we have the cunt Flynn was sleeping with. That'll make him squirm," Hugh said with a wicked chuckle. "Get Smith!" he shouted, enthralled with the amusing possibilities in his newest drunken fantasy.

The sound of running feet and the slamming of a door gave evidence that his orders had been heard. Smith arrived almost immediately; he must have been waiting nearby for instructions.

Smith averted his eyes from the woman on the billiard table, conscious of the peril in being party to such a gross outrage. Frank had filled him in on the Englishmen's latest stupidity; he didn't move from the doorway.

"What the hell is going on?" Hugh inquired, curtly, sitting like a squat potentate on the table. "Wasn't anyone watching the guns? What the fuck did we hire you for?"

Smith thought that he'd never seen a sorrier bunch of so-called men in his life. Not only did they have to tie up a woman to get sex, but they were stupid enough to pick the woman most likely to send them to their graves. "They came early," he said, his voice level. "No one saw them, no one

heard them. They're like shadows, you know that. And
Flynn's here now for your parley, along with Hazard Black, his
son, and a couple hundred men. This might be a good time to
reconsider your plans."

"Thank you for the update, Smith," Hugh said with the insufferable insolence that had made the English aristocrat
loathed in much of the world. "But I'm not concerned with
changing my plans. No red man or yellow devil can hold a candle to an Englishman. The British Empire covers the globe,
Smith. And there's a reason for that. An Englishman can't be
defeated."

"God Almighty, Hugh, you should be a politician," Nigel
said, sourly. "And you don't shoot any too straight if you recall.
So I wouldn't get too damned righteous about undefeated
Englishmen or someone might put a bullet through your fat
arse."

Hugh turned a venomous gaze on Nigel. "You've been
dragging your feet from the beginning. Someone might think
you've got a yellow streak down your back."

"Fine. You lead the attack on Flynn and Hazard then. I'd
like to see that fucking sight."

"That's why we've hired mercenaries." Hugh lifted his numerous chins, looked down his bulbous nose and glowered at
Nigel. "They're paid to shoot straight. We don't have to.
Boyden might have been thickheaded enough to put himself
in the middle of things, but I have no intention of leading any
damned charge."

"I'm relieved," Nigel murmured. "There won't be any
need to send another coffin back to England."

"Come, Smith," Hugh commanded, heaving himself off
the table and dropping heavily to the floor. "Let's go and parley with these curs. I think you'll find I have a very good hand
to play even without the Maxim guns." He turned to Nigel.
"And if you have the courage, come along."

"Ah'm comin'," Langley said, his words half-slurred.
"Wanna see that yellow devil Flynn checkmated."

"Watch and learn, my friends," Hugh asserted, arrogantly, moving toward the door. "An earl's son knows how to deal with the rabble. Put them in their place, Father always said, and keep them in their place with an iron heel."

As he reached the door of the billiard room, Langley in his wake, Hugh turned around. "Got the guts, Nigel? Or will you follow the boot-licking path of your grandfather. He knew how to make money, but he didn't know the first thing about honor."

"Fuck you, Mortimer. My grandfather knew as much about honor as your drunken forebears."

"If that's the case," Hugh retorted, waving his hand toward the hallway. "Here's your chance to show me your nerve."

Go, go, Jo silently urged, as if understanding with some sixth sense amidst the flurry of incomprehensible words and phrases flowing around her that they might be leaving. If she had enough time, perhaps she could free herself from her bonds. With supreme effort, she forced her mind to focus on that single thought. Freedom.

"Screw you, Mortimer. I'll show you nerve." Nigel stalked toward the door without a backward glance.

As the men moved down the corridor, the sound of their voices receding, Jo caught a glimpse of Frank in the blur of her vision, saw the door slowly shut.

Turning her head from side to side, she tried to concentrate. Was she alone . . . did she want to be alone—yes, yes . . . she *had* to be alone to escape. Listen, look . . . yes, the room was quiet. Everyone was gone. Twisting her body, looking upward to survey her bonds, she felt the billiard ball slip out and exhaled in relief from the violent, extreme, goading pressure.

Now to see if she could free herself.

Chapter

27

Flynn, Hazard and Trey with a large contingent of men were waiting at the Sun River ford when the Empire Cattle Company troop rode into view.

"None of them ride much," Hazard noted, observing the three Englishmen in the lead.

Flynn nodded in their direction. "Or do much of anything."

"Except make trouble." Trey lounged in the saddle, his silvery eyes alert.

"Not for long," Flynn murmured and nudged his paint forward.

The six men met midway between the armed ranks.

After destroying the trap that had been set for them, Flynn had only come to the parley to give a final warning. Or, depending on the circumstances, finish the job. "Those machine guns weren't part of the deal," he said, his dark gaze bland. "Other than that, I'm not sure there's anything to discuss."

"Perhaps one small thing," Hugh replied, silkily.

The fat Englishman sat his horse like a greenhorn, stiff and awkward, but his air of confidence was unmistakable.

"If you've got something to say, say it." Flynn tipped his head faintly. "Otherwise, we'll be getting back."

The two troops were twenty feet apart, lined up like cavalry, flanking wings left and right, everybody alert to any movement.

Hugh smiled, an oily, malevolent smile. "I have a friend of yours visiting."

Flynn looked at him, his dark eyes unwavering. "I don't play games."

"Very well. Her name is"—Hugh paused for effect—"dear me, I forgot to ask, but she was staying in your house in Helena when she accepted my invitation to visit. I believe she's a relative of Mr. Black."

Flynn slanted a glance at Hazard, a barely perceptible interchange.

"You must want something then." Flynn's voice was flat.

"Quite a lot actually."

"I'm listening."

"I want you off your land immediately. I want you in Helena by noon tomorrow. And if you do what you're told, you might see the bitch I have tied to my billiard table alive. Is that clear? Do you have any questions?"

"No." Flynn nodded. "We'll see you in Helena tomorrow." Easing his reins to the left, Flynn turned his paint and rode away, Hazard and Trey falling in beside him.

"What the fuck was that?" Langley exclaimed. "Why doesn't someone shoot them when we have the chance?" Fumbling for his revolver, he tried to draw it from his holster.

"For Christ's sake, you idiot," Hugh cried, putting his hand out to arrest Langley's fumbling. "Don't you see we have what we want? And everything fell into place, simple as can be. We have his damned land!" he crowed. Turning to Nigel, he offered him a superior look. "Now do you see how it's done? How a true aristocrat orders the world to his wishes?"

"You fucking idiot. Do you actually think Flynn Ito's going to turn over his land to you?"

"He will if he wants to see that woman alive again."

"What makes you think he gives a shit. Scores of women come to his ranch."

"Well, if he doesn't care, certainly her father will."

"Hazard Black isn't known for his benevolence to those who provoke him."

"Then, we'll have to persuade him. Maybe we'll send them her finger first if they don't comply. And then another finger and another if necessary, until they eventually see the merit in doing as they're told. It shouldn't be too difficult. You simply have no understanding of how to handle the lower orders, Nigel. That's your problem. You have to make it plain who's in charge, as the Mortimers have done since the time of William the Conqueror," he declared with an overbearing swagger. "My father will be pleased to learn we've added twenty-thousand acres to our holdings."

"Hear, hear," Langley intoned, even in his drunken stupor having recognized the words *twenty-thousand acres*. "I guess we'll show our families that we can manage a ranch and turn a profit."

"We'll send a telegram from Helena tomorrow," Hugh declared, his strutting satisfaction in direct proportion to the level of alcohol in his blood. "I expect our allowances will be increased accordingly."

While the two honorables were gloating over their victory on their ride home, Nigel was wondering whether he'd reach the ranch alive. He wasn't alone in his apprehension; Smith had already given orders for his men to be on full alert. Flynn Ito wasn't about to give up his land to God himself after fighting to keep it for so long. As for Hazard Black—he only hoped Hazard's vengeance didn't single him out as foreman to these idiots.

As soon as they reached the ranch and his employers were deep in their cups, he was packing his bedroll and hightailing it out of the territory. He'd heard the Holloways were looking for a foreman for their Colorado spread. Hopefully, that would be far enough away to escape Hazard's wrath.

Nigel kept looking over his shoulder, his plans having to do

with a swift return to England, disgraced or not. He'd promise
to stay on his parent's country estate and never go near
London again if he survived this disaster.

It required only the briefest of discussions once Flynn,
Hazard and their troop were out of sight.

"I'm going in for Jo," Flynn said. "My men and I know the
layout. Hold the Empire crew in the breaks just west of their
ranch. They have to come in slow and strung out there."

"We'll hold them," Hazard replied, each word unequivocal.

"Dead or alive," Trey said with a smile. "Although I'm
thinking that fat little fart who likes to give orders would be
better off—"

"Save him for me." Flynn's voice was sharp. "Don't forget."

And spurring his horse, he rode away with six of his men.

Flynn rode flat-out, his mount responding without benefit
of whip or spur, as though understanding the urgency of their
mission. The paint's ears dropped back; his stride lengthened
and he flew over the rough ground. His men kept pace, their
ponies prime bloodstock, their loyalty to Flynn absolute.

The Empire ranch was as familiar to Flynn as his own after
years of surveillance. He even knew where the billiard room
was, and he prayed during the seemingly endless ride, when
he hadn't prayed in years, when cynical and impious, he'd
given up asking the gods for help. He prayed to any god who
would listen: *Please, please, please, keep her safe.*

It was well known that Hugh Mortimer had been sent
abroad because he'd killed a woman, by accident it was said.
But rumor had it he liked violence with his sex and he'd been
warned off twice in Helena for hurting the girls in the brothels.

If he'd dared hurt Jo, God help him, Flynn vowed.

He would cut Hugh Mortimer into little pieces.

* * *

After deploying their forces in the thickets surrounding the breaks, Hazard gave orders to leave the Englishmen for Flynn. The rest were fair game.

"Although, I'd prefer the hired guns be eliminated first," he added. "We don't need their kind in the territory." It was a time of rough-and-ready vigilante justice, when the populace in the West looked askance at hired killers and dealt with them in a swift and summary fashion. Judges looked the other way and the army stayed clear of internal disputes, particularly if prominent citizens were involved.

Flynn heard the first shots faintly as he and his men approached the ranch from the low ground behind the stables. Screened by a stand of cottonwoods until they were within twenty yards of the buildings, Flynn dismounted at that point and said simply, "Follow me." His men knew what to do. They followed close behind as he sprinted across the stable yard. The shooting suddenly escalated in the west as they reached the back porch of the ranch house, indication that the battle was fully engaged.

Opening the door without pausing to reconnoiter, Flynn entered the house, his Colt poised. The back hall was deserted, not surprising with the number of men the English had brought with them to the parley. And household servants weren't a concern. Signaling his intent with a nod of his head, he loped down the hall, his men fanned out behind him.

He and Frank saw each other at the same time, but Flynn didn't slow his pace; he only tightened his finger on the trigger of his Colt.

The old man standing before a door as though guarding it, threw up his hands. "Don't shoot, for God's sake, don't shoot!" Panic rang through his voice. "I didn't do nothin'."

"Where is she?" Flynn already knew the answer, the man's fear patent, his last remark exposing his involvement.

"I didn't touch her, I swear." Frank pointed at the door. "She's in there."

"Is she alone?" If someone was guarding Jo, his entrance could endanger her.

"Yes, just her. They all left."

"If you're fucking with me, I'll kill you."

Frank knew he meant it. He also knew this was Flynn Ito glaring at him sure as hell. "I swear, she's alone. Tied up, sir. I didn't dare help her, but I was hopin'. It's a long story, sir; she'll be glad to see you."

Flynn's surprise showed for a flashing moment. How did the man know what Jo would like? But already shoving the door open, he dismissed useless speculation.

When he saw Jo trussed and naked, flagrantly on exhibit for the loathsome English, he came to a dead stop, inundated by a surge of fury so powerful he couldn't breathe.

Having turned at the sound of the door opening, she recognized him instantly, tears welling in her eyes. "Flynn!"

She was undeniably naked. Worse, she'd been naked, her legs spread wide, for who knows how long with those sadistic bastards. Quickly shutting the door, he told himself to breathe as though his brain required instructions in the presence of such heinous depravity. As he approached the table, he took note of the billiard ball, saw how wet it was and with what, observed the handle of the discarded pool cue, still dark with her essence.

She reeked of whiskey; she didn't like whiskey and her gaze was unfocused. He told himself they'd made her do what she did. He rationally understood that she hadn't been willing. But the ball was drenched, sticky and wet, and he knew why.

Forcing down the bile rising in his throat, he spoke as moderately as he could, as clearly with her understanding possibly compromised. "Your father's holding the Empire crew in the breaks. No one can hurt you now. You're safe." And then he quickly moved forward, carefully cut the ropes from her wrists and ankles, reddened and raw from her bonds. "Can you move?" He was almost afraid to ask, not sure he could deal with the answer.

She didn't immediately answer as though trying to understand what he'd said, and then she nodded and shutting her eyes, she suddenly began shaking.

"They're gone. It's over," Flynn whispered, gathering her into his arms. Gently raising her to a seated position, he quickly unbuttoned the top buttons on his linen shirt, jerked the garment off and dropped it over her head. Helping her to slide her arms into the sleeves, he lifted her off the table and holding her steady, set her on her feet. With relief, he saw that his shirt fell below her knees. He'd never realized he was so prudish. Scooping her up into his arms, he moved toward the door.

"I can walk."

"No."

The grim timbre of his voice alarmed her, her senses minutely attuned to male displeasure in the wake of her torment. "Are you angry?" she asked as a child might, anxious and fearful.

"No, not at all."

But she was conscious at some level of the effort it required for him to answer with grace.

"I just want you out of danger as soon as possible."

Again, that terrifying undercurrent of restraint in his voice.

His men were standing guard when he opened the door, Frank hovering nearby. Without pausing, Flynn nodded his head in the direction from which they'd come and swiftly moved away.

Frank ran to keep up. "Sir," he quavered, the uncertainty in his voice palpable. "Could we ride out with you?"

Not breaking stride, Flynn shot him a look. "We're moving too fast. But the English won't be back if that's what's worrying you. Although, I'd suggest you get out soon. I'm burning the place down."

The cold ruthlessness in Flynn's pronouncement brought Frank to a standstill, all the stories he'd heard about Flynn Ito suddenly brutally clear.

Jo plucked at Flynn's shoulder, her mind somehow distilling what was important from the brief conversation, Frank's pitiful expression jarring her senses. "His wife can't ride. She's too old. Flynn! She can't ride!"

Scowling, he came to a stop. "You trust him?"

She shook her head, as though clearing her thoughts. "Yes, yes . . . he helped me."

Flynn half-turned so he could see Frank. "Take the carriage!" he shouted. "The English won't be needing it! And head north—it's safer!"

"Thank you, sir!" A sudden smile wreathed Frank's face. "Thank you very much!"

But Flynn was already on the move, running.

The sound of battle had cleared the ranch of the few gun hands left behind and Flynn and his men rode away unmolested. Holding Jo across his lap, Flynn gave a wide berth to the hostilities, asking her the few questions he required answered, although cautious in his interrogation. He didn't wish to remind her unduly of her ordeal. When the small party was well past the breaks, he brought his horse to a halt. "Can you ride?" he asked her, finding the question repugnant but necessary.

She nodded, understanding what answer was needed to wipe the scowl from his face.

Without comment, he slid backward, deposited Jo in the saddle and dropped to the ground.

"My men will see that you get back to my ranch." He wanted to say, *I wish I had proper clothes for you,* but couldn't bring himself to refer to the circumstances of her near-nakedness. "It won't take long," he said instead.

She nodded, any attempt at framing thoughts into words difficult.

"I'll be back soon."

"Be careful," she blurted out and childlike, she reached out to him.

He patted her hand and set it back on her reins. He wasn't in the mood to be careful. He wanted to kill the English an inch at a time. Lifting his carbine from its scabbard, he smiled at her. "I'll be back before you miss me."

Then he slapped his paint on the rump and ran in the direction of the gunfire.

Chapter
28

When Flynn joined the battle, the Empire crew had been significantly reduced, their exposed position at the bottom of the ravine lethal to anyone who lifted his head above whatever hasty barricade they'd been able to throw up. There wasn't a man in Flynn's or Hazard's crew who wasn't a marksmen, their weapons first class. It was just a matter of time before the hired guns were picked off one by one.

The Empire had been harassing them for so many years, Flynn's crew harbored a real sense of personal vengeance. And this opportunity to shoot their paid mercenaries like fish in a bowl was gratifying.

Most of the Empire's local cowboys had managed to slip away, or perhaps the Sun River Ranch boys let them slip away. But the hired guns weren't faring as well, and of course, the English were being saved.

With fewer and fewer men left alive, the shooting eventually became sporadic, allowing Flynn the opportunity to find Hazard and assure him of Jo's safety.

Coming up on Hazard's makeshift redoubt, Flynn squatted down behind the fallen timber. "Jo's on her way to my ranch with six of my men. She needs rest."

"How badly was she hurt?" Hazard's voice was guarded; he knew about Hugh Mortimer—who didn't.

"Not too badly."

Flynn had taken a moment too long to reply. Hazard looked at him squarely. "Meaning what."

"She was tied up like they said." Flynn's expression turned grim. "I don't know the details, but she seemed reasonably calm, considering."

"We'll have to see if they're as calm when we deal with them," Hazard said, his voice chill. "You want Mortimer, I suppose."

Flynn nodded.

"And the others?"

Flynn shrugged. "It's up to you. I asked her"—he blew out a breath—"she talked some about what happened," he went on, tersely—"and I saw"—he grimaced—"you don't want to know. But the one called Nigel opted out, she said."

"One for you and one for me, then," Hazard declared. He didn't need any further details.

"I'm burning down the Empire tonight, so whatever that fellow Nigel wants to do . . . he'd better make up his mind fast."

"I'll see that he leaves Montana." Hazard's dark gaze was implacable.

"Good." The single word was softly uttered but infused with a brute finality. Flynn glanced toward the breaks. "I'm going down there. I'll see you when this is over."

Hazard quickly checked the rounds in his Colts. "I'll go with you."

By the time Flynn reached the boundary of the brush line, he and Hazard were no longer alone. Their men rimmed the alder-brush perimeter, weapons poised.

"Everyone but the English," Flynn ordered, the murmured command going down the line from man to man. Shortly after, he raised his hand, moved it forward in a swift arc and took off in a running zigzag. Launching himself over the rim of the ravine in seconds, he leaped and slid and plunged down the side of the dry gully, his Colts blazing, his men at his back.

The hired guns who tried to run were cut down. Those who stayed buried in their makeshift bunkers were ferreted out and killed. The rattle of small arms, the smell of gunpowder, the yells and screams of slaughter and command, the violent movement and milling free-for-all battle suddenly coming to a stop as abruptly as it had begun—every mercenary dead.

"We got 'im here, boss," McFee shouted. Pulled from their horses as they tried to flee, the English stood huddled together, guarded by a dozen men.

As Flynn walked up, he wondered if he was capable of killing a man in cold blood. The English looked desperately out of place, overdressed and flaccid, their silk shirts an incongruous note in the rugged landscape.

"Which one's Nigel?" Flynn's powerful nude torso glistened with sweat, his long hair swirled across his shoulders, his swords and Colts gleamed in the sunlight as he stood waiting, not completely sure it mattered who was who after what they'd done to Jo.

"Me . . . I am."

The voice trembled, as did the man and Flynn almost sighed in exasperation at the necessity of dealing with such useless creatures. But this man, Nigel, had been, if not kind, of service to Jo by his own cowardice. "Go," he said. "You're free to go."

Nigel's head swiveled from side to side as though his timidity would find some answer in the faces of the men surrounding him.

"I'd get the look out if I were you," Mc Fee said, holding up his thumb and swinging it to one side.

"Get him a horse," Flynn murmured. This was becoming more distasteful by the minute; the man was petrified. "Look,

you didn't personally take a hand in tormenting Miss Attenborough. That's the only reason I'm letting you go. Now, get
out; the time limit on this offer isn't indefinite."

Nigel finally seemed to understand or his paralysis lessened. In any event, he bolted for a horse, managed to get up
into the saddle and surrounded by Hazard's men, galloped
away.

"Now then," Flynn murmured, his mouth twisted in cheerless contemplation. "What are we going to do with you two?"

"You have no authority over us!" Hugh challenged, belli-
cose and defiant. "I demand you release us immediately!"

"I understand you were going to hang me."

Hugh's plump face was red with indignation, the pompous
conceit of twenty generations of Mortimers bred into his
blood and bone. "You're a renegade scoundrel! You deserve to
hang!"

His overweening presumption was staggering considering
his current status, Flynn thought. "Did Miss Attenborough
deserve her fate at your hands as well?" he asked with an icy
calm.

"I didn't hear her complaining." Hugh's smile was mali-
cious.

"I beg to differ with you, there." Fucking reptile; he was
making killing him easier by the second.

"I'll have you thrown in jail for what you've done today!"
Hugh's threats were pronounced with loud and lordly hauteur.
"My father will have you hung!"

"Hugh, for God's sake," Langley muttered, terror having
effectively sobered him. "Watch your tongue."

Turning his attention on Langley, Flynn softly inquired,
"Did *you* think Miss Attenborough was enjoying herself, Mr.
Phellps?"

Langley quailed under Flynn's harsh gaze. "I don't know.
Was damned drunk, you see—couldn't rightly say."

"I understand you were interested in Miss Attenborough's
feelings?"

"I—I . . . can't remember."

"She told me you were."

"Stop your cowering, Langley," Hugh ordered, churlishly. "Good God, this man is scum."

"While your family's title makes you what—stronger . . . richer . . . smarter?"

"It makes me a gentleman. Something you know nothing about," Hugh returned with a sneer.

"And gentlemen torture ladies. Is that right?"

"She was no lady."

Flynn struck Hugh with the flat of his hand in a blur of movement, the blow knocking him down.

"Now what do you milords say in circumstances like this?" Flynn drawled, watching Hugh struggle to come to his feet. "I demand satisfaction?"

Hugh's large nostrils flared, the rising red welt on his face striking against the whiteness of his skin. "Nobles don't duel with common rabble," he spat. "They horsewhip them!"

Flynn gazed at him, a merciless glint in his eyes. "You're a very stupid man."

"And you need to learn who your betters are," Hugh contemptuously retorted. Hugh Mortimer had never been able to control his temper, which accounted for the numerous public schools he'd been asked to leave and for the incident in the London brothel as well. That unfortunate quarrelsome pugnacity currently induced him to let slip the hidden derringer in his sleeve into his palm, sweep his arm upward and fire the twin barrels point blank at Flynn's face.

A collective gasp escaped the onlookers as Flynn ducked, seized his short sword and flung it hard.

Hugh staggered back, gagging, the ten-inch blade buried in his throat.

Flynn swung up from his crouch, a Colt in each hand.

And Langley slowly crumbled to the ground in a faint.

"The remittance men lack a certain honor," Hazard murmured, drily, sliding his revolver back in his holster. "But at least there's one less of them. What the hell are we going to do with this last one?" he added, nudging Langley's purple-shirted arm with his mocassin. "He's too pathetic to shoot."

"He'll probably drink himself to death soon enough anyway," Trey offered.

"Send him back. I don't care." Leaning over, Flynn retrieved his sword, wiped it clean on his trouser leg and slid it back into his belt. "I have a ranch to burn down."

Hours later when the Empire Cattle Company's buildings were no more than smoldering ash, Flynn offered his thanks to all the men who had come to help. The crews from other ranches started for home, their task complete, hoping the demise of the Empire would mean a peaceful future for them all.

The stars were out, the night wind cool where it blew in from the mountains, and only Flynn's and Hazard's men remained.

"I'll bring Jo back to Helena as soon as she's recuperated," Flynn said, standing with Hazard near the remains of the ranch house. "Or if she wishes to stay with me, we'll be down for a wedding." He spoke out of gallantry, his emotions in chaos—the events that had taken place in the billiard room demoralizing. But honor required he make such an offer and he made it.

"Jo shouldn't be moved now. I understand. If you'd like us to go back with you," Hazard offered.

"*No*, I mean, it's not necessary," Flynn added in a milder tone. He couldn't deal with company right now. Nor was he sure he could inflict himself on anyone else.

"Very well. I'll leave some men to serve as messengers should you have to reach us quickly." While Hazard recognized Flynn might wish to be alone, he wanted Jo to have advocates from her family should she want or need them.

"I don't anticipate trouble."

Hazard nodded. "I agree. Now if you're sure, we'll head back."

Everyone was on their best behavior. Even Trey was unusually reserved, Jo's abduction and captivity impossible to discuss without awkwardness.

Their farewells were muted and tactful.

And the two troops parted company at the Sun River ford.

Chapter

29

J o had been offered food and tea on Flynn's orders the moment she reached his house and afterward a bath had been
readied for her. Sobered by her food, she washed and soaked,
had fresh water brought in and had washed some more as
though she could scrub away the awful stench of the English.
As if so simple an act could remove the horror from her mind
and body and soul.

Eventually, in some small measure, it did. The security of
Flynn's home helped; the quiet solitude allowed her to recon-
cile the tumult in her brain into manageable areas of mindful
consideration.

And perhaps the English were dead by now.

Perhaps they could never harm anyone again.

But almost as quickly as she felt relief at the thought, she
questioned whether she wanted responsibility for another
person's death.

Now that she was still alive, she qualified, and in a position
to be benevolent. That wasn't always a certainty during the
torturous hours at the Empire ranch.

Suddenly feeling an acute and pervasive chill, she dressed,
with the help of a maid who found her some clothing that
would fit well enough to allow her to go out and sit in the sun.

She spent the rest of the afternoon in an uneasy fidget of activities, restless and fitful, skittish, needing constant variation to keep her mind distracted from the tumult of her emotions.

She ate the food the cook, Mrs. Beckworth, kept bringing her. Word of her ordeal having passed through the house like wildfire, every servant was solicitous, attending to her wishes with exactitude and sympathy. When she asked for some writing materials, she was brought four different kinds of paper and ink. After she wrote notes to her mother and Blaze and Daisy assuring them of her good health, a rider was immediately dispatched with the letters. The kitchen maid who'd helped her find clothes had carried a dozen different shirts of Flynn's to her before shyly offering one of her dresses instead.

She was shown into Flynn's library, extended an open invitation to make use of his extensive collection and for short periods she was able to thumb through one book or another. Until awful memories overwhelmed her once again and she was paralyzed with fear and self-reproach. With effort and conscious logic she brought herself back to the present, forced herself to look at each chair and table and drapery, assuring herself of her safe refuge, assuring herself of her blamelessness.

Throughout the afternoon, she fluctuated between trepidation and moments of calm, but when darkness fell and Flynn still hadn't returned, she found herself in a virtual state of panic over him, over her safety.

"Take a wee bit of hot tea, miss," the cook coaxed, having put a drop of laudanum in the sweetened drink. "Just a wee sip will calm your nerves."

When Jo finally agreed, sat down and drank some tea, she did feel better, stronger, less shaken and uncertain.

"Mr. Ito won't be hurt none, miss. I know that for a fact. He's got a guardian angel on his shoulder, he does. Right from when he was a little boy."

Jo's face lit up, the thought of Flynn as a child captivating. "You knew him then?"

"I been workin' here for more than twenty years, Miss. I knew him when he was just a wee tyke. Although," she added with a smile, "he weren't never too wee, not that one. He were bigger than me by the time he were ten."

Over the course of the next half hour, Jo sipped on her tea and Mrs. Beckworth answered all the questions put to her, relating numerous anecdotes from Flynn's youth: how he'd learned to ride and track like an Indian, how his father had begun teaching him mastery of the sword when he was very young, how his mother had insisted on half a day of school every day regardless of Flynn's laments, how he spoke five languages before he was eight—the Japanese of his father, his mother's Gaelic, English of course, and Absarokee and Nez Percé because his father had men working for him from both tribes.

Midway through a story of Flynn tracking his first Grizzly bear, Jo fell asleep. Smiling with satisfaction, the cook came to her feet, covered Jo where she lay in the big easy chair made for Flynn, then tiptoed out and shut the door.

When Flynn arrived shortly after, Mrs. Beckworth shushed him and pointed to the closed door of his library. "She's wore out, poor thing. Now don't go waking her up just yet. She needs her rest."

"I'll bathe first," he replied as though he were taking her advice, as though he wasn't relieved not to have to face Jo right now.

Once he'd bathed and dressed, he decided to have his supper before waking her. After he'd eaten and drunk more than he should, he walked by the library, went to his study instead and dropped into a chair near the window. Brooding and tormented, he looked at the star-lit sky with an unseeing gaze and drank some more.

Hours later the door opened. He looked up.

"Why didn't you wake me?" Still drowsy, Jo stood in the

doorway, gazing at him from beneath half-raised lashes, desperately wanting his comfort.

"I needed a drink." He tried to smile. "Go to bed. I'll be in later."

She could feel the distance in his voice as though he'd put up a wall in those few phrases. "When later?"

He tried to temper his tone, but the gruffness was unmistakable. "I don't know. It was a long day."

"For everyone."

He held her gaze for a moment, the minute anger noticeable in her softly uttered words. "Yeah . . . for everyone."

"Are you sulking?" He was even dressed in black as though in deference to his surliness. And she didn't deserve his anger.

"No." He took a small breath. "I'm drinking."

"You're obviously angry."

"No. I'm just tired."

Her brows rose fractionally. "Of me?"

"No," he said again, clipped and curt.

"Somehow I don't find your answers comforting. I was hoping you'd hold me." She winced as the words tumbled out, embarrassed to sound so imploring.

"I don't know if I can do that right now."

A flicker of outrage flared in her eyes, her moment of misgiving effectively squelched. "And why would that be?"

He didn't answer, the dead moment of silence deafening. "I don't know."

Her gaze narrowed. "I don't deserve this from you."

He scowled. "What the hell does that mean?"

"You blame me for what—being alive?"

"No, I don't."

"But you can't hold me."

He set his glass down, his gaze shuttered. "Not right now."

"You fucking bastard," she whispered.

He opened his mouth to speak, then shut it again.

"Smart choice."

"Don't push me," he muttered. "I'm not in the mood."

"What *are* you in the mood for? Some games like the English?" Her voice began to rise. "You're wondering if I enjoyed it, aren't you? Or how much I did? Maybe you'd like to see!" She reached for the buttons at the neckline of the maid's dress. "If these marks aren't good enough"—she thrust one of her raw wrists at him—"you can count my bruises and scratches and decide if I resisted enough, if I'm unsullied enough for your goddamned bloody ego!"

He started to rise, thought better of it, his own temper tightly curbed but unpredictable. "Stop it," he growled.

"No, you stop it, you damnable two-faced bastard!" She was shouting now, all the pent-up emotions she'd suppressed, her own uncertainties, boiling over. "You're not sure what to do with me, now, are you?" she cried, snatching up a book and hurling it at him. "You're not sure you can touch me again. You're not sure I'm pure enough, you intemperate fuck! Maybe I don't want you to touch me!" she screamed, advancing on him like one of the Furies. "Maybe I couldn't stand to have you touch me ever again!" On top of him now, she lunged at him, pummeling him with her fists, wanting to shatter his insufferable, unexpressed condemnation, wanting to hurt him as much as he'd hurt her.

Silently enduring her assault, he warded off her blows to his face, absorbing the rest without any visible reaction.

"Damn you, say something! Tell me about your new and convenient double standard! Tell me why you have the unmitigated gall to be resentful when *I* was the one forced to accept their abuse, you bastard! Still bloody mute?" she panted, breathless from the intensity of her attack. "Maybe this—will get a word—out of you!" Sweeping his scabbarded sword from a nearby table, she whirled it up over her head, and swung it downward.

He ripped it from her grasp bare inches from his head, coming to his feet in a surge of power. "Don't," he growled. "That was my father's."

They stood inches apart, breathing hard, furious, convulsed with rage.

"At least you can get up for something," she snapped.

"Now that I'm up, I'll bid you good night," he said through clenched teeth, his impulse to hit something almost irresistible.

"I'll raise you one," Jo rapped out. "I'll bid you good-bye."

"It's the middle of the night."

"Are you concerned for my welfare?" Her eyes were wild, insult in every syllable.

Enough to put his life at risk to save her, he thought, grimly. "Not any more," he bluntly said.

"If you're ever in Florence, look me up. Perhaps I can find you a virtuous woman to sleep with." Her smile was vicious. "You prefer that now, don't you?" And turning in a ripple of scented hair, she walked away.

He didn't reply or move; he didn't even move after the door shut on her. Jealous and judging, resentful, he stood victim to an uncertainty that encompassed a collective grievance more far-reaching than a lover's quarrel. A grievance that had to do with ownership and a level of possession he wasn't sure he even understood. And if he ever did, he suspected the fanatical sentiment wouldn't be commendable.

And she'd been wrong about the blame.

He didn't blame her.

He blamed himself for not knowing how to deal with what seemed an irreclaimable loss.

He was dead tired, probably half drunk too, but weary most of the violence that had been his life for so long that he wasn't sure his sensibilities were still human.

Was there any hope for peace?

If not, was he capable of continuing the twenty-odd years of struggle?

He didn't know.

Today had been his Armageddon of sorts, although he hadn't realized it at the time, Jo rescued, the campaign successful, the English gone. Where was his elation and triumph? Where was the satisfaction? Where was the sense of absolute victory? Instead he was more angry than he'd ever been and filled to choking with discontent.

The door opened, interrupting his poisoned contemplation and he looked up to see his cook, in robe and slippers, scowling at him. "She's leaving," Mrs Beckworth said, accusatory and tart. "In the black of night."

"I know." He finally moved, began walking toward the door. "I'll find her an escort."

But that was all he was capable of doing.

He couldn't speak to her; he wouldn't have known what to say.

But after rousing Hazard's men, he watched the preparations for Jo's departure from his darkened study, standing like a brooding shadow at the window.

And when they were gone, when Hazard's men and his daughter were no longer even a dark speck in the moonlight, he walked to the liquor table and poured himself another drink.

Slumped in the depths of a leather chair, he contemplated the amber liquid in his glass as though some relevant answer stirred in the Irish whiskey he drank because it reminded him of his mother.

No answers were forthcoming, of course, only chaotic, discordant questions, oppressive reminders of shortcomings and misdeeds, and the ugly memory of what he'd just done to Jo Attenborough because he couldn't help himself.

Chapter
30

Hazard wasn't surprised when Jo returned alone. She'd wanted to leave Flynn's, she said. And whether he believed her didn't matter right now because she was insistent the decision had been hers.

Perhaps he'd left his men behind because he'd had a premonition, or perhaps he understood how delicate and baffling the aftermath of evil could be.

Blaze was furious, not believing Jo's explanation for a minute after seeing her. "She's grossly unhappy. It's so obvious, I don't know how you can be so unruffled. She's hurting terribly."

He didn't argue with Blaze. What they felt personally didn't matter when it came to Jo's happiness. "Let's make her as comfortable as we can," he suggested. "Give her time to get over the horror of what she's endured. We'll deal with Flynn later."

"I should hope you'll deal with him! The man is as unfeeling as the despicable men at the Empire ranch! I won't have him in the house again! I mean it, Jon, don't look at me like that—I'm absolutely adamant!"

"I doubt he'll be in Helena anytime soon."

"Whenever he *should* come, if you must see him, do so

somewhere else. Jo is desperately unhappy and he is completely to blame—the disreputable cur." She made a small
moue of discontent. "Which brings to mind our son's intemperate amusements. These amorous diversions can leave a
great deal of unpleasantness in their wake—as you see. We
should talk to him and remind him of the consequences of his
flirtations."

"I'll talk to him," Hazard promised, although the women in
hot pursuit of their son were intent on satisfying their desires.
And unpleasantness was more likely to occur if Trey didn't ac-
commodate them than if he did. But he was more than willing
to make a case for a degree more discretion in his son's conduct.

That same day, Flynn called McFee into his study.

He hadn't slept, he was unshaven, and while not intoxicated, he'd obviously been drinking.

McFee kept his counsel, but he knew why Flynn looked
the way he did and if he had been in a position to give advice,
he would have told him to go after Hazard's daughter and
bring her back. Instead, he said, "Looks like you could use
some sleep, boss."

Flynn grunted in reply, ran his hands through his hair and
then looked up at McFee from the chair near the window
where he'd spent his time of late. "Do you feel like looking
after things for me for a while?"

Good, McFee thought, *he's going after her.* "Reckon I could."

"I'm going up into the mountains."

Shit. "For how long?"

Flynn shrugged. "I don't know. The Empire is finished, at
least until those in England make up their minds what to do. I
don't expect any trouble from anyone else. You should be able
to manage. You probably can do a better job than I."

McFee had been at the ranch from the start; he didn't argue
the point of his competence, but he did take issue with
Flynn's decision. "Bein' alone ain't all that good, I'm thinkin'."

Why don't you go south for a while and kick up your heels instead—a young fellow like you needs entertainment."

Flynn half smiled. "Thanks for the advice, but I'm not in the mood to be entertained. I'll be up on Blackduck if you need me."

McFee knew that meant he could come for him only if the most adverse circumstances arose, although Flynn was right, the coming months should be ones of relative calm. "When you leavin'?"

Flynn heaved himself up from the chair. "In about fifteen minutes."

"Don't stay too long, boss. You'll git moody."

Flynn's smile took effort. "Too late for that, but maybe some fresh mountain air will clear my head."

He rode away a short time later, his saddlebags packed with a change of clothes, some books, paper and brushes and ink, and enough food to supplement his hunting and fishing.

"He's as ornery as they come," Mrs. Beckworth muttered, standing beside McFee on the front porch. "You'd think he'd have more sense than to let her go when he wants her somethin' fierce."

"He's gonna go up in that cave o' his and live like a monk." McFee sighed. "Never could figger out what he did up there."

"It's like the Absarokee vision quests, I reckon. Some men have to talk to somethin' bigger than them. My ma used to always say, make up your own mind, girl, and don't take no guff from no one."

McFee smiled because Mrs. Beckworth was living proof of that personal philosophy. But then spirited independence was a common trait on the frontier. "I reckon I found my way out West for those same reasons," he said.

"Hell, half the territory did and the other half just ain't admittin' it."

McFee nodded his head in Flynn's direction, the horse and rider still visible in the distance. "How long do you reckon he's gonna stay up there?"

"He's missin' her somethin' terrible from the way he were drinkin'. He ain't a drinkin' man. So I'm guessin' two, three weeks and he's gonna be gettin' right anxious."

"Maybe just for any woman."

Mrs. Beckworth shook her head emphatically. "Oh, no, Mr. McFee, just any woman ain't gonna do a'tall for that one. He's head over heels and he don't even know it."

McFee smiled with genuine relief. "Well, that's right comfortin' to hear from the woman who been takin' care of him since he were a wee one."

"Mark my words, McFee. Three weeks on the outside and we'll be seein' that sweet boy agin'."

Chapter

31

For the next fortnight, the Braddock-Blacks did all they could to distract and amuse Jo. They entertained often—dinner parties, dances, musicales and literary soirees. The guest list always included several eligible bachelors interested in their daughter. And wearing the requisite gloves that conveniently covered the marks on her wrists, Jo did her best to be interested in turn.

She smiled until her face ached, danced until her feet hurt, conversed with so many men who were out to flatter her that she was tempted to believe that she was indeed the most beautiful woman in the world. And she ate and overate, Blaze's notion of solace having to do with food. But she couldn't fault her new family for their concern and she did her best to be pleasant at each and every entertainment that was launched.

Not a whisper of gossip had surfaced apropos of Jo's sojourn in the Sun River country, testament to Hazard's immense power. He'd made it clear to everyone involved in the Empire hostilities that Jo's captivity was not to be discussed.

It was enormous comfort to Jo not to have the added burden of public censure, for she was struggling daily with the effects. It surprised her: that inability to forget or efface those disastrous hours. She would have thought reason and logic could nicely set aside that horror and securely lock it away. But she discovered treacherous memory would slip by her defenses at the most inopportune moments and she'd find herself shivering in fear.

Each time Hazard saw his daughter so stricken, he rued the day he'd let that blond Englishman escape with his life. And one evening when Jo had abruptly excused herself from a dance and gone to her room, he and Trey discussed a remedy that would correct that error in judgment.

Two men were sent to England the next morning, their mission known only to Hazard and Trey.

But no amount of entertainment could assuage Jo's troubled spirits and one morning at breakfast she announced that she was returning to Florence.

"Not permanently, I hope," Blaze said, anxiously, setting down her coffee cup.

Jo smiled. "No, I just need a brief respite to gather my wits and restore my humor."

Even her smiles were wan, Hazard reflected, his concern creasing his forehead. "Would you like company? We could all go if you like." He worried she would sink into an all-consuming melancholy if she was alone in Florence. Lucy wouldn't be going, he knew for a fact. She and Ed Finnegan were inseparable and Ed was talking divorce, rumor had it.

"If you don't think me ungrateful, I'd like to go alone. Not for long," Jo added at Hazard's troubled expression.

"Plan on coming back for the holidays if not sooner," Hazard suggested. "You might enjoy our snowy Christmas."

"I'd like that. I will."

With that he had to be content. She was of age, independent and so unhappy, he couldn't begrudge her the move. "Have you told your mother?"

"I thought I would today. She's so busy she won't be without things to do while I'm gone." A vast understatement, Jo realized even as she spoke. "I'm afraid she's become a fixture in Helena. I feel as though I should apologize."

"Nonsense. We're all adults," Blaze replied, smiling. "Your mother can be very charming." There was no point in denigrating Lucy's love of society when so many other women shared her passion, and Ed Finnegan had monopolized her time so effectively of late, Lucy hadn't been an issue in their household. "Why don't we make a quick trip to Lucinda's and buy you some new things before you leave."

"Thank you, but I'm taking only one valise." Jo smiled. "You see, I'll be back in no time with nothing to wear."

"Good," Hazard said, warmly. "I like the sound of that. I'll have Sheldon wire some funds to Florence."

"That won't be necessary. You've been more than generous. I'm flush, Papa."

Hazard smiled, pleased when she called him Papa, her cheerful slang an optimistic note. "Tell her, darling," he remarked, turning to his wife. "Tell her there isn't a lady alive who can't use a bit more pin money."

"Listen to your father, dear," Blaze murmured. "And if you don't want to spend your pin money frivolously, you might think of a pretty little villa in the hills. We saw the most darling little country house. Tell her where it was, Jon, so she can look at it."

"It's south of Fiesole. I'll have Sheldon attend to it for you."

"Papa, no, for heaven's sake!"

"It won't hurt for him to see if it's available."

"Papa!" she chided, frowning. "That's outrageous!"

"We'll make arrangements for you at the Grand Hotel then." But Hazard was already planning to make the present owners an offer that would induce them to sell. He remembered the house and it was splendid.

Jo was shocked to see her mother dressed when she called on her shortly before one.

"I just have a minute, dear, before my afternoon ride," Lucy declared, straightening her bonnet in the mirror. "So don't sit down."

Her mother's tone of voice implied she went for a ride every afternoon, the concept sufficiently unsettling to the patterns of a lifetime that Jo's eyes widened in surprise.

"What is it dear?" Lucy inquired with perfectly arched brows. "Don't you like my new gown?"

"No, it's very pretty."

"Well, then—out with it." Lucy glanced at the clock.

"Ah, that is, I came by to tell you I'm leaving Helena."

Lucy pursed her lips and studied her daughter for a critical moment. "It's that awful man, Ito, isn't it? Didn't I tell you not to become involved with such a disreputable man. And now he's gone and you're wretched. I won't say I told you so, but you know very well I did."

Lucy knew nothing of Jo's captivity, only that she'd gone north to spend time with Flynn.

"I'm not wretched, Mother. I just miss Florence. I'll be back for the holidays."

Lucy rested her palms on her parasol handle and smiled faintly. "One has to be sensible about men, darling. Haven't I always said that?"

"Mother, have you conveniently forgotten the vain and egotistical Cosimo who was the least sensible choice of a man on the face of the earth?"

Lucy waved one hand in a dismissive gesture. "He was the merest bagatelle. I needed someone to pass the time."

Jo's gaze narrowed. "For fifteen years?"

Lucy sniffed. "Must you be so caviling? He was convenient."

"I heard Ed Finnegan is rumored to be divorcing his wife. Will he become your sensible selection?"

Lucy smiled. "Very much so, darling. He owns the bank, half the buildings downtown, a dozen ranches and I don't know how many mines. It makes one quite giddy just thinking about such lovely, lovely, sensible assets. And if he has one little foible like his obsession with punctuality," she added, glancing at the clock again. "I'm sure once we're married, I can temper that ridiculous trifle."

"If you're sure he's what you want, Mother, punctuality aside," Jo added with a smile, "then I'm pleased for you. I wish you all the best," she said with genuine fondness.

"And I shall scrutinize the eligible bachelors while you're away and have a wonderful list drawn up for you on your return. You're beautiful, a bit too educated, but never you mind," Lucy said with another small wave. "Your father is wealthy and prominent and I daresay, your mother will soon be as well. You will be quite a lovely catch, darling. What do you think about having your wedding in the cathedral? White roses, I think, masses of them and a Worth gown, dear"—she frowned—"we almost should order it before you leave." Taking a small breath, she waggled her fingers as though having resolved her dilemma. "I'll simply order one for you myself, I know what you look best in . . . and of course, we must have vast quantities of caviar and French champagne for the wedding banquet and I suppose some of that beef that everyone eats out here and Ed consumes out of all proportion to what most would consider a salubrious diet." Lucy was temperate in her selection of food, still maintaining her eighteen-year-old weight. "I forgot about an orchestra!" she exclaimed. "Oh, my goodness, I'm going to have to talk to Ed about that; he's the chairman of the symphony trust. Oh, sweetheart, isn't this exciting! You're going to have the wedding of the century!"

Jo chuckled softly. "And all I need is a bridegroom."

"Pshaw, darling, that's the least of our worries. The men will be clambering over each other in an effort to gain your attention when you return. Oh, dear, it's almost one and I have to run, my pet. You know how Ed is about his schedule and he's taking me to see his latest mine." She primped for a moment before the mirror, tucking a curl or two into her bonnet, adjusting the bow under her chin. "Now send me a note when you reach Florence." With a little wave, she briskly moved away and blowing Jo a kiss, opened the door and left.

Jo stood on the veranda of the Plantation House a short time later, surveying the familiar bustle of downtown with a touch of nostalgia. She was going to miss this frontier town after all, when only a few brief months ago, she'd arrived unwillingly, vowing to leave on the next train. Now she'd be leaving with sadness.

But she desperately needed to put some distance between herself and Flynn Ito. She had to be far enough away so that wanting him was no longer an option. So when she woke at night longing for his touch, his smile, the warmth of his body beside her, an ocean and a continent would separate her from her folly.

Florence would be peaceful. She had friends there. She had work if she wished because Father Alessandro had enough projects that needed completing to last her a lifetime. She enjoyed the intellectual discussions and arguments in the cafés; she'd missed the museums, the beauty of the city, perhaps more now than ever, the sense of safety an ancient city like Florence offered.

Shutting her eyes, she imagined the colorful Duomo bathed in sunlight and smiled.

How nice it would be to see it again.

Chapter
32

Like the legendary Miyamoto Musashi of Japan who had renounced the world in 1643 and had lived in a cave for the last years of his life, Flynn had climbed Blackduck Mountain to reflect on the road he'd been traveling and come to a better understanding of his life. Or if he was brutally honest with himself, to try to forget Jo.

He meditated and looked within himself, he painted in the Sumi-e Zen style of painting, using brush and ink in bold, confident strokes that reflected the philosophy of seizing the moment in life. He fished or hunted for what food he needed, but ate like an ascetic, the urgencies of a normal existence beyond him. He read and studied Musashi's discourses, reaffirming those principles he'd learned so long ago: From one thing know ten thousand things. The Middle Way, or the Way of no extremes, is the better way. What is sought is harmony among all things. It is the warrior's way to follow the paths of both the sword and the pen. And in the end, there are some who believe that even if you master the way of Heiho (the way of the warrior) it will be of no use.

When one has been led astray or filled with false conceptions, and cannot resolve these problems, this is *ku*—emptiness or illusion or true meaning.

He was here to discover the difference or the sameness. Whether one or all were correct.

And in those days on the mountain, Flynn lived in his sequestered, monkish world, pondering his prejudices and distorted points of view, struggling to find an honest heart and a straightforward spirit.

He asked himself what he wanted, what happiness meant to him?

He asked himself whether he was obliged to carry on his father and mother's dream, whether he could or even wished to?

He asked himself how important his family's mission when he was the last member of that family?

Who was he doing this for?

Until he'd met Jo he'd never questioned his world; he'd accepted it without thought of his connection to it or his future.

She'd changed all that.

It wasn't her intention, he knew, nor was it his. He'd tried to tell himself she was just more beautiful than most and more tantalizing, but he'd known from the beginning that she was important to his life in other ways. She made the sun shine brighter and the air seem purer; the world looked better, felt better, *was* better when she was around.

Truly.

He set down his brush, his ink painting of a sparrow on a branch unfinished. Rolling up his paper, he rinsed his brushes, stowed them away in their small cloth carrying packet and came to his feet. He looked around as though seeing his environment for the first time. The sun was brilliant, the birds were singing in all their colorful plumage, a slight breeze brought the scent of smoke from a campfire to his nostrils. Surveying the landscape spread out before him, he saw a thin plume of smoke in the southwest. One of his line camps, no doubt.

It was the thirty-fourth day since he'd left his ranch and he realized there is good and no evil when there is wisdom and reason. And he realized as well where the goodness in his life dwelled.

He packed up his books, and brushes and change of clothes and headed down the mountain, finally knowing what he wanted.

Knowing what he was going to do.

Chapter
33

"I didn't know if I'd be seeing you again," Hazard remarked, rising to greet Flynn in the club room of the Montana Club. "Sorry about the venue. Blaze is still angry."

"I don't blame her. I was hesitant about even approaching you."

"Whiskey?" Hazard queried, indicating a decanter on the table next to his chair.

Flynn nodded and took the chair Hazard waved him into. "I have to apologize, although the word is insufficient to convey my remorse."

"It was a messy situation. Difficult at best, horrendous in truth. Everyone responds to things like that in a different way. But Jo was damned unhappy. I hope you can do something about that. Not that I'm matchmaking, I wouldn't be so presumptuous, but she needs an explanation at least." He handed Flynn a drink.

"That's why I'm here. To apologize to her and ask for her hand in marriage if she'll have me after my stupidity." He smiled ruefully and gently swirled the liquor in his glass. "I've been living in a cave, trying to understand what I wanted, where I was going."

Hazard wasn't surprised; the Absarokee went on vision

quests, fasting for days until they saw and heard the spirits and found their way. "So have you decided?" His gaze was piercing, his voice sober. "Jo's fragile after what happened to her. You have to be sure."

"I'm absolutely sure. I've been miserable without her." Lifting the glass to his mouth, Flynn drained it.

"Nervous?"

"No—yes . . . not nervous, but contrite as hell and nervous about explaining to her. Is she available to see me today?"

"No."

Flynn met Hazard's gaze, something in his tone disturbing. "Will she be available soon?"

"She left for Florence two weeks ago."

"Alone?" It was the most frightening thought he'd ever had, that she might have found someone else.

Hazard nodded. "She'll be back for the holidays."

A wave of relief washed over him, quickly replaced by a restless impatience. "Christ, that's months away," Flynn muttered, frowning. "She's left the States by now, I suppose."

"She sailed from New York ten days ago."

"Alone?" He couldn't restrain himself. She could have met someone in transit; she was an impetuous woman.

Hazard smiled faintly. "As far as I know."

Flynn shot him a glance. "Don't bloody well fuck with me."

"It's the truth," Hazard calmly replied. "I can't be certain she's alone. She probably is, but with Jo, nothing's guaranteed, as you well know. But she didn't mention anyone in her last telegram from New York."

Flynn groaned, held out his glass and softly swore under his breath.

As Hazard was refilling Flynn's glass, Ed Finnegan walked into the room with a drink in his hand and nodding at the men, came over to join them.

"Haven't seen you in town lately, Flynn. Congratulations on ridding the territory of those hired guns. It's not good for respectable business. We all appreciate your work, there," he

said, reaching out and shaking Flynn's hand before he sat
down. "Can't say I miss those three useless excuses for
Englishmen, either. They were trouble every time they came
into town. The sporting ladies at Lily's are damned glad
they're gone as well."

"Didn't think you were spending time at Lily's anymore
with Lucy back in town," Hazard said, amusement in his gaze.

"Two different things, there, Hazard." Ed winked. "You
know that. We're both men of the world. Which reminds me,"
he added with a sly smile, "that son of yours is right friendly
with the women at Lily's—a great favorite, I hear—like his father before him." He lifted his glass in salute.

"That was a long time ago, Ed."

Ed smiled. "You know small towns. Who ever forgets. Like
when Lucy returned, she picked up right where she left off,"
Ed remarked. "It seemed like she'd never been gone."

"Except for my daughter," Hazard pleasantly noted.

Ed laughed. "That must have been a damned surprise."

"You might say so."

"She turned out to be a glorious young lady, didn't she,
though. Some lucky young man has snapped her up, apparently. Lucy tells me Jo is getting married when she returns—
big wedding . . . all the trimmings . . . Lucy's already tapping
my pockets for it," he sportively said. "Not that I mind.
Lucy's a charmer."

Flynn set his glass down with a bang. "Who's getting married?"

"Lucy's daughter, Jo. You're out of the picture, aren't you,
Flynn? That's what Lucy said. Must be someone here in town
from the sounds of it." He smiled. "To tell you the truth, I
didn't listen."

"If you'll excuse me." Flynn came to his feet, his jaw
clenched.

Hazard gave him a cautionary look. "Don't do anything
rash."

"I just remembered an appointment," Flynn said, brusquely.

"I'll talk to you later." He strode away, exiting the room like a bull on a rampage.

"He don't look like he's out of the picture," Ed murmured, watching Flynn stalk away.

Hazard's brows rose faintly. "He and Lucy might have conflicting opinions."

"She seemed right certain to me."

"I doubt she finds Flynn acceptable." Hazard tipped his head and smiled. "Unlike you."

Ed beamed. "Lucy's a real sweetheart. No hard feelings, between us, I hope, Hazard."

Hazard shook his head. "Not at all. Your wife might take issue, however."

"Not so long as she gets a right fair sum in a divorce settlement," Ed said, casually.

"So you and Mabel have talked about it. Gossip precedes you, of course."

"Hell, I know that." He smirked. "Just like I know about the choir director. So it'll be a fair settlement, if you know what I mean. More than any choir director could ever hope for. Actually, Lucy has two weddings to plan for." Ed's face turned a bright red. "You're the first to know. I just asked her right and proper last night."

"Congratulations." Hazard was almost as happy as Ed, although for different reasons. Lucy should cease to be a problem—not only for him, but for Blaze.

"Thank you." Ed grinned. "Hell, I'll drink to that," he said, draining his glass.

Hazard lifted his glass and drank his as well.

"To the joys of marriage," Ed remarked with a chuckle. "Again."

"As ever," Hazard softly said.

Chapter
34

Aman burst through her door without warning.
Lucy squealed, dropped her sherry glass and swore in a very unladylike fashion as the sherry spilled over her new gown.

"Tell me who Jo's marrying," Flynn growled, standing like a prophet of doom, dark and threatening in her doorway.

Distracted from her petulance by the sight of an unbelievably gorgeous man, Lucy surveyed Flynn from head to toe with a much practiced gaze. "You must be Mr. Ito. I didn't realize you were so beautiful. Do stop scowling at me and come in." She smiled. "And shut the door." Surely this tall, powerful, glorious man with long black hair and exquisite eyes that tilted up in the most delightful fashion could only be the dangerous and disreputable Mr. Ito.

If Flynn weren't in a towering rage, he might have been more wary of that tone of voice in a woman. But maddened by the desperation of his thoughts, he took no notice.

"Do come in and sit down"—Lucy patted the settee beside her—"and tell me what's brought you here in such a tumult."

Flynn stepped inside and shut the door, but he didn't move from the entrance. He wasn't in the mood to sit; he wanted his question answered. "I just saw Ed Finnegan at the Montana

242

Susan Johnson

Club and he said you're planning a wedding for Jo on her return."

"Dear, dear, you have such a glowering frown, Mr. Ito.
Could I get you a glass of sherry or whiskey, cognac perhaps?"

"No, nothing," he said, clipped and curt. "If you would be
so kind as to answer my question, I won't bother you further."

"You're no bother at all, Mr. Ito. On the contrary, do sit and
I'll tell you all about Jo." She waited then with the certainty of
a manipulator par excellence, her smile amiable and obliging.

Mr. Ito was dressed in the height of fashion, his frock coat
tailored to the inch, fitting his broad shoulders in the most intriguing way. She could almost feel those delicious muscles
that bulged beneath the fine broadcloth. A shame Ed didn't fit
a coat so well, she mused, but then he had all those lovely
mines as compensation. Although even mines didn't completely compensate for the strength of Mr. Ito's powerful legs
and, she silently sighed, the lovely way his form-fitting
trousers made one want to immediately take them off.

There was no question why Jo had been so enamored of
this magnificent man.

He was sinfully alluring.

Taking a small breath, she reminded herself of her splendid
prospects with Ed and curbed her covetous desires.

Even in his fretful, hot-tempered mood, Flynn knew that
assessing look in a woman's eyes and kept his distance. "I'm
in a bit of a hurry. If you could answer my question, I'd appreciate it."

"Do sit down," Lucy cajoled. "I'm not going to eat you
alive, although it's tempting," she said with a smile.

"No offense, ma'am, but I'm in love with your daughter."

"So I presumed with that unrelenting scowl. You may sit
over there," she indicated, pointing at a chair some distance
from her.

He sat.

"Now then, what do you wish to know?"

"Who is Jo marrying?"

"No one at the moment."

"But Ed said—"

"He doesn't listen. Did he say that as well?" Her brows rose. "We women aren't completely without intellect although there are times when such a pose is practical. Now, seriously, Mr. Ito"—Lucy's voice took on a chill briskness that couldn't have been improved on by a Spanish inquisitor intent on making some tortured soul recant—"exactly what are your assets? What can you offer my daughter?"

His moment of shock quickly overcome, Flynn understood what approach would serve him best. "I'm a wealthy man. My parents struck gold in Sixty-four and much of it is still in my bank account in Ed's bank. He'll vouch for me. I also own twenty-thousand acres of the best grazing land in Montana, ten-thousand head of cattle and a horse-breeding operation that nets a tidy sum every year. Your daughter won't go without. She's welcome to all I have."

My goodness, what outrageous generosity. But Lucy concealed her shock and said in a normal tone of voice. "You hurt her dreadfully, I understand. She may not want to see you." Although she'd personally drag her daughter back to Helena for the kind of fortune Mr. Ito was willing to bestow on her. "I could write to her and offer my support of you if you wish," she kindly offered.

"So she's not involved with someone else."

Lucy shook her head. "She was blue-deviled the entire fortnight she was here before she left. Poor girl, would hardly look at another man although they buzzed around her like bees." She had seen the phenomenon at Claudia's party so she could speak from experience although she would have been willing to improvise should it have been necessary. "Although," she said with a soft sigh, "dear Jo can be very obstinate and her coterie of friends in Florence is extensive. I can't guarantee she hasn't found someone of interest in Florence." Perhaps it would be best to send Mr. Ito abroad immediately, rather than wait until Jo returned. In her experience, men's interests could be fickle and a handsome, wealthy man like Mr. Ito surely had legions of women in pursuit. "If I might suggest, perhaps you should go to Florence and press your suit in person."

"Where is she staying?" he asked, without hesitation.

"The Grand Hotel."

He instantly came to his feet and bowed. "Thank you, very much, Mrs. Attenborough. I appreciate your help." He smiled, bowed once again and bid her adieu.

As the door closed on him, Lucy sat in a mild daze. He had bowed in such a civilized manner and actually said, adieu, his accent as good as any Frenchman's. How gallant he was and of course, beautiful beyond words and rich as a pasha.

Whoever had described him as disreputable and dangerous should have their head examined. He was a consummate gentleman. And if he'd killed all those men people said he had, well, they must surely have deserved it.

She would ask Ed directly he arrived just exactly how much money Mr. Ito had in his bank.

But right now, she must write to Jo posthaste. And she would tell her in no uncertain terms, that if she didn't agree to marry Mr. Ito, she would disown her on the spot.

Chapter
35

Flynn had never been abroad before. He'd been to San Francisco often and now New York. But Helena was enough of a microcosm of the world with the population of the gold camps and resulting mines having been drawn from far and wide that he well understood the practicalities of le beau monde.

If one were sufficiently wealthy, most anything was available—for a price.

Including a suite beside Jo's in the Grand Hotel—hastily vacated by its occupant, the direction of Father Alessandro, the cafés Miss Attenborough frequented and even the names of some of her acquaintances . . . in this case, male acquaintances. Flynn was unconcerned with her female friends.

The extent of his rudeness to her at his ranch made him wary of directly approaching her. She might refuse to see him. He would reconnoiter first, a long-standing practice for a man of his background.

It was midafternoon. He'd begin with Father Alessandro.

The curate was a small, elderly man, he discovered, who spent his afternoons cultivating his flower garden. And perhaps without actually acknowledging the fact that he'd been anxious, he was able to dismiss Father Alessandro as a rival.

He surveyed the first of the half-dozen cafés suggested to him from afar, but there were few patrons at that time of day and none of them was Jo. He'd look again when the establishments began to fill; café society was most active from late afternoon through evening. He was optimistic about finding her, if not now, later tonight, when she returned to her suite.

But she didn't appear at any of her usual haunts, although he kept close watch. He returned to the Monastery of San Marco, thinking she might be there. He even walked through two museums she'd mentioned as her favorites without success. As the hours passed and he wasn't able to locate her, his frustration escalated. She hadn't come back to her suite; he had the maid look when he returned to the hotel. And she didn't sleep in her room.

He knew because he sat in the alcove opposite her door all night.

By morning, nearly insane with jealousy, he called on Father Alessandro, only waiting for him to leave morning matins before accosting him in the monastery courtyard. Flynn was hoping the curate might know her whereabouts.

When he approached the elderly man, Father Alessandro looked up. "So you've come," he said, gruffly.

"You know who I am?"

"Yes, of course, the samurai."

Even dressed in well-tailored clothes, he was conspicuous, apparently. "Jo spoke of me?"

"Yes, on more than one occasion."

Father Alessandro's brusque manner, his tone, his critical gaze was disconcerting. Had she said he was a brute? No doubt from the look in the man's eyes. Although he couldn't argue with her assessment. "I came to apologize to Jo, but I can't seem to find her. Do you know where she might be? Is she out of the city?"

"What makes you think she wants to see you?"

"I don't expect she does."

The priest didn't speak for a moment, surveying Flynn

from head to foot, his mouth pursed. "She's at the Grand Hotel," he offered, finally.

He must have passed muster—no devil's horns visible— Flynn thought, but the priest's answer had been grudging. He was careful to reply with courtesy. "As I understand, she hasn't been there recently."

"She has many friends. She may be with them."

That was the damnable problem, particularly if a male friend was involved, but he could hardly speak of his jealousy to this man of God. "I'll just have to wait, then. Thank you for your time."

"If I see her, I'll tell her you're in Florence."

For a fleeting moment, Flynn wanted to say, *No, no, don't tell her. She might run*. But he said instead, "Thank you, I'd appreciate it." And bowing faintly, he began walking away.

"She might be with the Americans from Boston."

Flynn spun around, his heart beating wildly.

"The Montgomerys have a home near the Boboli Gardens. I'm not sure I should be telling you this," he added, a note of censure in his voice.

"I'm forever in your debt," Flynn said with profound gratitude. He unconsciously bowed as his father had, his hands palms together at chest level. He smiled. "Forgive me, a holdover from childhood. You don't know how happy you've made me."

And then he ran.

Immediately returning to the hotel, he talked to the friendly concierge and received directions to the Montgomerys. They were a wealthy expatriate American family, the concierge explained, with grown children—he named the daughter and two sons—all of them longtime residents of Florence, art collectors and dilettante writers. Their home had once been a ducal palace, he added with suitable reverence.

Flynn thanked him, tried not to think about wealthy men who were art collectors when Jo had spoken so often of her fascination with the art of Florence and chose to walk rather than take a carriage. He preferred being as inconspicuous as possible as he approached.

His caution was unnecessary however, because several blocks short of the address he'd been given, he saw Jo.

And his temper instantly flared.

She and another woman were seated at an outside café table surrounded by four men and she was laughing. Everyone was laughing. They were all drinking their morning coffee and enjoying the sunshine, the morning papers spread out on the long wooden table. She wore a pretty green-striped gown, her hat hung from its ribbon on her chair back, her parasol was tipped against the table and she was enjoying herself without him.

In a flash of a second, his anger turned to misery.

What had he thought? That he could arrive in Florence, say forgive me and she'd fall into his arms? Had he lost his mind completely? Had he spent so long in the wilderness that he'd forgotten there were bustling cities filled with bright, intelligent people who led interesting and engrossing lives? That Jo had only recently left such a city and had returned after a few brief months to pick up the threads of that existence. She knew all these people; you could see they were friends of long-standing—their camaraderie playful, intimate. The two women touched each other when they laughed, and nodded their heads together and flirted with the men with a light-hearted gaiety.

When Jo spoke, everyone leaned forward to listen and when she laughed, she threw back her head so the merry, jubilant sound soared into the sunlit sky. And he couldn't help but notice how the men took particular notice of her as though she were a queen and they her court. Her dress was too form-fitting, he silently grumbled, as though he had the right, as though he'd suddenly become her duenna. And her beauty was so striking, pedestrians slowed as they walked by to look at her.

Like the most doleful wretch he watched from afar, listening to the tenor of the party's laughter, the rhythm of their
conversation, too distant to hear the words, but painfully
aware of the demonstrable affection and pleasure exchanged.
The other woman took out a letter, read from it briefly, then
passed it around and they all perused it and made jovial com-
ments that made them laugh again, the correspondent apparently known to them all.

He'd never felt so lonely.

Not even on the mountaintop for thirty-four days.

He stayed there, like a pariah, watching from the shelter of
an apartment portico, until the party rose from the table and
strolled away, the ladies arm in arm with two men each—as
though one wasn't enough.

Eaten with jealousy, stricken with gloom, cheerless and
grieving, he had to face the unbearable truth.

He'd lost her.

He wandered the streets of Florence aimlessly for hours,
his thoughts in turmoil, every beat of his heart an ache of sadness, feeling more alone than ever. Maybe he shouldn't have
left his ranch and the familiar pattern of his life. At least he
knew what to expect in the Sun River country, the sameness if
not comforting, recognizable, the home he'd helped build, the
ranch he'd grown up on, the men he worked alongside familiar and predictable. If he'd had no particular intimacy in his
life since his parents died, he hadn't expected any. Hadn't
wanted any.

And then because of Jo, he'd become aware of a raw, all-
pervasive emptiness in his soul.

Because of Jo, he'd learned the misery of solitude.

He spent the night in his suite, hoping in some irrational
way that Jo would return, that someone would tell her he was
there and he'd hear a knock on his door. He'd been drinking,
he hadn't slept for days or perhaps his thinking would have

been less fantastical. But she didn't come back to the hotel, the knock on his door remained a dream and he watched the sunrise slowly lighten the sky, sunk in the blackest despair.

With the bright light of morning, his thinking cleared, or perhaps he finally gave up hope, and forced himself to face the truth. He'd come to Florence too late; worse, he'd driven Jo away with a brutality he still recalled with horror. He really didn't deserve her. The wealthy men at that café table, the laughing, kind, attentive men who collected art and wrote pretty phrases were what she wanted. He didn't blame her.

His journey had been a wishful dream from the beginning. And dreams had a habit of dissolving into nothingness. The real world consisted of his Sun River Ranch, his horses and cattle and work—the only things he'd ever known and now he didn't know if he wanted them anymore. He sighed, a lonely future the only surety in his life. Suppressing his melancholy with willful determination, he forced himself to move as well, quickly washing and dressing, packing his valise, having the concierge arrange for a carriage to take him to the train station.

A short time later, he settled back against the leather seat of the barouche and shut his eyes. The beauty of Florence offended him, Jo's happiness offended him, the fruitlessness of his quest offended him the most.

What a bitter end to a journey begun with such hope.

Chapter
36

Making his way down the busy, crowded train platform, Flynn heard her laughter before he saw her. Jo was standing with the same people she'd been with yesterday, he noticed, her tall, slender form suddenly visible as the flow of passengers shifted. She wore a different gown, rose-colored and bright. She must be staying with them for some time since she'd brought her luggage, he reflected, disconsolately. Linked arm in arm with one of the men, she looked up and spoke to him. Suddenly, the man bent low, brushed her cheek with a kiss and then whispered in her ear.

Flynn's stomach twisted in envy.

And as if the sight of Jo and her new lover wasn't awful enough, he thought, swearing under his breath, he was obliged to walk past them to reach his rail carriage. Although, the press of passengers might be to his advantage; he might be able to pass by undetected if he moved far enough to the left and put the crowd between himself and Jo.

Keeping to the far edge of the platform, using his valise as nominal buffer, he moved through the crowd, feeling like a fugitive trying to escape the carabiniere. Out of the corner of his eye, he caught a glimmer of Jo's rose-colored gown in passing, unconsciously lengthening his stride at the sight. Moving

by as swiftly as possible, he was just beginning to allow himself to relax, having put considerable distance between them
when Jo's voice rang out above the din of the crowd.

"Flynn!"

Was he deceiving himself or was there elation in the sound?
Or was that accusation in the intensity of her voice?

For a breath-held second he continued walking, not sure he
could face her condemnation, not sure he had the heart to be
rebuked in such a public arena, before all her friends. And
then he turned because he would willingly grasp at straws for
her.

She was running toward him when he looked up and if it
were possible to measure hope by the size of the lump in one's
throat, he was calibrating that belief to an excessive degree.

This man who had learned to charm at a very young age,
who was known to have countless women in pursuit because
of that charm, this man who had until a few short months ago
considered himself enthusiastically single, now waited for the
great love of his life, breath held and unsure.

Jo stopped running when she saw he hadn't opened his
arms to her or even dropped his valise. He was just standing
there, his expression unreadable. Slowing to a more sedate
pace, cautioning herself to less fevered emotions, she reached
him a few moments later, her gaze as uncertain as his. "What
are you doing here?"

Now was his opportunity to apologize, but the man she'd
been kissing had followed her and was standing a few feet
away, his brows drawn together in a frown.

"Who's he?" Flynn asked, gruffly, when he shouldn't have,
and nodded his head toward the man.

Jo swiveled around, then swiveled back. "A friend," she
said, a new coolness in her voice. "Why are you in Florence?"

There—the accusation he'd feared. "I came to see you." It
was the truth and friend or no friend, frowning or not, there
was no reason he should lie to her.

"Why didn't you call on me then?"

"I couldn't find you."

"I'm at the Grand Hotel."

"Not really," he said, tipping his head faintly toward the dilettante American. "You've been with them."

The man moved closer, took Jo's hand in his, his frown deepening as he gazed at Flynn. "The train will be leaving soon," he said to Jo and then looked at Flynn. "If you'll excuse us."

She shook off his hand. "In a minute, Charles."

He lifted his chin a fraction and stared at Flynn. "You must be the samurai."

Flynn felt his spine stiffen at the disparagement in the man's voice. "Yes," he said, "among other things."

"And what other things might those be?"

"Charles, for heaven's sake," Jo exclaimed, her expression fretful.

"I understand you're handy with the sword. I fence."

Flynn wanted to laugh, but he understood such a response would be unsuitable. Jo hadn't left yet. She was still only inches away and she'd chided the man. Three points for his side. Now wasn't the time to take tactless issue with a man who fenced. "Congratulations," Flynn said, instead. "I understand it requires great skill."

Jo slanted a look up at him, and for a moment he thought he caught a glimmer of amusement in her eyes.

"Our team at Harvard took all-conference three years running."

"Congratulations again."

Charles's gaze narrowed, understanding he had a rival. "Tell him you have to leave, Jo."

Flynn almost smiled at the sudden stubborn set of her chin, but he was caution itself in his current equivocal position.

"Why don't I say good-bye to you here, Charles. I'll see you all on your return."

For a taut moment, Charles Montgomery's gaze flicked between Flynn and Jo, his mouth twitched faintly and then ap-

parently, too well mannered to make a scene, he said with a
forced smile, "We won't be gone long."

"Good. Say hello to Maribelle for me."

"We'll be back the end of the week."

Jo smiled. "Splendid. I'll see you then."

He had no choice, short of starting a scuffle with Flynn, and
understanding that, he bowed stiffly and took his leave.

Flynn grinned. "I thought I might have to hit a fencer for
the first time in my life."

Jo tried not to smile and didn't succeed. "He really is a very
good fencer, darling." She instantly raised her hand to her
mouth as though she could smother the unwanted word.

He set down his valise, suddenly realizing he'd been given
leave to stay. "Can I assume you and Charles are not—"

"No, we're not and you needn't look so smug . . . nor so
damned cocksure either. I'm expecting considerable penance
and hours of apology from you for what you thought of me.
That wiped that smile off your face, I see," she said.

"I shall willingly do whatever you wish to put myself in
your good graces once again," he said, suave and ingratiating,
and if he hadn't smiled at the last, his gallantry would have
been seen as the pink of good manners.

"Bloody right you will and neither that unctuous flattery
nor that seductively wicked look are likely to *put* you in my
good graces, Mr. Ito."

"I understand, ma'am," he said with the most implausible
obsequiousness.

"It's miss and you're beginning to annoy me," she tartly
said.

"You won't be miss for long. I hope I haven't spoken too
plainly and annoyed you again."

"You presume too much, Mr. Ito," she crisply said, but her
heart was beating at a vastly accelerated pace and billowing
clouds of sunshine seemed to be flooding the huge, shadowed
train shed.

"I came halfway across the world to apologize most profoundly for my stupidity and rudeness and then make you my wife. And as you may know, darling"—his grin was roguish—"I usually get what I want."

"And as you know, *darling,*" she purred, tempted to throw herself into his arms without a single penance, but not yet lost to all reason, "I get what I want *first.*"

"Yes, yes, absolutely yes." Cognizant of his great joy and gratitude, his loneliness had instantly vanished at her utterance of that first darling, he spoke with great sincerity. "You first, of course . . . always."

"In that case"—she glanced around—"Could we go somewhere else?"

"We can go wherever you like, the mountains of Peru, the Valley of the Gods, Mount Fuji, the Champs Élysées. Or might I suggest something closer because right now I'd like to go someplace where I could hold you tight and sleep for a week. I haven't slept much lately."

"You too? I haven't slept through the night—"

"Since you left," he finished.

She laughed. "Yes. I have huge black circles under my eyes. See here, I look a fright."

She didn't, of course. She looked outrageously beautiful, her eyes glowing, her smile heart-stopping, the crane brooch he'd given her that first night in Helena prominently displayed on her collar. He touched it lightly.

"I always wear it," she said.

Why hadn't he seen it yesterday? If he had, it would have changed everything. He would have swept her away from her friends and carried her off because he would have known. "I saw you at the café with your friends yesterday, but I didn't see this."

"Your mistake . . . and you would have left me today." The thought was so frightening, she took his hand and held on tightly and all thought of penances vanished.

"You looked so happy with them, laughing, and animated, everyone so proper and acceptable—I thought you'd found what you wanted. I thought I'd lost you."

She shook her head. "I was miserable. I have been for a very long time. But now I'm not, definitely not," she whispered, leaning into him, inhaling the familiar pine-scented cologne he wore. "I was thinking, maybe we should look into this loss of sleep of ours . . ."

"Find a way to deal with it," he murmured, pulling her closer, dipping his head, brushing her lips with his. "You could marry me and then we could sleep together every night."

"Now there's an idea . . ."

"We have to talk to Father Alessandro, then. I'm not taking any chances this time that we might argue over something stupid—"

"Very stupid," she said with a touch of pique.

"Ridiculously stupid, I agree. I must have been insane."

"Well, you had reason," she murmured, offering him a forgiving smile.

"Thank you for your understanding." Feeling relatively safe in her affections once again, he released her, reached down and picked up his valise. "We're getting married before we do anything else," he declared, the fact that he might have lost her forever still frighteningly real. He began to draw her away.

She pulled back. "Isn't a proposal generally required?"

Dropping his valise with a thud, he sank to one knee and gazing up at her as the rush of passengers around them ground to a halt, he took her hand and said in a deep, clear voice, "I've loved you from the first moment I saw you, Miss Attenborough, from the very first second. I was a fool not to have asked you then. In the interest of rectifying that gross error in judgment, would you do me the honor of becoming my wife? Will you marry me and not only make me the happiest of men, but gratify the curiosity of all these people watching us?"

She grinned. "Yes, Mr. Ito, I'd love to marry you."

Quickly rising to his feet, Flynn pulled her into his arms and kissed her soundly.

A loud cheer went up and much clapping of hands ensued and they accepted heartfelt congratulations from all the smiling strangers surrounding them. And then Flynn said with courtesy and grace, "If you'll excuse us, we have a wedding to go to."

They walked away amidst a gaudy charivari of hurrahs and congratulations and amused smiles.

"I'm serious about getting married first," he said, his grip tightening on her hand. "You don't know what hell I've been through since you left."

"Since you practically threw me out, you mean."

He grimaced. "Let me offer you another of several thousand apologies I intend to make for my barbarous behavior that night."

"Accepted." She ticked off an imaginary check in the air. "Four thousand nine hundred, ninety-eight to go."

"I really feel terrible."

He looked so sad and contrite, she was able to say without a qualm and mean it, "I know."

"There was no excuse for my behavior. Not any in the world."

"You're here, now, darling and I'm happy. I don't want to talk about any of that—" Her voice trailed off. She didn't want to remember that night at his ranch, nor the reasons for their anger. "Not now, not when we're together again." She smiled. "I'd rather plan a wedding."

He understood, the ugly memories of that night were so debilitating he couldn't think of them without feeling a wave of remorse. "As long as the wedding plans have a contingency for speed," he said with a smile. "I've been suffering without you too long. I can't wait."

She grinned. "I think that's my line. But don't worry, Father Alessandro will arrange things," she said. "He can do anything."

Chapter
37

In this case, Father Alessandro had a marriage license drawn up swiftly, the bishop signed it and twenty minutes later, Flynn and Jo were married in the chapel of the San Marco monastery. Father Alessandro officiated, the bride and groom were beaming, and the witnesses agreed later that the couple were so deeply in love, they didn't hear a word of the service.

When Father Alessandro pronounced them man and wife, they looked at each other in the candlelight, their eyes bright with tears.

"You're crying," Jo whispered.

"It's the candle smoke," Flynn said, swiping his fist over his eyes.

"Me, too. Candle smoke always does that to me."

He laughed softly. "I'll have to take care of that now that you're mine."

She nodded her head. "You're mine too, don't forget."

He grinned. "Are you sure that's how it works?"

"Flynn!"

Father Alessandro cleared his throat, not wishing to referee an argument so soon after the wedding. He recognized that obstinate look in Jo's eyes, having seen it numerous times before—the first time when she was four and told him in no uncertain terms that she was not lost, she was smelling the flowers.

"Thank you for expediting everything, for your kindness and support," Flynn interposed, shaking the curate's hand, preferring not to seriously debate degrees of possession at the moment. He'd not quite come to terms with them himself.

"I wish you both all the happiness in the world." Father Alessandro had tears in his eyes as well, gazing at the young woman he'd helped raise, pleased she'd found the love she deserved.

"I'll take good care of Jo, Father. She's my world."

"I don't need taking care of," she retorted, force of habit difficult to break. "Tell him, Sandro. I can take care of myself."

"It's my hope you take care of each other," the curate diplomatically replied.

Tactfully changing the subject, Flynn said, "Father, we'd like you to join us for our wedding breakfast."

Jo shot Flynn a surprised look. "You didn't say anything about a breakfast."

"Everyone has a wedding breakfast," he replied with a smile. "I thought you knew."

She beamed and immediately declared, "We have to go to Giacosa! You'll love it, darling. He'll love it, won't he, Sandro!"

And so it was decided. They dined outside under the shade of flowering vines and were feted by the entire restaurant for their newlywed status. It was a lovely wedding day, sunny and warm; it was a splendid wedding feast and they ate and drank and basked in the blissful enchantment of their love and the absolute perfection of their world.

On their return to the hotel, Flynn bought her a ring from one of the jewelry stalls on the Ponte Vecchio. "You decide," he said and she picked out a square-cut emerald the jeweler claimed had come from a Spanish Infanta. She admired it and enthused over it all the way back to the hotel, waving it in front of him, holding her hand out before her, twisting it this way and that so the gem caught the light, telling him he shouldn't have spent so much, making him enormously happy he could buy her presents.

And when they walked into her suite and she saw all the flowers, she squealed with delight. "How did you do it? How, how, how?" she cried, throwing her arms around him, causing the maid who was carrying in a bottle of wine to almost drop it.

"Just set it down anywhere," Flynn said, nodding at the maid over Jo's head. "That will be all."

And the minute the door closed, he grinned at her and said, "You're so much fun to buy things for . . . such enthusiasm."

"We're not all stoic warrior-monks," she retorted, grinning. "So tell me"—she waved her hand at the flowers, baskets and vases of them, the fragrance scenting the suite—"how did you do this when you never left my side?"

"I sent a message from the restaurant."

"For that, too?" She indicated a large package on one of the few tables not occupied by a vase of flowers.

He nodded and unlacing her arms from around his waist, turned her and gave her a little nudge toward the package. "See if you like it."

When she'd unwrapped the present, she discovered a beautiful scale model of the Duomo, every detail precise, the various components lifting apart so the interior could be viewed, each fresco and altar and column lovingly approximated. "It's gorgeous," she whispered. "I've never had such a lovely gift." She'd had very few gifts in her life. Lucy wasn't ungenerous, just unthinking.

"I saw it yesterday when I was wandering the streets and I know how much you love Florence. I thought wherever we are, you'll have this as a remembrance."

His tone had suddenly changed and looking up from the model, she turned to him. "What do you mean *wherever* we are?"

He held out his hand and a tiny shiver of fear struck her. He looked so grave. When she went to him, he sat down, pulled her onto his lap and kissed her gently.

"You're frightening me, Flynn," she said, a moment later, her voice hushed, her eyes dark with apprehension. "You're not dying of something?"

He smiled and she felt better. "That's only in operas."

She thought of the battle with the Empire. That hadn't been an opera, but very real and if he hadn't been so serious, she would have mentioned it. But she didn't want to argue— not now . . . with his mood so alarming. "Tell me what you meant when you said *wherever,*" she said, trying not to show her fear.

"I don't know if I want to go back to Montana, that's all."

She was instantly relieved. "We'll stay here for a time then. It doesn't make any difference to me."

"I don't know if I ever want to go back," he said, softly.

"Oh." It was the smallest of exhalations.

"I started training as a warrior when I was very young," he quietly explained, his words subdued. "It seems as though I've been fighting all my life. I'm tired. My enemies are all dead. My family's gone. I want peace. I want a normal life." His dark gaze held hers for a poignant moment. "Now that I have you, I want it even more. You are my Kwannon, my goddess of mercy."

"You were going back though, when I saw you at the station."

"I'm not sure I would have gotten there. I might have gone somewhere else."

"What about the ranch?"

"I left McFee with power of attorney and a half interest. But if you want to go back," he said, quietly, his gaze open, "we will."

"I'd like to go back from time to time—to see Mother and Hazard and my family. Would you mind?" She was being as cautious as he, trying to read his expression, his feelings.

"I just want to be with you. Somewhere, I don't care where

as long as I don't have to prove myself to every man with a gun and an attitude." He wanted to say, *Do you know how many men I've killed?* but he couldn't without seeing forever the look of horror that would appear on her face. So he said instead, "I've been fighting since I was sixteen. I don't have anything more to prove."

"Should we stay in Florence for a time?"

He smiled. "With Charles?"

"He'll get over it."

"Why not stay then," he agreed, because he could tell she wished to. And he could deal with Charles well enough. "Just make sure you explain to him that I don't want to fence with him," he said, smiling.

She grinned. "Done. Hazard bought me a villa that I haven't lived in because I think I wanted to go back and find you, although I didn't realize that until just now," she said, finally understanding why she'd been reluctant to settle down. "Would you like to stay there? It has the advantage of being an hour away from Charles."

"No more need be said. The villa it is." Flynn smiled. "First thing tomorrow."

"Because we have to admire all these flowers today."

"And tonight—among other things."

"Umm . . . whenever I hear that tone of voice I get all tingly."

"Do you get tingly in any special place?"

"It depends what you mean by special?"

"As in specially *mine,*" he said, hushed and low.

"As long as what I want of yours is *mine,*" she answered with a smile, as possessive as he, as independent.

"I can see we're going to have to negotiate this issue of ownership delicately."

"Delicate is good," she said, grinning, shifting her bottom faintly on his thighs.

His dark gaze was amused. "Is there anything that's not good for you?"

"Not when you're around."

His brows drew together in mild reproof. "Perhaps you'd like to rephrase that, now that you're a married woman."

"You're my everything, always and only." She grinned. "Better?"

"Much."

"I'm relieved. Since this is supposed to be our honeymoon," she said with a considering look.

He offered her a rueful smile, his fierce jealousy resistant to reason. "Forgive me. I'm completely at fault."

"Perhaps you could show me the degree of your contrition in a more physical fashion," she murmured. "A personal gesture, as it were, to show your devotion."

"I'm not getting on my knees again."

"Not ever?"

The way she pronounced the words made him immediately change his mind. "You want me on my knees? You need but say the word, darling. But if that's what you want, you have a great deal too many petticoats and other sundry articles of clothing in the way."

She instantly slid from his lap and lifted her skirts and petticoats. "Even now?"

He laughed. "Haste is no longer a requirement. We have all the time in the world."

"Which fact does not, however, negate the need for speed right now"—her brows rose—"if you please."

His mouth lifted in a slow, lazy smile. "Why don't I play lady's maid and dispose of all those unnecessary clothes. You're not going to be needing them anyway."

"Ummm . . . what a delicious thought. Are we going to spend our honeymoon in bed?"

"Isn't that what a honeymoon is?"

"According to some women of my acquaintance, honeymoons are for shopping and sightseeing."

"Then their husbands must have very lovely mistresses."

Suddenly recalling Flynn's former life of dissipation, she

turned a darkling look on him. "Which you will never have—is that clear?"

"Why would I want one when I have you?"

"I would prefer a more definitive reply. One that contains the word *no* or *none* or *never.*"

Reaching out, he unclasped her hands from her skirts and pulled her close. "I will never have a mistress," he said, softly. "My word on it."

"Thank you." She made a moue. "I should be more sophisticated, I know," she said with a little sigh. "But in that regard, I'm terribly ungenerous."

"We're both of the same mind. You need not explain to me. In fact, I'm sure I'm even more ungenerous than you."

"So we will be in each other's pockets."

He grinned. "And other places as well."

"Libertine"—she pulled her hands away—"I thought we were being serious."

"I am serious."

She held his gaze for a potent moment. "How serious?"

"Whatever you want, darling," he said without hesitation.

It stopped her for a moment—that casual unbridled license. "You're only rash with me, right?"

He understood it was going to be a matter of serious negotiation—this mutual jealousy. "I am only rash with you," he said with utter simplicity.

Her face lit up with delight, her smile piquant. "In that case, I'd like to make love on the balcony with the sun and breeze and the great blue sky above us."

"Now?" It was midday and the square below was bustling with activity, not to mention the various other nearby balconies that might be occupied.

"A balcony has always seemed so romantic—I've always wanted to . . . well—"

"Expose yourself?" he said with a grin.

"And you've always been discreet?" she countered, her raised brows offering challenge.

Discreet was not a word ordinarily applied to Flynn Ito and
his amorous escapades as they both knew.

"Not entirely," he answered, carefully succinct, glancing at
the balcony through the half-opened doors.

"We could leave our clothes on."

His mouth twitched into a smile. "I see."

"Well—will you?"

"Of course," he said.

"Why didn't you say that right away?"

"No reason." He was still smiling.

"You're highly aggravating for a man on his honeymoon."

"And you're sweet as sugar candy," he said, agreeably, beginning to unbutton his frock coat.

"What are you doing?"

"Taking off my coat. No one's likely to take issue with me"—
his brows flickered in amusement—"for various reasons, one
of which is my extreme generosity to the concierge. I don't see
why we should have sex with our clothes on."

"Flynn! Don't you dare!"

"You started it." He kicked off his shoes.

"Well, I'm stopping it right now!"

"Do you know how tantalizing you look when you stamp
your foot like that? It makes me very lustful," he said with a
grin, dropping his frock coat to the floor, his waistcoat following a second later.

"Flynn! I'm not going out there naked!"

"You have no sense of adventure." He pulled his shirt over
his head and dropped it atop his other discarded clothing.

"I know too many people here!"

"Believe me, no one will say a word to you." He was unbuttoning his trousers with swift, facile movements.

"To my face, you mean."

"What else did you think I meant. They won't." He slid his
trousers and underwear down, stepped out of them and pulled
off his socks. "Now, then," he said standing up, "let me help
you undress."

Jo ran—not very far, as it turned out. Flynn was faster, stronger and in truth as intemperate as his reputation alleged. He disrobed his new bride with only a few minor scratches and bruised shins while gaining a new appreciation for his wife's extensive repertoire of Italian curses.

But her fury transmuted after a time, her struggles quieted and while it wouldn't be fair to say her sexual needs were paramount in that eventual capitulation, or that Flynn's powerful nude body and blatant arousal were prime incentives— certainly they were strong inducement. But he kissed her too—over and over again—everywhere and whispered heated words of love that quickened her senses and kindled her ready desires.

It was really quite impossible to long deny Flynn's very agreeable charms.

"Don't think you can always have your way with me," she whispered, twining her arms around his neck, her nude body melting against him, "just because I happen to find tall, dark, handsome men particularly sensual and enticing."

"I would never presume to think that," he said, grinning.

"Are you being impertinent?"

"Not in the least. But if you had a moment to indulge me," he murmured, pushing her gently backward, "I feel sure I could further entice you."

"What makes you think I wish you to?" But she didn't resist his gentle pressure.

"The flush on your cheeks," he whispered, brushing his knuckles over her face as they slowly moved backward, "and your stiff little nipples," he added, touching one taut crest with the lightest of pressures. "And of course—this," he murmured, slipping his finger into her throbbing slit, bringing it up drenched, sliding it up her throat as he eased her against the wall. "You seem—well . . . cordially disposed . . ."

"To be enticed."

His smile was cheeky. "Or fucked," he said, his fingers curling over her shoulders, his body leaning into hers.

His blunt suggestion spiked through her brain, his rigid erection pressed hard against her and an answering flare of desire curled downward—pulsing, liquid, flame-hot, urgent. She moaned softly.

"Soon, darling," he whispered, exerting pressure on her inner thighs with his palm, gently spreading her legs. "You can have it all." Bending his legs to adjust his height to hers, he guided the crest of his erection to her heated cleft and entered her with a swift upward thrust of his hips.

She exhaled in a low, breathy sigh as he buried his rigid length inside her, and when he lifted her legs around his waist and leaned into her, holding her hard against the wall so he had better leverage, so he could plunge deeper, she clutched at his shoulders and sobbed and cried out his name and climaxed before he'd established a decent rhythm.

"It's been so long," she whispered in the way of an apology, the words warm on his throat.

"Good, that's good, perfect," he murmured, her celibacy gratifying, his penis surging higher as though in reward for her good behavior. Mildly shocked at the overwhelming pleasure he felt at her disclosure, he'd not thought himself so punctilious. Sliding his hands under her bottom, he slowly drew her toward him, filling her, stretching her, moving in her with deft finesse and exquisite deliberation, as though in compensation for her constancy, wanting to make her as happy as she'd made him. And midway through one of her fierce, panting, tempestuous orgasms, he carried her outside because she was past noticing anything other than the surging fever pitch of ravenous desire.

The sun was warm on their bodies, the bustling square three stories below them, their neighbors if any, partially shielded by conveniently placed topiary. And the outside wall offered solid support for Flynn who was holding his bride impaled on his erection.

Although vaguely aware of the sun and the breeze and the

warmth of the stone wall against her back, Jo's inflamed senses were more conscious of the hot, pulsing core of her body, of the acute, riveting thrust and withdrawal of Flynn's engorged penis, of the blissful silken friction of flesh on flesh, of the tremulous, aching, all-consuming need rippling up her vagina. Eyes shut, her cheek resting in the hollow between Flynn's neck and shoulder, she clung to him, while he held her bottom and thighs cupped in his arms and kept her captive to the deep, slow unrelenting rhythm of his lower body.

She came under the hot sun and he did and they did in a series of furious, raging orgasms that only came to an end when they collapsed breathless and gasping on the chaise.

"Sorry," he panted as she lay atop him. "My arms—gave out . . ."

She shook her head, wanting to demur, unable to speak.

His chest heaving, Flynn reached out and plucked a bottle of water from a basket of fruit and wine and amenities set on a low table. Uncorking it with his teeth, he poured the water over his head and down Jo's back.

"Ummm . . . more," she whispered.

"Water or sex?" he panted, pouring a draft into his mouth.

"Water." Her head lifted fractionally from his chest. "And you're going to get us thrown out of Florence." But her voice was teasing.

"There's no one around—at least three floors up," he said with a grin, pouring another bottle of water over them. "And we're moving to Fiesole tomorrow."

Her brows rose faintly. "How reassuring."

"None of this was an issue a few moments ago." His gaze was amused.

"We can't all be level-headed in the throes of passion."

He laughed. "Hardly. Nor would I want *you* to be."

Her smile was impish. "How fortunate."

"I'm the fortunate one to have found you again."

His voice had taken on a sudden seriousness and she

touched his cheek as though in reassurance. "Thank you for coming to find me. I don't know what I would have done without you."

"Nor I," he softly said. "I went up in the mountains after you left." He glanced at the buildings surrounding them. "And discovered"—he paused and took a small breath—"that all I needed was you beside me."

"I'm glad," she simply said, the words insufficient for the overwhelming gratitude she felt. But his mood had visibly altered and he'd looked startled a moment ago when he'd looked around, as though suddenly realizing where he was. "You must miss the wilderness, here in the city."

"At times."

"This may not be enough for you then." She lifted her hand. "With the congestion and throngs."

"Fiesole will be different."

"Or somewhere else."

"Yes." He stroked her back lightly. "Perhaps a place with trees and mountains someday."

"So it's not the ranch you want to leave." Bracing her arms on his chest, she looked at him directly.

"Not exactly," he said, not sure how much to say—what she could understand, if anyone could understand what his life had been.

"It's the constant battles, no doubt."

He nodded. "I'm not fighting for the survival of a clan like your father, or attempting to maintain an age-old culture or tribal lands. I'm only taking up arms to save myself and my land and I'm not sure it's worth the personal cost. I couldn't even guarantee your safety in the Sun River country." *Or mine,* he thought, which was more likely at risk.

"Then there's no reason to go back. Don't even consider it. I'm content wherever you are."

"Thank you. The sun feels good, doesn't it?"

"Yes, wonderful," she answered, understanding he'd prefer not discussing the subject.

"Would you like some more water?" He held out the bottle.

"There's something else I'd rather have," she softly said.

His smile was pure seduction. "Let me guess . . ."

And perplexities and vexing quandaries were set aside for more pleasant endeavors.

They spent the day in the grand gilded bed and then the evening and very late that night, Jo fell asleep in Flynn's arms, her ravenous desires at last, sated.

He wasn't sure if his ever would be. Restless, his thoughts in ferment, he gently eased her from his embrace and rose from the bed. Walking to the opened balcony doors, he stood in the moonlight, looking out on the city, the solitude and quiet muting his disquietude. He breathed in the balmy night air, mindlessly counted the few lighted windows in the square, wondered if he was meant to live in a city like this. He didn't know. There was so much he didn't know, cut adrift from his home.

He'd become a ronin, a wanderer, like his father.

Would he find another home someday as his father had? Would he return to the Sun River Ranch if lasting peace was achieved? Would he ever take up the swords he'd put away? Would he ever fight again now that he had a wife?

The riddles of the universe were rarely so easily revealed as he well knew, and after a time, no nearer to understanding, he returned to the bed, leaned back against the ornate headboard and kept watch on the woman he loved.

What he did know was that he was lost without her.

And content when she was near.

It was enough.

Much later that night, Jo woke, and looking up, saw him gazing at her.

He smiled. "Go back to sleep."

"You should too," she murmured, drowsily, snuggling closer to his warmth.

"I'm taking pleasure in having you beside me," he murmured, touching her cheek lightly. "I'll sleep later."

"I don't know how you can stay awake," she whispered, already dozing off again.

He smiled.

Practicing a thousand days is said to be discipline; practicing ten thousand days is said to be refining. This should be carefully studied, Musashi had said.

He was a samurai.

He could stay awake and guard the woman he loved.

Epilogue

The newlyweds spent a year in Fiesole and then moved to Paris where their first child was born. The Empire Cattle Company was no more, the investors having cut their losses and sold out. McFee and Flynn had purchased the land; peace had finally come to the Sun River country and McFee sent monthly reports to Flynn wherever he was.

Lucy was in Paris with her husband Ed Finnegan when Flynn and Jo's daughter was born. She'd brought the baby a lavish layette, taken one look at her new granddaughter and decided she was much too young to be a grandmother. But she'd admired the baby from a distance, proclaiming her very beautiful and then spent the rest of her Parisian holiday shopping.

Hazard and Blaze came to visit their first grandchild shortly after Lucy left and stayed for a month. On one of their first evenings in the city, Hazard and Flynn had a moment of quiet after everyone had gone to sleep. Sitting over brandies in the library, Hazard brought up a subject that couldn't be discussed in a letter or telegram. "I sent some of my men to England awhile back to take care of that Phellps fellow," he remarked.

"My men came home and told me they were too late. Seems he'd been sliced up some before he died."

Flynn nodded. "I got to him first."

"Then the matter was settled," Hazard said, softly.

"He deserved it." Flynn met Hazard's gaze. "You saw what they were like."

"Yes. Despicable men—cowards who had others do their fighting."

"I put my swords away after that."

"For good?" Hazard watched his son-in-law closely.

Flynn shrugged. "For now, at least." He smiled faintly. "I have this urge to see the world and Jo indulges me."

"McFee's doing a good job as you know, and there's still too many witless fools trying to make a name for themselves with a gun." Hazard smiled. "Enjoy your travels."

A son was born to Jo and Flynn in a small village north of Kyoto two years later and they stayed in Japan until the baby was old enough to travel. Flynn studied with his father's Kendo school and in the refining of his samurai skills, he also found a greater degree of peace. For the next several years, the small family journeyed the world, meeting with the Braddock-Blacks or Lucy from time to time at various locales, coming back to the villa in Fiesole when they felt the need for a more permanent home, enjoying the sweetness of life together.

Jo and Flynn's love only deepened with the years, their happiness and contentment a constant delight to two souls who had once questioned the reality of such tender sentiments as love.

"I'm really glad you rode into town for Stewart Warner's dinner," Jo would say on occasion, gratified or amazed, sometimes fearful of the unfathomable workings of fate.

"I would have found you wherever you were," Flynn would always reply, with an unruffled certainty and strength of conviction that invariably calmed her. "We are like a force of nature, you and I—our spirits would have met somewhere in the world. Even sitting quietly and doing nothing," he said, the words of the Zenrin poem echoing in his ears, "it would have happened."

Please turn the page for an exciting preview of
THE FOREVER KISS by Thea Devine,
a summer 2003 paperback release from Brava.

It was the blood. That gypsy blood pounding through her body that would never let anything go. And it was the house, Ducas's house, a magnet, with the gas and candlelit windows that beckoned deep in the night, especially when the Sangbournes were entertaining.

They were always entertaining. Lady Sangbourne had an insatiable need to surround herself with people all the time, with fascinating people. People about whom you could find out things if you were clever enough and if you followed the lure of your gypsy blood.

Oh, there was something about the way it thrummed deep within her, blotting out her mother's every attempt to turn her into the lady her father wanted her to be.

But then, her father didn't know that her mother was a frequent visitor to Sangbourne Manor, because he himself was such an infrequent visitor to the house in Cheshamshire.

And this he didn't need to know—that his exotic, alluring Gaetana was frequently the entertainment. They feasted on her, the wild gypsy dancer, as they gossiped about her, she who had enticed an earl and held him still in her thrall. They paid her to come to the Manor and dance for them, and she

went, following the call of her nature, and in spite of the fact
the earl kept her like a queen.

It was the blood. It could not be denied. Not in her mother,
not in her. And so Gaetana danced, giving herself to whatever
voluptuous pleasures were on the menu on any given evening
at Sangbourne Manor, and giving herself to the earl at his
command.

Gaetana on the inside and Angene, her changeling daughter, on the outside, looking in, squirreling away secrets.

So many secrets. Her gypsy blood reveled in the secrets.
Secrets were knowledge, secrets were power, and Angene
knew someday the power would come in very handy.

And besides, what else had she to do until Ducas came back
from the war? Dear God, Ducas, throwing himself in harm's
way in a godforsaken country thousands of miles away for no
reason she could ever understand.

Ducas, with his persistent tongue and honeyed promises.

Her body twinged just thinking of it. It was the blood; no
decent woman would even conceive of doing what she in-
tended to do when Ducas returned.

And he would return. There was not a doubt in her mind.
And then . . . and then—she would become his mistress and
enslave him forever, the way her mother had captivated the
earl.

The thought made her breathless.

How stupid of him to go to war. It wasn't his war. And it was
so far away that it could take years to return. The idea of
it yawned like an abyss, dark as the night that enfolded her.
Perhaps that was why she so loved the night; there was always
the promise of a new day, and with it, Ducas's return.

But until that day, it was the house that drew her, and the
sense that at night she could be close to him by just touching
the cold stone walls, and by learning everything she could
about those who peopled his life.

By lurking in the shadows . . .

It was the blood: there was a turbulence in her that could

not be tempered by all the good breeding of the man who had sired her, nor by a hundred lessons with the best tutors in deportment and manners her mother had employed.

She was what she was; daughter of a gypsy dancer and an aristocratic earl, and the fact she was creeping along the outer walls of Sangbourne Manor was proof enough which part of her held sway.

And then there were the secrets, the delicious sensual secrets about the games that adults played.

Games that quickened her blood, because she and Ducas had played at playing those games, had skirted the ultimate conquest and surrender, with the full understanding that someday, somehow, it would happen.

But for now, she moved noiselessly through the trees and into the bushes that fronted the windows of the grand parlor where the games would begin.

The dining first, hours of it, with five or six courses of elegantly prepared food and the best china and silver; they began early in the country, on the evenings when they played their games. After dinner, the men would retreat for port and polite conversation as the tension and anticipation escalated to an unbearable degree. And finally the men would join the ladies for the evening's entertainment—this night, Gaetana, the gypsy, well-paid for her sensual dances, for her time, for her body.

A never-ending fascination, watching the aristocracy as they ate, drank, eyed each other, flirted, paired off, disappeared; sometimes they imported girls from the village to service the gentlemen while the ladies went off with the goat-boys and shepherds into the fields.

Or they would hire high-priced courtesans for a more elegant and willful seduction.

Or they took each other up and off in private rooms in a variety of interesting combinations.

All of this, Angene knew. And the queen of all this rampant lasciviousness was Ducas's mother.

Gaetana would not talk about her, nor anything that went on at Sangbourne Manor. Secrets were safe at the Manor, kept beyond the grave in a devil's bargain. No one would tell, ever, about the things that went on there, weekend-long things, forbidden things.

Things, perhaps, Ducas had been a part of. Things, because of that, Angene had to know, since she was certain they were things that would give her the power she needed to convince him to become her lover, forever. She was a bastard child; she wanted nothing more.

As she peered into the tall, multi-paned windows of the dimly lit grand parlor, she saw her mother dancing to a wildly strumming guitar, her skirts held high, her feet and legs bared to all. And the look on her face—the transcending look of joy that she could finally be herself, even among these heathens who had no idea of her life, her lore, her heritage.

It didn't matter. She did not need to pretend in these wild hours. She could follow the dictates of her heart, her blood, and no one would tell.

In that curious honor among deviants, her mother's secret was safe.

Angene was the only one who knew—and even she harbored a tumultuous desire to be among these libertine people, her hair, her skirts, her desire flowing free.

If only Ducas would return; Ducas understood her. Handsome, reckless Ducas with that irresistible combination of haughty aristocrat and primitive stable boy—and that tongue, that insatiable, demanding tongue . . .

But wait—her mother's voluptuous dance was finished, and the guests—four couples in all, excluding Lord and Lady Sangbourne, were clapping loudly and appreciatively.

She knew what came next in this sexual quadrille; every country weekend almost seemed to be a set piece. In tonight's little play, the lights would dim, a gentleman would rise and select the lady of his choice, who was not his wife, and away they would go into the shadows to explore the unfettered nature of men and the naked response of women.

Lady Sangbourne directed the scene, standing tall and slender in the center of the room, dressed in her habitual green, with her long thick hair that deliberately grazed her waist bound away from her narrow face; did she not know how much men loved long hair to curtain their sins? But she was always the last to go into the shadows.

She knew everything, Lady Sangbourne, and didn't blink an eye as her husband chose his companion for the night . . .

Gaetana?

Angene's heart sank. This she had never witnessed before, this wholesale taking of her mother, in spite of her allegiance and her love for the earl. But none of that ever counted here. And certainly not tonight, if her mother's expression were any indication.

The air was thick with expendable lust, and every last guest only wanted that evanescent moment of surrender. Instinctively Angene understood that the crux of the evening was the pleasure point, nothing more, nothing less, and not even her mother was immune to the call of her blood.

She sank against the wall, her heart pounding painfully. This reality was not pretty. But then, wasn't it what she wanted for herself? To give herself wholly and completely to Ducas, and to live, outside constraints, as the love of his life forever?

Was there a forever when it came to the nature of men?

Would *she* entertain Ducas's friends and companions, and would he just as cavalierly hand her over to whoever wanted her for a night? Was this the life she wanted to commit to, in her overwhelming desire to possess Ducas?

It did not bear thinking about . . . she couldn't. He might be dead for all she knew, on some foreign battlefield, dead with no remains to be buried and mourned over . . . and this was worse than anything that might come of their life together.

Oh, dear Lord—Ducas . . .

Silence descended, the curious silence of the deep dark night, where the merest rustle of a leaf could set the blood thrumming. Not a star burned; the moon drifted behind a tail of clouds; every detail of the landscape merged into another so that there was only the flat black of nothingness around her.

There was nowhere to move, nothing to see that could guide her back home. She was a prisoner of the dark, caught in that abyss of emptiness, that cold black hole she so feared, and there was nothing she could do but curl up against the cold stone walls of Sangbourne Manor until daylight.

The howling of a dog awakened her.

Dawn. Cold. Wet. Dank.

Jingling. A rasping, rolling sound. Horses. A carriage emerging out of the fog that hovered just beyond the drive in front of Sangbourne Manor.

Dreaming. Too early in the morning for visitors . . . and besides, they were all still tumbled in their ruttish rest.

If she moved quickly, she could get back to the house before her mother returned.

Only, limbs stiff from the cold. Can't move. Not yet. Slowly, slowly . . . no sound—if anyone caught her here, her mother would abandon her to the wolves . . . the carriage door opening—who . . . ?

A stranger. Wait—someone leaning on him . . .

Slowly easing out of the carriage—was it? The stranger, giving him a cane. A familiar stance, a bend of the body, the rumble of a word, a familiar voice . . .

Oh, God—Ducas . . . *Ducas?* As if she'd conjured him with her thoughts. Injured? Maimed? Oh, mighty lord in heaven, he must not see her here, not like this, not now . . . there could be no explanation, ever, for her skulking around his house.

She ducked into the bushes, watched him walk slowly and painfully on the arm of the stranger up to the front door.

A jangling bell in the distance. Scurry of footsteps. The

door opening. She couldn't see anything—it couldn't be him, could it?

But it must be . . . a word, a welcome, and he entered the house.

Thank heaven there was fog—while they were all occupied by the surprise of his return, she could slip and slide away without anyone noticing.

But dear heaven, this was so unexpected; she didn't know what to think, what to do.

But you don't have to do anything.

Ducas is home . . .

And here is a second preview that will whet your appetite for
WILDE THING by Janelle Denison,
a July 2003 release from Brava.

He had *bad boy* written all over him, and Liz Adams wanted him in the worst possible way. From his rumpled sable hair and striking, seductive blue eyes, to that lean, honed body she'd imagined naked and aroused, he exuded raw sex appeal and brought her feminine instincts to keen awareness like no other man had in a very long time.

And she was completely and totally in lust with her gorgeous, head-turning customer who'd recently started frequenting her café, The Daily Grind, in the evenings. He'd become a pleasant, visual distraction to other responsibilities and worries that had been weighing heavily on her mind lately.

He lifted his head from the latest best-seller he was reading, and from across the room their eyes met briefly and she caught a glimpse of the to-die-for grin that lifted the corner of his sensual mouth. An undeniable warmth and excitement stirred within her, and she had to resist the urge to close the distance between them, rip his black t-shirt and tight jeans off his long, muscled body, and have her wicked way with him. On the counter top, on one of the couches in the sitting area, or even the floor. She wasn't picky about the *where* part of her fantasy.

Picking up a damp towel, she wiped down the stainless

steel espresso machine and let out a wistful sigh that con-
veyed two long years of suppressed desires. She'd recently
turned thirty-one, and she swore she was hitting her sexual
prime, because for the past few weeks she'd been *craving* sex.
Ever since *he'd* strolled into her coffee house and jump-started
her libido and fueled her nightly dreams with carnal, sinful
fantasies.

Undoubtedly, it had been too long since she'd felt the exquisite caress of a man's mouth sliding across her sensitized
flesh. Too long since she'd experienced the delicious heat of a
hard, strong body covering hers, the silken texture and erotic
friction of him sliding deep in a slow, grinding rhythm. Those
realistic sensations were something no artificially enhanced
sex toy could duplicate, and she missed that kind of physical
connection with a flesh and blood man.

But as much as her fantasy man tempted her, everything
from that black leather jacket he wore, to his come-hither eyes
and self-confidence, screamed *rebel*. And she'd vowed after
her marriage to Trevor she'd never fall for another man who
was wild and reckless and had the ability to leave her devas-
tated in the process.

Unfortunately, despite being burned by one bad boy who'd
turned out to be bad to the extreme, she couldn't help her attraction to the kind of man who had a bit of an edge to him. A
take-charge kind of man who was decisive and straightforward,
yet unpredictable, with a sense of reckless adventure. That
Harley-Davidson motorcycle *he* rode told her a lot about the
man, that he was secure in his masculinity, didn't like to be
constrained by rules, and was untamable, intrepid, and daring,
as well.

Even knowing he was most likely all wrong for her, that
those qualities could only lead to trouble and heartache, she
still wanted him. *Badly.*

"Mind if I make myself a chilled mocha before you finish
cleaning up?"

The sound of Mona Owen's voice snapped Liz out of her

private thoughts and jolted her back to reality and the stocking and clean-up still awaiting her attention. She glanced at her good friend and owner of The Last Word, a new and used bookstore that directly connected to her café, and caught Mona eyeing the last of the drink mix in the blender.

Liz grinned, having grown used to Mona's tendency to mooch off leftovers near closing time. "Sure. Help yourself."

Mona tossed ice into the concoction, switched the blender on for a few seconds, then poured the icy drink into a plastic cup and added a straw. "I've been meaning to ask you if you've heard from your cousin Valerie yet?"

The reminder of Valerie's vanishing act tossed everything else from Liz's mind except worry, and a helpless feeling that had grown with each passing day without any contact from her cousin. "I haven't heard a word from her since she left me that vague note Friday night." And all the message had said was that she was going to a weekend work party with a new boyfriend who was a client she met through The Ultimate Fantasy, the phone sex place where she worked.

While Valerie had always possessed a wild, reckless streak, and it really wasn't out of the ordinary for her to do something as frivolous as to take off with a boyfriend for a getaway, Liz found the whole situation too disturbing, and worrisome. It just wasn't like her cousin to go so long without getting in touch, especially since they shared an apartment together, even if to leave a brief message on their phone recorder. And here it was Tuesday evening, and Liz had yet to hear from her.

Liz knew Valerie enjoyed her unconventional occupation, but there had been other aspects of her job that her cousin had mentioned that concerned Liz, and made her fairly certain that the phone sex business was a front for a much larger operation dealing in prostitution and other sexual escapades. Her biggest fear was that Valerie had gotten herself involved in something illegal, or even dangerous, with this man she'd taken off with.

"Are you thinking about contacting the police?" Mona

asked, apparently sensing Liz's distress over her cousin's disappearance.

"I already tried that." Grabbing the steaming pitcher, she
dunked it into the hot, soapy water in the sink and took out her
frustration in scrubbing the stainless steel pot. "I spoke with an
officer, but once I told him about the note Valerie left stating
she was off on her own free will, he said at this point there wasn't
any evidence of foul play to warrant an investigation, and all I
could do was file a missing person's report on her behalf."

And with every day that passed without a word from her
cousin, Liz's desperation grew. So far, she'd been able to keep
Valerie's vanishing act from her aunt and uncle who'd moved
from Chicago to Southern California a year ago and had asked
Liz to look after Valerie. The last thing Liz wanted to do was
apprise them of the sort of career their daughter had chosen,
but if her cousin didn't show up soon, she'd have no choice
but to inform them of the less than ideal circumstances.

Not wanting to shell-shock her aunt and uncle with the
news that Valerie indulged in phone sex for a living unless she
absolutely had to, Liz had opted to pursue her cousin's absence herself, in the only way she knew how. And knowing
she needed to tell someone of her plan, she decided to make
Mona that person.

She bit her bottom lip and gathered the fortitude to spill
her secret. "I applied at the same phone sex company where
Valerie was working," she said, the reasons for her actions self-
explanatory. "I have an appointment for an interview at The
Ultimate Fantasy tomorrow morning at eleven."

Concern creased Mona's dark brows. "Do you think that's
safe or smart?"

Liz didn't want to directly respond to that question, because she knew the answer would be a resounding *no*, and she
wasn't about to give up on the idea. "It's the only way I can
think of to get inside information on Valerie or where she
might be and with whom."

Mona shook her head, her expression adamant. "I don't think this is something you should do on your own."

Liz dragged her fingers through her hair and sighed. "The police aren't willing to get involved, so I don't have much of a choice, not if I want to find Valerie or get in touch with her."

Her friend was quiet for a few moments while she considered Liz's idea, her gaze focused on something out in the lounge area. Then a bright smile spread across her face. "Why don't you hire Steve Wilde?"

Liz frowned in confusion as she filled a basket with scones and another tray with gourmet cookies. "Who?"

Mona pitched her empty plastic cup into the trash and hooked her thumb toward her fantasy man. "Steve Wilde. The guy you've been lusting after for the past month. And don't bother denying it. I've been watching the two of you, and when you're not ogling him, his eyes are following you. And from my astute observations, that lingering gaze of his is hungry for more than just your pastries." She gave Liz a playful but encouraging wink.

Wilde. God, even his last name insinuated trouble of the most sensual variety. Her gaze strayed back to the lounge just as he unfolded his big, lean body from his chair and shrugged into his well-worn leather jacket, causing the muscles in his arms and across his chest to shift temptingly as he moved. Her pulse quickened with female appreciation. He was so compelling, his magnetism so potent, she couldn't help but respond to his stunning good looks.

He picked up his book and keys from the coffee table and glanced up, his disarming gaze locking with hers—as bold, direct, and unapologetically sexual as the man himself. He tipped his head in acknowledgment, causing a lock of unruly sable hair to fall across his brow, accentuating his rakish appearance. The private, sinful grin he graced her with literally stole her breath and sent her hormones into an overwhelming frenzy of sexual longing. Her breasts swelled and tightened, her nipples tingled, and a surge of liquid desire settled in intimate places.

Oh, yeah, he was most definitely trouble personified.

He exited the café, leaving her with more than enough new stimulating material to fuel another night of erotic mind candy. She returned her attention to Mona. "So, tell me, how do *you* know his name?"

Her friend snagged a biscotti from the glass jar on the counter and munched into the baked treat. "He's come into The Last Word to purchase a few books, and we've talked a time or two."

Which essentially meant Mona not only knew his name, but his age, marital status, and occupation, as well.

Finishing off her cookie, Mona licked the crumbs from her fingers. "And knowing the attraction between the two of you is mutual, I'm thinking it's time you took off that gold band you wear on your finger that makes men think you're taken, and take a walk on the *Wilde* side."

"Ha-ha. Very funny," Liz said, though the idea was one she'd already considered . . . in her fantasies.

"I'm being completely serious." Mona's tone reflected just how resolute she was. "At least about taking that ring off your finger and putting yourself back on the market. There's a time and place to shed everything . . . your ring, your clothes, your inhibitions . . ." she added meaningfully.

The lights overhead glimmered off the gold band Liz had worn since Trevor's death, mocking her solitary, abstinent lifestyle—of her own choosing, she reminded herself. She was still struggling to dig herself out of the financial mess her late husband had left her in when he'd died two years ago, and she didn't want or need the complication of a binding relationship. Not when her focus was on her café and seeing her savings account back in the black.

Feeling useless resentments clawing their way to the surface, she redirected their conversation back to their original topic. "You mentioned hiring Steve Wilde. What for?"

"Because while he might have all the markings of a bad boy, he's definitely one of the good guys. He's a private detective with his own agency, and I'm betting he can help you out with Valerie." Excitement infused Mona's voice. "At the very least, he can offer advice or follow up on your cousin's disappearance without you putting yourself at risk."

So, he was a good guy with a bad boy demeanor, a combination Liz found much too intriguing. "It's not like I have a lot of extra money to pay a private investigator. You know that." She'd spent the past two years on a tight budget while Trevor's debts had drained a huge portion of her savings. "I could barely afford to have the alternator on my car fixed, let alone a PI's professional services."

Mona seemed undeterred by her lack of funds. "Maybe Mr. Wilde would be willing to work out a payment plan of some sort. If you're really lucky, he'll take his services out in trade," she offered with a sly smile, leaving no doubt in Liz's mind what her friend meant. "I have his business card back in my shop if you're interested."

Interested in his services or paying him in trade, Liz wondered wickedly. She shivered, unable to stem the fiery sensations rippling through her at the thought of being a slave to Steve Wilde's every sexual whim. Not that she believed he'd agree to such a shameless proposition. But it did make for a nice fantasy to add to her growing collection.

On a business level, she supposed an initial consultation with Mr. Wilde couldn't hurt, and any free advice he might impart could only help her in her search to find her cousin.

"I'm interested," she said to Mona, and realizing how those simple words could be misconstrued, she followed that up with a quick, "In his business card."

"Of course." Amusement and satisfaction flashed in Mona's eyes. "I'll be right back."

Liz watched her friend trek across the short distance to her bookstore, anticipation making her heart pound hard in her chest. She swore that contacting Steve Wilde—the object of her fondest, most carnal dreams—had nothing to do with her attraction to him, and her interest was strictly professional.

Her mind accepted the lecture. Unfortunately, her neglected body wasn't completely convinced.

Steve Wilde wasn't a man easily shocked. Yet he couldn't have been more stunned when his secretary, Beverly, announced that Liz Adams was there at his agency to see him. Seconds later, the woman who'd occupied too much of his thoughts lately appeared in his office, her vivid green gaze tentatively meeting his from across the room.

She looked incredibly sexy. He'd only seen her in her work uniform of jeans, t-shirt, and a bib apron that tied around her neck and waist. Nothing overtly suggestive or clingy, but he'd seen enough of her coming and going to know that she had the kind of full, luscious figure he liked on a woman. And the thigh-length, form-fitting cocoa colored skirt and matching blouse she was currently wearing confirmed a knock-out, head-turning shape he couldn't help but appreciate and admire.

Unlike his brother Eric who was drawn to a woman's derriere, and Adrian who went for long, shapely legs, Steve was first and foremost a breast man; he liked them full and firm, and preferred more than a dainty handful to fondle and play with. The "V" neckline of Liz's blouse dipped low, giving him a glimpse of an ample amount of cleavage that made his mouth water and his fingers itch to touch. He assumed she was wearing a bra with no padding, because he could see the faint outline of her nipples pressing against the silky fabric of her top. He imagined the velvet texture of those stiff crests in his mouth, against his tongue, and felt a rush of pulsing heat spiral straight to his groin.

He gave a barely perceptible nod to his secretary, and Beverly quietly closed the door as Liz continued to walk into his office. The skirt she wore accentuated the indentation of her waist and the provocative sway of her shapely hips. From there, he took the liberty of continuing the sensual journey, taking in the curvaceous outline of her thighs, and long, lightly tanned legs designed to wrap around a man's hips and clench him tight in the throes of passion.

God, he just wanted to eat her up, inch by delectable inch—from her soft, glossy lips all the way down to those pink painted toenails peeking from the opening of her heeled sandals, and everywhere in between.

Much to his delight, there was nothing dainty, delicate, or petite about her. No, she was a well-built woman with a voluptuous body made for hot, hard, lusty sex. Which was just the way he liked his physical encounters, though it had been too long since he'd been with a woman who matched his sexual appetite and could fulfill his needs and demands in the bedroom.

Shaking off his surprise at Liz's impromptu visit, along with the thrum of arousal taking up residence within him, he stood and casually rounded his desk to greet her. "You're Liz, from The Daily Grind." He held out his hand and waited for her to acknowledge the gesture.

"That's correct." With a slow, sensual smile that made him feel sucker-punched, she slipped her palm against his, allowing his long fingers to envelop her hand in the superior strength of his grip.

Her flesh was warm and soft, but her handshake was firm and confident. As for the instantaneous chemistry that leapt between them at first touch, well, that was nothing short of a simmering heat just waiting for the right flame to ignite their attraction into a blazing inferno.

She didn't try and tug her hand away when he lingered and brazenly brushed his thumb along her skin. Rather, she maintained eye contact and waited until he chose to release her, confirming his first impression of her at the café that she was a strong, independent woman who was secure in her femininity and had no problem giving as good as she got when it came to the battle of the sexes.

He liked those unique qualities about her, and knew he'd

found a woman with enough tenacity and daring to keep him stimulated physically, as well as intellectually. A rare feat and challenge he'd more than welcome, if it wasn't for the ring encircling her left hand finger that gave the impression she belonged to someone else.

As soon as he let go of her hand, she said, "I hope you don't mind, but Mona gave me your card."

Ahh, Mona, the chatty, albeit friendly woman from The Last Word who enjoyed prying information from her customers. "I'll have to thank her for the business." Though he'd always thought of Liz in terms of pure, unadulterated pleasure. The kind that made him wake up sweating in the dark of night, his muscles rigid and his cock granite hard from erotic images of Liz beneath him, her body soft and inviting and just as tight as his own fist stroking his erection.

Before his libido reacted to the nightly, obsessive dreams that plagued him, he leaned his backside against his desk and crossed his arms over his chest. "What can I do for you, Mrs. Adams?"

"Actually, it's *Ms.* Adams," she clarified.

He glanced at the ring she was absently twisting around her finger. Since she'd come to him and was in his territory, he figured he had every right to ask frank, personal questions. "So, you're unmarried and single?"

She nodded, causing her silky, shoulder-length blond hair to brush along her jawline. "Yes, to both."

She didn't give an explanation for the band she wore that indicated otherwise, but he'd just learned all he needed to know to give him the incentive to pursue her on a more intimate level. With less than two feet of space separating them, there was no denying the awareness between them, and their attraction was something he had no qualms about using to get what he wanted.

And what he desired was *her.*